Lance Clarke

Thirty Days

First published on ebook Kindle 2012-04-01

Copyright © Lance Clarke 2012

Lance Clarke asserts the moral right to be identified as the author of this work

The catalogue record for this book is available from the British Library

ISBN 978-1-291-06003-4

www.publishnation.co.uk

This book is dedicated to a decent US air force lieutenant colonel I worked with in NATO and showed me that there was more to leadership than wearing rank badges. We only ever disagreed on the matter of the American Dream; he, because he was full of American true grit, loyalty to the flag and optimism, me, because I am a European and have history on my side!

Acknowledgements

This story was written years ago when my wife Jean was terminally ill and I wrote several books whilst tending to her. We talked about an upcoming American election and how we had seen political tactics develop over the years, on both sides of the Atlantic. The views of a much respected erstwhile American military boss in NATO came to the fore in our discussions and it was easy to develop a character who felt the same way he did.

Jean was a good proof reader and this helped us through the difficult last years.

My thanks too, to the legion of other friends and work colleagues who also did some proof reading and helped me to locate a tin mine in Arizona and a tribe of American Indians. I am also grateful to the internet that enables armchair authors to research information about all sorts of things without leaving their front door.

All writers need an apprentice-piece and I guess this is mine. It is a short easy read, but, as well as entertaining the reader it should sow seeds of doubt along the way, especially in the minds of those who care about national governance and the pernicious effect of the political spin-doctors.

Do we get the governing system we deserve?

LC

"....to secure these rights, Governments are instituted by men, deriving their just powers from the consent of the governed."

American Declaration of Independence

Prologue

Senator Randolph Kinz sat at the window of his Washington office looking at his favourite view of Capitol Hill.   On the oak desk in front of him was a pad of good quality, vellum writing paper, a MONTBLANC fountain pen, given to him some ten years ago by a geologist he much admired, and a small silver plated revolver.

His eyes welled with tears. It was not meant to happen like this. The deaths were a catastrophe and now he had to own up to his part in it all.   He felt ashamed and sick to the stomach as most decent men feel, when they are tempted to act on impulse or against their better judgement and things go terribly wrong.   Only this time his actions had cost lives.

Kinz wiped his forehead and slowly unscrewed the top of his fountain pen. His eyes ran over its black shape, edged with gold plate. After all these years he was tempted to read the small printing on the nib – but he knew that this was simply a human tendency to play for time; his time!

The pen was perfectly weighted and balanced and he wrote steadily. He had stylish handwriting and was always commended on it.   The former president would receive his personal notes with delight and state out loud, "It's from Randolph again, I'd recognise that hand anywhere." Kinz had worshipped him. He was uncomplicated, fiercely independent, honest and had an absolute lack of arrogance; this was a bit like a description of Benjamin Franklyn, but it fitted.

The current president wouldn't even recognise his own handwriting!

Kinz looked over his shoulder towards a small television in the corner of his study. It showed President Brannigan waving to an enthusiastic crowd, probably stage-managed by loyal Republicans, as they cheered him on to victory in the upcoming Presidential Election. Brannigan's vice-presidency had been insidious behind the scenes that led to the disastrous Iraq debacle and many other dumb policies that beleaguered the hapless former president. Kinz was angry and bitter that Brannigan would be the last man to read his words – but he was an honest man and it had to be done, lest anyone else be blamed.

After about twenty minutes writing he signed the last page of three, wrote neatly on the envelope before sealing it and propping it up against his crystal ink well. He then sat back in his chair and carefully put the top back on his fountain pen. It was a nice office, full of memories, pictures and his extensive library of books on American political and cultural history. He got up and removed a classical music CD from its cover and put it on the player; the sound of Mozart wafted around the office. Then he poured himself a large single malt whisky, his favourite, Glen Livet. He sipped it. Never gulp good whisky he had told his acolytes. When he finished and the flavour of the spirit had filled his senses and the alcohol flowed into his veins he sat down and reached for the revolver.

The gun was shiny silver and had mother of pearl inlays in the handle. It was not a very practical firearm, but it felt good in his hands. It was only when he was loading the sixth bullet in the chamber that he realised what he was doing and laughed out loud. He poured some more whisky then, despite all his good advice, gulped it down in one before putting the empty glass next to the envelope on the desk that bore the inscription:

CONFIDENTIAL DO NOT OPEN

Personal for the attention of President Jake Brannigan

Then he laughed out loud again; he had loaded six bullets when he only needed one! That seemed to sum up his judgement pretty well.

He was still laughing when he raised the revolver to his temple and fired a single shot.

Chapter One

Ginny Grivas stomped around her New York studio apartment, located between First and Fifth Avenue, walking distance from Central Park. She was gathering up countless wine bottles and pizza boxes, throwing them into a large black plastic bag with more energy than the task demanded. She had argued with her Dad again. He was the redoubtable Democrat senator who had faced down President Clinton when he had got himself into such a dreadful situation in the Monica Lewinsky affair. He had been in such a rage and said things that thereafter consigned him to a political wilderness. Clinton survived and he didn't. It wasn't fair, he would keep saying. His bitterness affected everyone at home, at work and even amongst his most patient friends and his family.

All except Ginny that is; she was a loveable, playful and yet feisty young lady. Above all she was surprisingly mature for her nineteen years. It didn't surprise her that the Clinton situation had affected him as much as it had. In many ways she understood and although she didn't like it, put up with his mood swings and general malaise. Ginny knew where she was going in life and had her own views. It always surprised and amused her that her father believed it was right to say what he thought and yet balked when he received it from others, particularly his offspring. Her older brother and sister were in thrall of him; she wasn't. She spurned the traditional education route for richer Americans, the Ivy League universities, and law school then a life in politics. Her father's comments about her wanting to enjoy life and avoid hard work pinged off her like split peas off a rhinoceros hide. But for all that, there was something in her that made her want to show him what she could do.

It was for this reason that she had picked political science as her core subject to study at the Hope College, on the North Side of New York City. She loved it, immersing herself in the different streams that the subject offered. But most of all, it was the psychology of mainstream American politics and leadership, and the eventual effect on ordinary people who committed their very lives to the fortunes of the Democrat and Republican parties, that interested her most of all. In nearly all US educational establishments the bright and intellectual were creamed off early and served long apprenticeships working their way through internships in the political jungle, on their way to developing their primary skills as attorneys at law or businessmen.

But Ginny had a mind of her own and spurned the 'good ole boy' approach to political thinking; it didn't make her popular. That was why she had jumped with excitement when she received a strange call, from the Senator Randolph Kinz, who she knew well, offering her a chance to make a political video in the company of five other teenagers who were the offspring of US senators. The subject matter was to be of their own choice, expressing the views of young people of America on the 'state of the nation' prior to the presidential election just over one month away. He was very persuasive.

She would receive details in the post of where to go to meet her companions and should be prepared to be away for thirty days, during which time she should contact no one. Ginny wasted no time and made arrangements to explain her absence with her College and then wrote a short letter to her parents. She had been advised in the call that she was to give it to the two guides who would meet her. The letter would be sent to them within twenty-four hours.

The next day Ginny bubbled with anticipation as she received in the post the directions to the rendezvous point. She was told to travel to La Guardia airport, just outside New York City and

2

fly to Dulles airport, Washington D.C. Once there she should head to the car park, A1, next to terminal two. There she would see a small coach with a thin orange stripe down the middle and should join the others for a journey that would take two to three days to a secret location.

Her bags were packed already and she lost no time in getting a taxi to her local airport. It would cost her a bundle, but what the heck! She hardly noticed what was going on around her as she made her way through the crowded concourse at La Guardia airport - her head was buzzing with excitement. She quickly located the right airline desk and purchased a ticket to Washington then walked to an adjacent newsagent and bought papers and magazines to help the time pass quickly.

The journey took no time at all and the papers and magazines remained largely unread. After landing, Ginny crossed Dulles airport to terminal two and looked around her for car park A1. At first she couldn't find it, but then saw the signs and followed them. It was quite a walk, so she decided to take an airport bus. It arrived at the car park entrance and she easily spotted the coach with the orange stripe parked at the far end of the car park and she could just about make out a group of young people. As she drew closer, she became both excited and delighted. Ginny knew every one of the teenagers, but she was especially pleased to see Clem Johnson. She liked him whilst they were at the same High School, and this turned to a deeper attraction when they went to summer camp a year later. They parted to go their separate ways to new Colleges, but the attraction remained.

Clem Johnson heard an odd sound and sat bolt upright in bed, his head throbbing from a hangover induced by the previous night's beer drinking and watching four hours of recorded football games at a friend's apartment just off Marrie Avenue SW, Washington D.C. The cover on the video box had described the contents as, 'the best touch downs of the season'. Halfway through, he and his friends had become so bored they finished a couple of boxes of beer and had fallen asleep. He staggered back home to his flat just off Rhode Island Avenue NW, at about three in the morning.

It was now almost ten o'clock, his mouth tasted like glue and his eyes were sticky and hard to open. He tried to concentrate on the noise that was doing its best to penetrate his aching head and realised that it was the answer-phone loudspeaker.

Wearily he got up went to the bathroom and poured a glass of water which he drank almost in one swallow – he felt his body slowly re-hydrate. Then he went to his living room and pushed the glowing red button on the phone and listened to the message. It was Senator Randolph Kinz's voice and it sounded cultured, pleasant and a long way from his Tucson roots. He had known the senator, who was a friend of the family, since first grade and liked him a lot. Kinz was the only adult he had been able to have a damned good political argument with. It wasn't easy being a teenage Democrat in a family of Republicans.

Early on in his education Clem harboured an intense interest in politics. It was Senator Kinz that he had to thank for that. They discussed many things at family barbecues and Clem's appetite was well and truly whetted for discussion and inquiry – the two important elements needed to succeed in politics. Then he joined High School and College debating societies, attended student forums that discussed issues and passed resolutions in an attempt to get within touching distance of the presidency of the student senate. He was recognised as being a bright and energetic student, but somehow he never quite reached the peak when debating. Clem was popular with his peers who recognised that he was really very smart. But although he fashioned his arguments well, he lacked one thing: stagecraft. Other candidates always managed to pip him to the post because they polished their product and spun it for all it was worth, parsing language to win at all costs, whereas honest Clem just wanted to tell it as it was. He often regretted his lack of style; he had the product, but not the wrapping.

Nevertheless, he had enormous self-confidence and in his sophomore year at college, chose to develop a hobby that would enable him to concentrate on his presentation and follow his love of political debate; photography and video making. He then used his new skills to interview and record viewpoints and this made him more independent of mind and far more inquisitive as his experience grew. From then on his Republican politics hung by a very loose thread.

His father disliked his son's 'inquiring mind' and told him so. Clem tried to argue back, but it was no use. He now had a number of Democrat friends and despaired to hear his father insult them, calling them a party of giveaways and pinkos, or referring to East Texans as 'yellow dog Democrats', who reputedly would only vote for a yellow dog rather than a Republican; what kind of politics was that? Clem hated the pantomime of politics. Unsurprisingly, exasperated and needing an intellectual haven, he took refuge with the family friend, Senator Randolph Kinz.

Inevitably, he got to know more about Senator Kinz than he did his own father who was aloof, opinionated and simply not around. Kinz was affable, interesting and passionate about American history; he cared about his country. But he was no fool. He recognised it had its faults, but always skilfully managed to counter Clem's Democrat ideals with the hard facts of life, deftly and sometimes annoyingly leading him back to a straight line of logic as he saw it. Kinz was a skilled negotiator and masterful debater and Clem soaked up his stories and political knowledge.

Senator Kinz was not just a politician, he was an academic who knew his American history back to front; above all, he fervently believed in the 'American Dream' - he always had. He told Clem that when he was younger this had led to some spirited arguments with his fellow college students and even his family, but he held true to his beliefs all his life. He believed that the American dream was almost Darwinian, that capitalism was a way of life as old as history of man, and although it had evolved beyond mere trading of clay pots, it was up to governments to control it. Clem always got the feeling that Kinz was not so much arguing with him, but trying to teach him the truth as he saw it.

Kinz said he was not an apologist for the chaos that American capitalism caused, but that inevitably it was all for the best, especially when viewed against the history and actions of other countries that had so appallingly failed their people. On the other hand, he was able to take a neutral viewpoint on some major issues, particularly where US interests had such a bad effect on Third World countries, or, to his enormous disappointment, the creation of financial behemoths that were beginning to creak at the seams.

Against Clem's statements about capitalist greed, he conceded that the position the US held in the world was indeed one of monopoly and self interest. But, he stubbornly contended this that was a price that had to be paid. Capitalism was like a giant house of cards that had to be continuously re-stacked to avoid a total collapse that would be in no one's interest. Then he would argue about the 'American Dream' again.

The most repetitive statement that Kinz made was that he believed in his heart that the DNA spiral that formed the American psyche, its very heartbeat, was the spirit of its people. People who, throughout history, had come to the country to work hard, be ingenious and push back boundaries. Along the way some of their peers would have been exploited, but equally their struggle to survive gave them character. It was indeed very Darwinian he had said, somewhat earnestly, but in the end the best plants push up to meet the sunshine – and that was the truth of it!

So, here he was, hung-over and a little light headed, receiving a message from his favourite senator. He had to listen to the message twice. Astonishingly, Clem was being offered a chance to put together a political video in which six teenagers, sons and daughters of US senators, would express their political views of the state of the nation, from the perspective of young people, prior to the upcoming presidential election. Kinz explained that it was to be frank and honest and would receive the widest distribution throughout the US in double quick time. Clem couldn't believe his ears and for a moment swore that he would never drink again. This was such a good opportunity to get into producing and directing films. He guessed that Kinz had chosen him because of his video skills and was excited beyond belief.

Kinz asked him to wipe the message from the telephone and he did so, making notes of where to go and what to pack.

He couldn't get out of the door fast enough.

Chapter Two

Senator Randolph Kinz stood in his library and reached out instinctively to touch some of his favourite books. This always made him feel good. He had a fine collection of work and had read all nine hundred and thirty four books. He knew where to turn to find his favourite passages in each of them. The smell of the cedar wood shelves made him want to close his eyes and drift back to his college days, where he could study and debate for as long as he wanted.

He swallowed another mouthful of single malt Scotch whisky and wondered whether it was his sagacity that kept bringing him back to his library to ponder on the fate of the country he loved or current events. Swirling the spirit around the crystal glass with his index finger, he pointed it at the shelves, talking to an imaginary bunch of college students.

"No, boys and girls, no! America has always had the ability to handle difficult situations and where necessary withdraw and reinvent itself. It's all here, read it yourselves," he said with a sweep of his arm along the line of books and he wobbled unsteadily on his feet.

It was too. There was every kind of failure and success and he had analysed them all: the Republicans of the early thirties, contemplating the ruins of the supposed Coolidge-Hoover prosperity, the Wall Street crash, the assassination of President Kennedy, Vietnam, the scandal of Watergate and the yearning that he had had in his heart for President Nixon to leave office – and he had damned well told him so. There were so many bad things to offset the many achievements and successes of his cherished America he thought that he had seen it all. But now things were getting even worse and this hurt him a lot.

Kinz was livid. He had worked in politics all his life, but had never seen such a crass and incompetent administration. Not since he had winced at the sound of car horns sounding outside the White House for the impeachment of Nixon had he felt so let down by politics. Just like Vietnam, American boys were still coming home in body bags from Iraq; just like Vietnam towns throughout the US were beginning to question the purpose of the war; just like Vietnam there were stories of American atrocities - in the minority of actions taken in warfare - occasioned by incompetence at the top or through frustration and stupidity by troops under too much pressure, overshadowing acts of bravery and kindness elsewhere. Only this time the majority of the American public seemed to believe all that was said to them by the administration.

There were few meaningful marches or protests. No one called for the Abu Grabe prison at Guantanemo Bay to close; few cared about the inmates held for years without proof of guilt or a fair trial; few cared about the dirty deals being done to redress the balance in world steel and oil production; and few cared about the unemployment that was now rife in large parts of the US as the economy faltered. Opposition from within government brave enough to blow whistles found themselves quickly removed from office or soiled by innuendo, whispering campaigns or scandal, facing years ahead to prove their innocence.

This was a world away from the content and spirit of the American Declaration of Independence that Kinz had ingrained on his very soul.

The US had the economy to worry about as well. Rising prices and unemployment fuelled unrest in poorer areas, but he was astounded that this was blamed on insurrection and outside influence. He couldn't believe how the US political 'spin' departments deftly exploited and controlled the media to court people fortunate to be unaffected by one crisis or another, whilst ignoring others. All the while, the press office created diversions to take the plebeians' minds off internal troubles.

9

Kinz sat in his leather wing-backed chair and fingered the file in front of him on the coffee table. He waited for his visitor with uncontrolled emotion. Today was special. Today he would make plans to wake up the American people and show them how muddled, selfish and easily led they had become. He would show them how they needed to take a good hard look at their famous Declaration of Independence, especially the Jefferson line, "....to secure these rights, Governments are instituted by men, deriving their just powers from the consent of the governed."

The American people needed to see for themselves just how little attention was paid to their consent to the actions of their government, led by a bad President: Jake Brannigan.

Kinz was a rich man and would spend as much as was needed to take the American people on a journey that would show them the truth.

Just then there was a knock at the door and Kinz's housekeeper put her head timidly around the door

"Senator Kinz, there's a Mr Quantock to see you, sir, shall I show him in?"

"Yes, Margaret, please do show him in and can we have a couple of cups of coffee my dear?" he replied with a smile. She nodded and a few minutes later showed him into the room.

Quantock was a senior man in a rather nondescript home security office of the FBI. Kinz was aware though that he had a distinguished past and had been a very good operator. It had come to his attention that he did not like the current administration; it was an unusual and unwise move, but he made contact with him socially. Kinz understood Quantock had no career to speak of. Circumstances made him the right man to use.

Quantock strode into the room. He was a tall, well built, but gangly man, square jawed and with dark well cut hair. His suit fitted immaculately, he wore a matching blue shirt and tie and his shoes shone. Here was a man of confidence and detail; he looked every inch the 'All American Male'.

"Senator Kinz, nice to see you again sir. What can I do for you?" he said, as he thrust out a strong hand.

Kinz shook his hand firmly and regarded him for a second before responding. Just then Margaret came in with the coffee and Kinz beckoned her to put the tray on the coffee table and leave. She did so as quietly as she had entered.

Quantock sat down. "Black no sugar," he said without being asked, as Kinz inclined a manicured hand towards the tray, "keeps me alert, sir!"

Kinz smiled and poured the coffee. Then he passed the cup and saucer to Quantock, poured his own coffee and let it cool whilst he got straight to the point. To emphasise the seriousness, he brought his hand down on the arm of his leather chair with a loud thump.

"Dan, if I may call you that, we have talked briefly outside the government environment and I know you to be a patriot; I also know your sad background. I want to give you a chance to do something exciting that will call on all your excellent skills and help our country to get out of these difficult times. I want you to help me to influence the next presidential election."

Quantock looked shocked and put his cup and saucer down.

Kinz leaned forward and touched his arm. "Let me explain. The fact of life is that I am a God-fearing American and loyal as you care to think. But both you and I know – and don't try to deny it Dan – that the president is an ass. If all the leaks are true from my military insiders, he will soon take us on another military adventure, we can all see it coming. He is set on personality politics to get himself re-elected, instead of dealing with the issues that currently threaten our way of life: unemployment, economic collapse and so on. Would you believe it, my contacts in the Oval Office tell me that if our problems do not get solved within a year then there might even

11

be talk of secession by some states? Can you really believe that? Dan, people are hurting, but tragically, those that aren't hurting cannot see what's going on and some of them will for sure vote the sonofabitch back into office. We can't have that. We just can't! Don't you agree?"

He sat back in his chair exhausted with his tirade and gripped the arms of his chair with his hands until the knuckles showed white.

Quantock regarded him carefully, but neither agreed or disagreed and said, inquiringly, "what did you have in mind sir?"

"Don't worry Dan, I'm not suggesting we assassinate him. I would like to hang him, but that is not my style I promise you. No, I want to put a scam in place that will force him to act stupidly, you know, the way he normally does, driven by personality rather than common sense." He paused, leaned forward and added, "Anyway, you didn't answer my question. Do you agree or not?"

This was a difficult situation to be in and Quantock felt ill at ease and didn't know what to say.

Kinz understood and continued. "Look, I know it's not easy. You feel that if you agree and tell me so then that's just plain treason. If you don't agree then it's still treason and you are duty bound to tell the president; of course I will deny everything. Anyway, he is likely to tell you that he already knows that I am a troublesome meddling old fool and take it with a pinch of salt. Nothing new there then!"

Quantock smiled at the offer of this 'get out of jail free' card. He had heard of Kinz's reputation for being cantankerous and yet persuasive in the extreme, but knew too just how much the old man was revered as a loyal American of the old political school - virtually the father of the Senate. He was clearly now intrigued – and it showed. Kinz sensed that he had won the day and went in for the kill.

"Dan, let's focus on a real good reason for you to help me shall we? Rumour has it that he sidelined you a while ago because of that, well, that incident. You owe him nothing other than the fact that, for better or worse, he is your President. But should you decide to leave here and inform him of my feelings you need to consider that he is unlikely to even grant you an audience to do so."

Quantock's expression hardened and he looked beyond Kinz's face and into space – this was no joke and he wasn't laughing.

Kinz continued, "Dan, let me say this again - you owe Brannigan nothing. Now then, I have a plan in this file." He pressed home his advantage by tapping a blue folder in front of him. "This will trigger all President Brannigan's worst characteristics. Don't worry, as I say it doesn't involve assassination, violence or intimidation. It's just an honest to goodness scam."

He paused for effect. Quantock's silence didn't bother him at all, the longer the man was silent the more chance he had of convincing him of his plan.

"I want the president to think that six young teenagers, the offspring of US senators have been kidnapped by Arab insurgents. They will of course be perfectly okay. The idea is to encourage them to agree to make a secret video to be screened immediately before the final days of the upcoming presidential election. It will be a kind of 'state of the nation' as seen through the eyes of young people. They will be told to write letters to their parents and these will be posted within twenty-four hours to let them know they are okay – only they will be withheld. The resulting parental worry, and remember they are all senators, will turn to fury and as the scene unfolds Brannigan's press office and his spin-doctors will swing into action. Clues will be discovered, implicating a middle-eastern plot, and knowing the voracious appetite of the president's press office for over egging detail, they'll make a lot out of it. It is as predictable as night follows day. I want this to take place during the next thirty days before the election."

Quantock broke his silence, "And then?" he said.

"He doesn't panic, that's not his style. But what he will do for sure is to make political capital out of the situation. I have studied him closely and I am sure that he will see that this is a situation that will have sufficient traction with voters to turn their heads towards him and away from the realities of everyday life – most of which I might add are down to his poor administration. I am confident that he will rattle his sabre and make several fiery speeches and when the nation is wound up tighter than a bowstring, the kids will show up with their political video asking what all the fuss is about. He will look stupid and he will have to reverse all his actions. My hope is that the young people will be seen to be the only ones worrying about the things that matter to us all, that is to say our problems at home and he will feel compelled to stand down as president. I have chosen the kids with care; they are smart and know their political onions! I want you to help me organise this Dan. I am giving you now," and he handed Quantock a small envelope, "a letter saying that I am the only one responsible. You will be in no danger whatsoever."

He paused for effect, "I'm in God's waiting room Dan, what need have I of worries about blame or guilt? What do you say?"

Quantock read the letter and it did indeed place the responsibility totally on Kinz's shoulders. He reached for an envelope on a coffee table next to his chair.

"Oh, and I thought that you might need a little something to help to make it all worth while – there will of course be a lot of work and this is a kind of, well, payment for a job that I know that you will do well!"

He passed Quantock an A5 envelope that felt heavy; inside were bundles of hundred dollar bills.

"Can I go away and read your file sir? I've listened carefully to what you said and regard you as one of America's leading loyal senators. I know that you would not do anything like this if it were not absolutely vital for the nation. I just want to study the modus operandi. Can I do that sir?" said Quantock.

Kinz regarded him with a smile. He had to trust him. It may lead to success or it may lead to a knock on the door from the FBI. He had to take the chance.

"You still haven't said whether or not you agree with my views, leaving aside the plan?" said Kinz.

Quantock automatically looked left and right. "For what it's worth sir, I totally agree with your summation. I have the same fears as you and feel just as frustrated. I am a cautious man sir. I just want to read your plan, and, to be honest, be real sure that there is no trail back to me. I'm sure you understand."

He weighed the envelope full of money as he spoke and at the same time tapped the blue folder in front of him.

Kinz regarded him with respect. "Take the file Dan. Read it. I have worked out every detail. There is a bank account with ample funds that can be used to fund the scam, but, oh, please always pay cash - what's left over you can have. I am a rich man with no one to give it to."

Quantock took the folder then stood up slowly.

"I'll be on my way Senator. This has been a very interesting conversation. I'll read the plan tonight. You will know by mid-day tomorrow whether or not it is flawed and my possible role, if at all. If it is not something that I feel I can undertake, then I will return it to you to shred, along with this money. I don't want what I cannot earn. We will then say nothing more about the proposal. If it has merit then you can rest assured, I will do the job."

He held out his hand and Kinz shook it hard. Then he left and Kinz turned to look out of the window. He was beaming. Quantock's reaction had been just what he wanted. The scam had to work – it just had to. Kinz reached for a bottle of single malt Scotch whisky and decided that he would eat out tonight.

Alice's hash house on Greenwich Street was an old fashioned coffee and eats place frequented since time immemorial by New York taxi drivers. Other people were welcome of course, but the raucous language, shouting, insults and general playful mayhem meant that they were unlikely to go there for a quiet doughnut and coffee. Alice had long since died. She founded the place in the nineteen thirties when the food was simple, in other words anything that came to hand and the coffee cheap and plentiful.

As the country's fortunes changed so did Alice's place. Most of her money went to charity when she died and a small business consortium now ran the infamous coffee and eats place. Her picture hung above the kitchen hatchway. The equipment was now state of the art and a wide range of drinks and foodstuff was served. The most important element though was the staff – as always – and they bantered and controlled the unruly clientele with the skill and humour. In the current political climate their skills were needed more than ever.

But today was unusual. It seemed as though everyone had got out of bed the wrong way. The waitresses were quiet and grumpy and the customers were more argumentative than usual.

Two Hispanic taxi drivers argued about whether President Brannigan was of Irish or Spanish descent. This irritated a table nearby who thought that there were more important things to worry about. A large fat truck driver sat by the doorway. He always ate lunch at Alice's and was renowned for his double portions. Today he was in early and his table was crowded with what looked like a bucket of coffee and a dustbin of doughnuts each one despatched in only two bites.

The noisiest area was in front of the television, which was perched precariously on a kind of cantilevered shelf, placed in the corner of the dining area. A large contingent of taxi drivers, about eight in all, sat yelling at the screen. The subject was not a ball game, but politics. A female reporter dressed in a smart day suit, was outlining the situation in Philadelphia where steelworkers had been laid off yet again. Her voice was shrill and her smile out of place in the circumstances. It was part of a political documentary that included similar scenes from other parts of the country, such as Pittsburgh and Ohio. But this was a particularly harrowing report of hopelessness in the face of economics. Workers interviewed were critical of the government and in particular the increasing lack of welfare and medical support. One man said he would've been better off in China and was thinking of emigrating and this caused the taxi drivers to laugh for the first time that morning and yell even more.

"Hey, Donna, turn up the goddamned sound I can't hear the lies clear enough!" said the fat man.

Everyone laughed again.

"Yeah, y'know what, I heard that the president has said he's gonna start telling the truth. He says it's easier than having to try and remember what he said the last time!"

The diners laughed some more, but this time the tone was ugly.

Donna the supervisor obliged and turned up the volume using the television remote control. She noticed the anger in their humour and was glad of the jokes that lightened the mood a little.

It wasn't to last.

The television scene switched to presidential spokesperson, another young and attractive girl clutching a clipboard, better suited to auditioning for a movie than political journalism. She explained the temporary blip in world trade and said that the government was doing all it could. Things would get better. It might have worked had she not given a simpering and patronising smile. That was enough for one of the taxi drivers. He threw a doughnut at the screen and it bounced off leaving a smear of jam not unlike a trail of blood.

Donna shouted, "Hey Mikey, that ain't nice, I gotta clean it all off now, ya jerk. Give me a break huh?"

The mood was changing and the men yelled abuse at the female figure on the television newsreel, who was drivelling on about balanced economies the changing world environment with cheap imports from China and India. Then she made a big mistake. She had been briefed to suggest that the unrest was an unwelcome addition to the nation's problems, particularly in the Middle East, but instead exceeded her brief and blamed it on trade union and political agitators.

This was too much for the fat man by the door. His face reddened and he stood up, visibly shaking and pointed at the television. He was a member of the Teamster Union and well aware that Social Security, the minimum wage and other things dear to unions were under threat from Republicans in Washington; he was rough, but not stupid. Past promises of a bright future had seduced men away from union membership and now look where they were.

"Goddamned prissy whore, what does she know about real life!"

For a brief moment there was silence.

"My kid brother came back from Iraq last year in a body bag. My sister's husband has been outta work for ten months and the kids are sick. I may lose my job soon because fuel's costin' a fortune and all she does is to blame imports from China and the unions. What the hell does she know about life, she's only a damned schoolgirl? Stoopid bitch!"

He screamed and threw more doughnuts at the screen.

The other diners were now just as mad and his words and actions inflamed the situation. Many of them were in a similar precarious situation regarding future employment or the fate of their businesses and this touched a raw nerve. It was as much as they could take. They too threw food at the television and screamed ugly abuse. The waitresses fled behind the counter. A couple of decent men tried to urge calm and they were punched to the ground. Then all hell broke lose. Some men fought and others simply vented their rage by breaking furniture and windows.

The fat man tipped over his table and screamed like a mad man. There were sparks of electricity as lights were ripped from walls and the television exploded as a coffee jug hit it square in the middle of the screen bringing the presidential spokeswoman's platitudes to an explosive end. An enormous cheer filled the room. The waitresses retreated even further into the kitchen area and Donna hurriedly telephoned the police.

An hour later several police cars with their blue lights blinking sat outside Alice's. A dozen men were standing handcuffed in the park lot looking unashamed and angry, as though it was all right to trash a diner and they were being punished for nothing. Ambulance medics, tended to the wounds of the guilty as well as the blameless. People stood and stared at the damage and were speechless that such a thing should happen.

On his way home back to Washington from a meeting, Dan Quantock, FBI, stopped to see what all the fuss was about. He parked his car, showed his pass to a policeman and stood watching the television and radio film crews interviewing local people. After a few minutes he had heard enough.

He wondered just how many other Americans would trash their workplace or leisure facilities like this, in the face of frustration and anger about their lot in life. Were things really this bad? If the US administration didn't do something and quickly, the nation would surely end up in melt down?

Once that started, it would take an awful lot of stopping.

Chapter Three

Fred Spiker, the US Chief of Staff walked slowly down the long corridor from the far right of the White House towards the Oval Office. The carpet felt soft underfoot and the air was scented from the recent attention of the housekeeping staff. Several people recognised him instantly and smiled and bade him good morning. He was a popular man. Everyone knew that he had been personally selected by President Brannigan and that it was difficult to dent his loyalty. Spiker was good at dealing with the hoary apparatus of the party. He was an affable man who charmed all those whom he met. Brannigan had chosen well.

Spiker did not relish today's conversation with the president. Most of the state business had been concluded in earlier meetings, but he had indicated, perhaps more forcibly than usual, that he needed to discuss several other matters of a sensitive nature. But would the president listen? It was unlikely, he thought, but he had to try. Despite Spiker's ability and experience gained in the pharmaceutical industry and many non-executive director positions, he found Brannigan particularly difficult to deal with. He was a bully, there was no doubt about that, but like most bullies once you get used to them you cope or fight back. In Brannigan's case it was difficult because he simply never fully listened and asked such stupid questions. Right from his junior days, Spiker had always hated briefing superiors who asked questions that moved the debate so far out of the mainstream and into such remote pools of stupidity that all hope is lost in attempting to reach any sensible conclusion. Like legions of others in similar situations in commercial and government life, the only way to combat this was to be blunt and highlight the foolishness in such comments – but then no one would dare do that to Brannigan.

He closed in on the office door and whilst the president's personal assistant went into the office to announce him he breathed deeply, as he always did, and visualised Brannigan small and weak sitting in a large chair ready to be told what to do by Spiker. Then he entered the office and as he did so he saw the man and the image immediately disintegrated in his mind – so much for visualisation!

Brannigan barked, "Fred, come in and sit down. Now what are these issues you wanted to discuss with me? I need you to be quick now, I've got a delegation from the Democrats who want to moan about this and that."

Spiker took another breath and positioned his thoughts before he began.

"Mr President, thank you for your time, sir. I'll be blunt. I am concerned over some issues and, it has to be said, some others in the Republican Party are too."

He paused and Brannigan absentmindedly grabbed a cigar as he always did in such situations. As expected, he concentrated on treating the cigar to the usual protocols, as Spiker was about to speak. It was a disarming ritual and would continue throughout briefings or discussions that Brannigan did not want to particularly focus on. The effect of this lack of attention was always to dispirit the other person and put them off guard. It rarely failed.

Nonetheless, Spiker was an old hand and concentrated hard.

"Firstly, it's the religious issue sir, you know full well that it is causing some anxiety, we, well, we're being accused and I believe understandably, as being a party of white Christians."

It was a new tactic. He paused for effect instead of letting his voice trail off or to try a push on with a detailed description of the issue.

"What do you mean, Fred? Now don't tell me that people don't want me to talk to the Catholic League, the Baptists, Seventh Day Adventists and the like," he blew out rings of smoke from his newly lit cigar, "we get a chunk o' votes from these guys Fred, millions in fact. Many of our policies have survived as a result, including my presidency."

Spiker was ready. "Yes, I know Mr President, but they punch with greater weight than they ought. In fact, it has been evident that several issues, in addition to the abortion and gay rights topics, have been eased through the Senate. People are beginning to criticise this administration for creating a kind of theocracy and some in political circles are saying that the religious lobby is now horse trading rather than lobbying. Sir, they're playing the parties against each other and their appeal to their respective congregations means that they have the upper hand. That's a serious charge sir, and one we need to either rebut or, well, or do something about. Sir."

The word, 'sir', weakly fell off the end of the sentence.

Brannigan, held the smoke in his mouth for a long time then let it out slowly.

"Fred, Fred, my main man. If we were Democrats we would rely on the votes from the unions, so where's the problem with the religious vote? We're all God fearing Americans, aren't we? Frankly, I think you're reading too much into this."

Then he added, as if to catch Spiker out, "And anyway, just who is doing all this talking?"

"I don't think that's the issue, Sir. Look, it's plain and simple. The majority of those who would damage your chances are making hay on this and it's feeding your political enemies. I can walk away from this – if it was the only thing I had to worry about."

Brannigan growled at the innuendo in Spiker's comments.

"What other stuff then Fred?" he said, holding his cigar like a dart and pointing it straight at Spiker.

Spiker dug deep and brought out another hoary old chestnut.

"The economy is doing badly, Sir. Unemployment is rising especially in areas of manufacturing where there is enormous pressure from Asia. The rot started when the South Koreans sold a steel plant to the Indians, then the Chinese bid for and won one, as well as two more major oil companies together with their drilling rights in the Pacific. The space programme has been shelved and jobs are going there too, despite promises Republicans made a few years back about men on the moon. We also have the ongoing saga of Iraq which promises to be a second Vietnam."

"Get to the damned point Fred!" barked the president.

For once, Spiker hit back and he stood up to make his point.

"Okay then. Given all this strife and the administration's courting of the religious lobby, the working man feels left out of government. You remember that bit, "by the people, of the people" and so on? Well, our researchers tell us that many people feel disenfranchised."

Spiker struggled to keep his voice calm, and continued, "Put simply, sir, the people are fed up, now they are fed up with being fed up. There are other consequences too. It has allowed the hate groups, and by the way sir, you know we have almost three hundred in the US, to have a field day? There is positive evidence that they are recruiting dissenters like mad. More worryingly, our old friends the secessionists of South Carolina are at it again. They preach secession from a federal government that doesn't listen and is robbing them blind in taxes. Bleeding the federal states to pay for the President's mistakes is what they are saying. Sir, before you tell me this is all baloney, I want you to read these reports from the FBI."

He carefully slid the folder across the shiny table towards Brannigan. "You are not a Roman Emperor, Sir," he said emphasising the word, *Sir,* "you have the facility to obtain good intelligence and be forewarned. We have an efficient political field organisation bequeathed to us by your predecessor, so we should use it to be more proactive than just replicating spin from the Oval Office. There is no reason why we can't deal with this, but we must do so as a team. We need to tackle the religious issue, the economy, including our energy needs, medi-care and the emergence of the Asian market. And we need to tell people we are doing it now. That's it – period. Now I know that this is not what you want to hear and I for one am not prepared to suffer your ire just because I am being loyal. So I will take my leave and, well, I'll catch up with you later, *Sir*."

Without waiting for a reply Spiker turned away from the president, who was by now frowning and stubbing out his cigar, and he left the office.

Brannigan read the content of the file, turning the pages slowly, skim reading instead of taking in all the information carefully. There were speeches and rallies in promotion of secession with the Confederate flag much in evidence. On all the occasions in the report the venues were inconspicuous, fairgrounds, barbecues or college balls, but the reported air of rebellion was in the air. He read the list of rabble-rousers and recognised half the names as being, as one of his predecessors termed it, loony tunes. The trouble with loony tunes is that they eventually play a melody that everyone listens to. He closed the file with a flourish and pushed it to the centre of the desk.

The veins stood out on his forehead and neck and he drummed his fingers.

Then without using the intercom he yelled, "Alice, get me Sadie Burrows, now…!"

Ralph Anderson and Martin Adams sat in a New York bar watching two girls dressed only in thongs revolve around poles that reached from floor to ceiling. Neon lights flashed and mirrors showed the girl's images from several different angles. About twenty men sat around the stage at small tables and shouted enthusiastically at the girls.

Ralph and Martin's table was littered with glasses and bottles, evidence of a night spent on a real 'bender'. Although they joked and kidded each other they were a little subdued. Their last assignment in Chile had been a real mess. It was their fault; no one else's and they knew that. But it didn't make it any easier to swallow.

The mission had been simple enough: get to ex-Army Colonel Gonzales Zamora, now in his early seventies, and stop him from going public about US intervention in Chile back in the 1970s. He had been General Pinochet's aide de camp and as such had been privy to the machinations, which led to the overthrow of President Allende's socialist government. Although this unsavoury episode was well known it was now largely forgotten; what was known, was subject to 'controlled information'. Zamora had developed a conscience, having spent considerable sums of US dollars, and was about to become a thorn in the American 'politically correct under-belly.' He had been side-lined and funded for years to keep him out of trouble, but had now taken religion and wanted to reveal all before he arrived at the 'pearly gates'. Rumour had it that he was about to name names in the current US administration; those who had a key role in the overthrow of President Allende of Chile and the instatement of General Pinochet in his place.

The US government simply did not want any more information to leak out and cause embarrassment. They wanted the situation dead and buried – and that went for Zamora too.

Martin and Ralph had been chosen for the task of eliminating Zamora because they were good at their job. They worked on the margins of the CIA, not in mainstream work, doing the really dirty work that no one else wanted to do. They were not quite official agents and yet were paid by the CIA none-the-less.

They were intelligent, but rough, and often lawless, convinced their membership of this elite club gave them a 'licence to kill'. But they got the job done and that was what was needed. Quick work and no untidy audit trails.

The plan had been straightforward. Enter Zamora's house, smother him and make it look like a heart attack. But Ralph's newly acquired drug habit made him sloppy. His attention to detail, especially timing, was poor and no sooner had the evil deed been done than the house-keeper and nurse arrived back to discover the agents at work.

There was no option but to strangle the women. Then they panicked and called up their overseas agency and asked for 'cleaners' urgently. These people could be relied upon to clean up any situation wherever and whatever without delay and leaving no clues whatsoever. They did what needed to be done then melted away without further contact or reference to anyone.

The housekeeper's body was placed in bed with Zamora's and the nurse's body in her own bed. Then, after making adjustments to the butane gas tank controls the house was set alight. It worked and the Chilean coroner recorded 'death by misadventure' on all three of them. Only Zamora's physician expressed surprise, especially at the antics of a man in his eighties with no prostate in bed with his housekeeper. Apart from this lone voice the mission was judged a success – but only just!

Agents Adams and Anderson had been suspended by an embarrassed and irate Head of the CIA, but some said it was on Brannigan's direct orders. It was one close call too many for a new US President keen to keep his credentials untainted.

Ralph turned his gaze from the pole dancers and looked at Martin through bleary eyes and said, "Who does the Godamned dirty work buddy? Tell me that man? Go on buddy just you tell me?"

Martin regarded his friend through less bleary eyes and said, "Well, heck we do Ralphy baby, we do. Don't you worry buddy we'll soon be on the up – we stick together don't we?"

Ralph slapped his friend on the shoulder and said, "Sure we do, sure thing!" Then he reached into his inside jacket pocket and pulled out an oblong shaped silver box. It was what he called his Coke Kit. He opened it and took out a packet of white powder, sprinkled it on the glass table and then moved the powder into lines using a razor blade from the box. He rolled a ten-dollar bill into a tube and snorted the cocaine. When he had finished he sat back and looked at the ceiling – he was in a different world. His body filled with beautiful euphoria and he floated through wavy clouds. It was the best feeling in the world.

Martin regarded him with amusement. After about fifteen minutes he said, "For Chris' sake man, you'll have no nostrils left in ten years," and he laughed. "If our esteemed masters knew you were a coke addict there would certainly be no way back, sideways or forwards or what," he failed to finish the sentence in any sensible form, lifting a bottle of beer to his lips. He swallowed half of it in one go.

Ralph looked angry and said, "Aw, shit, slack off man. What kinda job have we gotten into anyway?" He sneezed. "That FBI guy, who wants to be called Mr No-Name, more likes no-balls if you ask me. Anyway, who cares?" He then sat back in his chair and contemplated the ceiling again. The music thumped out a repetitive tune and the girls twirled round the poles, coloured lights playing on their bodies.

Martin knew Ralph was as high as a kite and if he told him to go and tango with a tiger he would. It was becoming more difficult being his buddy, but hell, what else was there in life? All the same, he pondered on what Ralph had said. They had for sure gotten themselves a really boring baby sitting job, with a lot of preparatory work beforehand. Mr No-Name had told him the senator who was planning it: Senator Randolph Kinz. Apparently, this man was not afraid of owning the strange programme. That intrigued Martin a lot. It was really very odd indeed and somehow it didn't feel right. His previous jobs had rarely had any identified owner of a project, either as a person or a department. But it was better than nothing and it did get them out of the spotlight of the Chile fiasco. It was also clean and tidy and very well paid - he could do with some of that.

Ralph swayed left and right then sat up straight staring at one of the pole dancers who had just finished wrapping herself around a pole. She was dressed only in a soft leather pink thong. He beckoned her over. The house-style was that the girls would dance for the punters and they would in turn put dollar bills in the edges of the thongs. They would then withdraw to their dressing rooms and the show goes on.

Ralph took out his wallet and Martin had to stop him taking out several bills instead of just one.

"Hey honey, you want some dough, here look lots of dollars, c'mon, let's put it in your thongy thing eh?" and he smiled like an imbecile.

Unwisely she proffered her hip for the money. Ralph placed the note carefully inside and blew her a kiss.

"Want some more honey?" He said, proffering his open wallet.

She stayed where she was and pouted at him. Then he took out another ten-dollar bill and put that in the front of her thong. Only this time he hooked his index finger tightly around the thong strap. She was trapped. This man was obviously as high as a kite and unpredictable, and she could neither retire nor was it safe to stay.

"You can go honey, but leave this iddy biddy thing. With my dollar bills I damn near bought the factory that made it. Go on you can go now." He laughed out loud at her predicament.

"Please sir, I have to go now. Let go please?" she said and pulled away from him. But his grip was secure and it only served to pull her costume away from her body. This delighted the other punters who urged Ralph on. The dancer looked for the bouncers, but to her horror they were at the far end of the hall talking to some troublemakers. Ralph began to pull harder and the thong became contorted as they both tugged at it. He fixed the girl with a glazed look.

"Honey, I just want my money's worth. Now what do you think twenty dollars is worth?"

"At least a peek!" shouted some men from a nearby table.

Martin laughed, but kept a close eye on his friend, uncertain as to his next move.

Ralph smiled like an imbecile. "See now honey, these boys here are not stupid! I've been watchin' you intently. I wanna know – are you a natural blonde?" and he laughed, so did the other men.

Sensing what was coming the girl squirmed and pleaded again, "Sir don't be silly, let me go please?"

"Aw, c'mon, give old Ralphey a peek at yer beaver then I promise to go home like a good boy."

He began to pull the thong away from her body. It was made of strong stuff and didn't break. She wriggled some more and before she knew it they were both engaged in a tug of war with the small thong, which by now covered almost nothing at all. From that moment all dignity was lost and they both pulled like mad, she to keep the thong and Ralph to remove it.

By now the audience was yelling support and Ralph was in his element. Only extreme fits of cocaine-induced giggles prevented the girl from losing the battle.

"Just a peek honey, just a peek?" Ralph said through gasps of laughter. Then he added to a cheering audience, "Hey boys, just what I thought, the dame's a red-head!"

The audience howled with laughter and hooted support for Ralph's efforts. The dancer screamed and at last the bouncers saw what was happening and rushed over. Ralph felt a sudden bang on the back of his head and the world went grey. The dancer, freed from Ralph's oafishness, rushed to her dressing room crying. His head buzzed like a thousand ringing bells and through the numbness of the sound he heard Martin's voice.

"Whoa boys, just a misunderstanding and a little excitement. Here's a little something on account," and he threw down a handful of dollar bills on the table, "my friend here has been under a lot of strain and anyway he ain't so smart. I'll just take him home to sober up and he'll be back in the mornin' to apologise. We'll just go now eh?"

The bouncers picked up the money and signalled for them both to leave. Martin had no doubt that to refuse would lead to a severe beating. He half dragged the slightly unconscious, but babbling, laughing Ralph out of the bar. The fresh air hit them both like a steam train. Ralph regained consciousness almost immediately and he shook his head.

Eventually a taxi stopped for them and they fell into the back.

Martin sat back and turned to Ralph and said seriously, "Hey buddy, you're a bad boy. I'm always havin' to dig you outta situations! You and your damned cocaine and sexual curiosity!"

He didn't know whether to laugh or get mad. Years of experience as Ralph's friend and co-worker had taught him that neither option worked.

Ralph looked at him through bleary eyes and just smiled. Then he said, "Yeah man, you're right," he started to giggle hysterically again, " 'n y'know what? I lied man. To my bestest buddy damned I lied. She weren't no Godamned red-head man. Y'know that?"

Martin looked perplexed.

Ralph stopped giggling, just about catching his breath.

"She weren't no red-head at all. She shaved man – she shaved!"

They both burst into uncontrollable laughter.

Dan Quantock got back to his office and poured a large black coffee from a pot that was simmering on his side table. He was fazed by the hash-house incident earlier in the day and it made him think long and hard about the 'Plan'. He liked and respected Kinz, everyone did, but thought him a kind of 'Mary Poppins' Senator. He was not in the real world, like Quantock, who had to shuffle human cards into some kind of playable hand, dealing with winners and losers, but most of all understanding that politics is a game and like cards relies of a deal of luck. But, he was right about a lot of things. The country was in a parlous state and more importantly, everyone who worked on Capitol Hill despaired of Brannigan's antics. The trouble was, like all despots he was crafty and fleet of foot, he had his coterie and was watertight when it came to batting off criticism – someone else was always to blame. And as far as party politics was concerned, you were either inside or outside – nothing in between. Quantock used to think about the interests of the nation, but now, well, heck, he thought only of himself. Why not?

The US was taking on a sadly dysfunctional form, with political and economic strife at home and worrying involvement in spats outside its borders. All of which was tainted by US interest in oil and a neurotic fear of nascent Asian economies with their cheap labour and endless supply of raw materials. Funny old thing – but when other players hold better poker hands than you it makes sense to make friends not blow them out of the water! Secondly, US capitalism was unused to subtlety and there were no current plans that intelligently addressed the challenge; only talk of protectionism, cartels and political chicanery.

Quantock didn't really give a damn. It was true that he did hold a grudge against Brannigan but he also wanted a bit more excitement in his life. Being on the 'outside' of the action as he had been forced to be for a number of years now, was boring. Kinz's plan was a bit whacky, but what intrigued him was the way that the old boy had plotted everything in such clear and precise detail. Every part of the plan was outlined in the brief and he could find no flaws. All he had to do was make arrangements. Everything was funded and all dealings, except the one bank account that Quantock would operate, were to be in cash. Importantly, nothing at all would be traceable back to him and Kinz would even provide a letter owning up to be the person responsible for the actions. It seemed foolproof. He trusted Kinz, even if he didn't trust anyone else.

Quantock went over the details in his mind, again and again. It all seemed so clear. After a while he daydreamed of the fall of President Brannigan. He disliked this man more than anything else. Bringing Brannigan down satisfied his soul and might even do immense good for the nation. That was quite a deal - he may get some cash, some kudos and an even better job in the end.

He decided that he would go ahead and informed a delighted Kinz who sent him more money and details of a bank account that he could use. As luck would have it a CIA colleague had told him about the plight of two 'bozos' as he described them, who had recently got themselves into a spot of bother. They didn't know what to do with them and wanted them out of sight for a while. Kinz's plan needed two 'baby-sitters' and these boys fitted the bill.

It didn't take long to use his Ivy League connections and, after spinning them a story, arrange a meeting with two men called Martin Anderson and Ralph Adams; they sounded like a comedy duo. That was not however what their records showed. They were men who were able to mete out violence to order as part of their work, without conscience or concern and as such worked on the margins of acceptability in the CIA. They had a reputation for being loose cannons, but were regarded as highly intelligent, if a little weird. The screw up in South America had been a rare one off event. Unfortunately, in the CIA you don't get too many chances.

After meeting the pair of them and introducing himself as 'Mr No-Name', he saw what his friend had meant about them being 'a little strange'. Unfortunately, he let his disdain show and they regarded each other with mild hostility as he outlined the project. It was 'take it or leave it' with the emphasis on 'take it'. The large amounts of cash kept them smiling and they canned their mutual suspicions.

Quantock gave them their plans and cash to do the preparation and operational work, and allow sufficient for themselves. He also let them have a cell phone and a number to call in an emergency or to provide feedback on the progress of the mission.

All they had to do was to follow the plan.

Dulles airport was bright and cloudless and rang with the whooping and yelling of six teenagers as they greeted each other in various ways. JoAnne Dempster, blonde and bubbly, screeched and kissed everyone, including a surprised but nevertheless delighted bystander waiting for a pick up truck. Her ample figure was exaggerated by a tight fitting white blouse and blue stretch pants. Matt Dawson, tall and gangly in baggy clothes, wearing a baseball cap on back to front, was reserved and quiet, but he beamed at the sight of Clem, his old summer camp buddy. Jon Masters a ginger headed bright faced young man kidded around and kept saying to everyone, "Hey, look at you!" when confronted by a friend some six to nine months older than when he had last seen them. He was a handsome young boy and knew it. Dressed like the Midnight Cowboy in jeans, hide jacket and a flamboyant cowboy hat, he had a way of sauntering rather than walking. Only Walt Danberry remained reserved and aloof. He had always been the bookish, philosophical type, given to smart remarks at someone else's expense; he knew everything, or at least that was what he believed. He was old for his age and his round face, brown bushy hair and dark rimmed spectacles set him apart from his friends.

Walt turned to the others and with the kind of pomposity his friends were used to, said, "Hi guys. This is quite a group and quite a project. I'm real glad I was chosen, because I have a great deal to offer."

Then he turned to Matt, smiled sarcastically and said, "Boy, you must have improved your political science grades a lot Matt?"

Matt smiled slowly. "No idea what you're talking about Walt? My grades were so good I had lots of time to spend in the out-field."

Walt smiled patronisingly and Clem stepped in just like he used to do at summer camp. "Hey guys, let's go see the tour guides over there?"

He pointed to two men dressed in black T-shirts and jeans leaning against the front of a small shabby looking coach. The men saw them coming around the side and came to meet them. The taller of the two smiled broadly.

"Hi there. My name is Martin Adams and this is my partner Ralph Anderson." They exchanged names and handshakes with the teenagers and waited for them to calm down.

"Look guys, we need to talk before we set off," said Martin, "you need to stack your gear in the rear of the coach first of all. Before you do that, and this is important, give Ralph the letters you were instructed to write to your folks. He will take 'em to the airport post office and post them to a contact who will make sure they get sent out after twenty-four hours. We don't want mom and pop getting worried about you! We are in for a long journey, about two or three days in all."

There was a low groan from the teenagers and he smiled and continued, "But it will be worth it. When you get to where we are going – top secret I'm afraid so don't ask – you will find good quarters and very good sound and vision equipment to make the video show. I know the equipment is good guys, I bought it myself!"

He handed some pictures of the equipment to Clem who yelped with delight, not wanting to let them leave his hands as his friends clamoured to take a look. Martin continued, "One more thing guys, hand over your cell phones please." There was another low groan. "Yeah, I know, it's a pain, just like school huh? But it is essential that there are no mistakes or contact with the outside world. This way we remove all temptation. I'm sure you understand that the operation must not, repeat not be compromised. If that happens then, well, we may as well all just go home, end of story. Okay?"

The teenagers obediently did as they were told and the second man, Ralph, collected all the cell phones, and then nonchalantly waved an arm at the airport car park. "Say goodbye to all contact with the rest of the world guys!" They got onto the coach and after it stopped briefly to allow Ralph to post the letters to the parents and return, settled in for the long journey. Only Walt tried to get more information out of Ralph and he was curtly reminded that he would be briefed fully a lot later, but until that happened he should not ask again. Walt just smiled in his patronising way, which rattled Ralph, who made his mind up not to like the snot nosed academic. For his part, Ralph smiled inwardly as he tapped his jacket in which the letters to the parents remained.

The coach drove smoothly out of the airport complex and navigated the mid morning traffic with ease. After a while they were soon just outside Washington on the Interstate Highway 81 heading Southwest then drove on past Front Royal, Harrisonburg and Staunton, Virginia. Just after a junction where Highway 60 connects, the coach took a left down a minor road.

After about four hours total driving since leaving Dulles airport the coach stopped at the rear of a car park to a gas station and store just outside the town of Lynchburg. They welcomed the break, but Martin made an unusual appeal.

"Look guys, I know you could probably do with a break, but we need to keep our route as secret as possible. I know it sounds kinda crazy. The idea is that no one should know where you are going, not even your parents, and we don't want anyone who might know you to spot you by chance and spill the beans. The work needs to be carried out speedily and without any interference, so we need to stay out of the public eye. I chose this car park because there is a women's and men's bathroom out back."

Martin pointed to the rear of the gas station car park. "Now it ain't very pretty, but if you're bursting for a pee I guess that it's the best sight in the world!"

The teenagers laughed.

He continued, "So, please get out quick, jettison fuel and get back on board the coach beside us, not this one. Don't ask questions now, let's go, as quickly as you can if you please! This is your tour guide speaking!"

They murmured their acceptance, one or two claiming to be bursting and beyond care. Walt added, "A secret pee station, well, what do you know!"

Ralph was beginning to dislike him; Martin noticed this and felt very uneasy; he touched his arm and said, "Cool, man, cool!" Then he changed the subject adding, "Good job on the coach buddy where'd'you pick it up?"

Ralph smiled wryly and went along with the change of direction. "Yeah, not bad at all. Twenty thousand dollars. I bought it in Kankakee, Illinois and got some replacement plates, two sets in fact. It's a fourteen-seat Chevrolet with a Collins body. The six point five litre diesel engine is automatic, of course, and should be easy for us to drive with, say, three hour shifts. We'll get about five hundred and fifty miles at least for each tank of fuel. That makes, let me see, about ten hours motoring, meaning," and he reached into his top pocket for a piece of paper which he peered at, "let's see, meaning about four stops over about two to three days tops. It has some nice extras like a decent radio and air conditioning. It's gonna be a long trip! I really can't wait to get to the 'baby sitting centre'."

He shrugged his shoulders and then gathered his wits. He had a job to do and needed to get on with it. Just as the kids reached the washrooms he shouted after them, "What do you say to case of cool Cokes, guys?"

They all smiled and gave him thumbs up. Ralph watched them go into the rest rooms, turned to Martin smiled and pulled a scowling face. Martin thumped his shoulder and said, "Go do your thing, buddy!"

Then Ralph hunched his shoulders and deliberately shuffled towards the front of the drug store. He was a swarthy man, with black hair and moustache. His name, Anderson, came from his American father and his dark sharp features from his Turkish mother. Unsurprisingly, to an American public worried by the threat of terrorism for almost a decade, the customers in the filling station store viewed a man with middle-eastern appearance and strange mannerisms with considerable suspicion.

He went to the soft drinks machine and stood peering at the writing, pretending not to understand it. In his hands he held a set of prayer beads and fiddled with them constantly, mumbling to himself as he did so.

"Water, water?" He said aggressively with a thick accent.

A large middle aged woman dressed in a blue gingham dress sitting on a chair in the corner of the store, grimaced, turned towards him and said, "Behind the counter, boy, the counter, over there!" She gestured towards a small queue of people being served by a girl with hair piled up and a face full of cheap make-up.

Ralph kicked the machine hard and it rattled loudly. The people in the store turned round and looked at him. He glared at them, and then shuffled towards the stack of mineral water bottles covered in cling film. He picked up two packs and walked towards the front of the counter, ignoring the line. As he did so, a large young man, wearing a NYC T-shirt and a baseball hat moved out of the line to block his way.

"Say buddy, get in line?" said the young man.

But as he raised his arm Ralph came up close and before he could defend himself he was head-butted. The young man fell backwards with his face covered in blood from his bleeding nose and the people around him screamed. Without further ado Ralph muttered something unintelligible, drew some dollar bills out of his pocket and after waving them around he selected a fifty-dollar bill and threw it on the counter.

Then he strode out of the store. As he did so he smiled, laughed and thought to himself, "Today, American theatre in Lynchburg, tomorrow Shakespeare in London town, you Oscar winning actor you!"

Martin was just finished helping Clem and Matt move the bags to the more modern second coach. When all the bags were removed except JoAnne's, Martin told Clem to settle the kids down. As Clem walked away, Martin looked both ways then; sure that he was not seen, he threw an old thumbed Arabic copy of the Koran under one of the seats.

Ginny and JoAnne came up to him and enquired about their bags and Martin seemed perplexed, "I think we have them all?" he said.

"Hell no, sir, there's mine!" said JoAnne, and she hopped onto the coach, grabbed her rucksack and threw it to Martin. He caught it quickly and put it down. Then he held out his hand to her as she got out of the coach.

JoAnne said, "Well thank you Mr Tour Guide!" took his hand and stepped down.

As she did so she yelped in pain, "Ouch, what was that?"

There was a small cut on her hand that was bleeding.

"Oh Jeez, I'm so sorry. I had my sorority ring fixed the other day and it has a rough edge, it must have cut you. Can I get you a Band-Aid?"

"Hell, no," JoAnne said, "it's only a small cut and no problem I have some in my pack." Then she put her finger in her mouth, picked up her rucksack and headed for the other coach.

Martin waited until he was alone then, unseen, wiped the blood off his finger and on to the seat nearest the coach door; there was enough to leave a mark. Then he joined the others who had by now found spaces in the second coach.

A few minutes later Ralph came round the corner, this time head up and smiling, not the shuffling suspicious character he had seemed a few minutes ago. He got into the driver's seat, threw the packs of water bottles onto the seat beside him then switched on the engine, revved it up and turned to the passengers.

"Hell, guys, you know what? The people around here are just about the most unfriendly I have ever seen in my entire life! You better believe it! Maybe this is a kind of 'X' Files set?"

He looked around with a mock-frightened face, "Say, the place may be full of gooks and ghosties, who eat strangers alive, oooooer!" Then he turned and looked over his shoulder, "Oh no, my God, here they come!"

As Ralph said that, he gunned the coach forward, it skidded around the edge of the drug store, spraying stones and a lot of dust everywhere, some of the stones and grit shot trough the air and hit the store window with loud cracks. Then, partly out of surprise and partly because they were rising to his jibes about ghosties, the girls screamed and the boys let out yells and they were forced down or off their seats by the swerving of the coach.

Unknown to the teenagers, the shoppers in the store, already upset by the violence, heard the sound of the speeding coach and screams of the passengers. A woman standing by the window put her hand to her mouth and, as she tried to peer through the clouds of dust, said quietly to herself, "Oh, my, dear, my!"

Ralph smiled as they drove away, first due south on Highway 29, then, to shake off any possible chasers he picked his way through small roads via Eden and Christiansburg back onto the Interstate 81. A scene of violence and suspicion had been created that would provide sufficient grist for the press mill.

He smiled. It was a job well done!

The teenagers were breathless with laughter in the back of the coach. After a bit more joking and moving around of bags and coats to the spare seats they settled back for a long journey. Matt and Walt sat alone, with Jon and JoAnne, and Clem and Ginny side by side. They left the two front rows empty for Martin and Ralph. The second coach was much more comfortable and had air-conditioning. At least their bottoms didn't slip and slide on cheap plastic seat covers and the seats were padded. A small foldable armrest made for a more snug fit. In the back of the coach they could see a supply of blankets and pillows. Ralph switched on the radio and selected

Megarock Kicking Country on 105.7 FM, the name amused him; it was the kind of foot tapping music that made everyone feel energised – even if it wasn't quite their style. He yelled at them to look into a brown box, which contained some cookies and doughnuts. They fell around laughing as they wrestled to get to the box. Ralph couldn't help noticing JoAnne's shapely body in the rear view mirror; his lack of concentration let the coach drive into the gravel area between the road and the verge and he jerked it back into line. Martin glared at him.

The teenagers then settled down to talk, listen to their CD players or play with Game-boys and generally mooch around. Walt was using his lap top to type out something lengthy whilst at the same time trying to explain to JoAnne in the seat in front of him, that Lynchburg was named after a Quaker judge called Lynch. He delighted in explaining that Mr Lynch dispensed his own kind of justice, usually summary and usually at the end of a rope; hence the name given thereafter to lynching. By the time he had explained that there had been over five thousand lynchings in the Deep South between eighteen ninety-eight and nineteen twenty-three, she had dozed off against Jon's shoulder. Some people were simply not made for small talk!

Clem couldn't doze. This was no boondoggle for him. This was serious work and a chance to do something really important. He was going to lead this project and he was determined to do it well. His video skills were going to be tested to the full as well as those of producing and directing. Most important of all he knew he could encourage and lead the debate to bring out of his friends just what American youth really thought about the plight of the nation and its place in the world. In the quietness of his own thoughts his vision was already taking form; people would have to listen even if they didn't like what was being said - Kinz had given him such a great opportunity. He just could not wait to get to the destination.

42

Clem watched as the coach turned left and right, changing roads and heading, more or less in a south-westerly direction. At times he wondered if the driver actually knew where he was going. It was picturesque scenery with mountains rising and falling and patches of pine forest. After a few hours the girls reminded everyone that it was approaching dusk and they had only eaten breakfast and snacks, and what was more they needed a 'pee-break'. This encouraged taunts from the boys about why they never chose girls to be in their gang or how can you be a fighter pilot with a diaper on? The girls ignored the remarks and demanded a stopover. In truth, everyone wanted a break and Ralph stopped the coach by a patch of woodland on top of a hill that sat between two mountains. It was a beautiful dusk evening in autumn and the orange sky looked was breathtaking. The boys headed east and the girls west, but not without the inevitable teasing and cries of "we're watchin' you". When they returned they all stretched their limbs and were about to get on the coach when Martin stopped them, hands raised.

"As your assigned tour leader, ladies and gentlemen, I am here to inform you that it's chow-time!"

Then Ralph came around from behind the coach with a large wicker basket that he put next to a picnic table that now stood by the rear wheels. He flamboyantly opened it to reveal fruit, buns, canned frankfurters, sweet biscuits, chocolates and much more. He lit a couple of barbecue torches to brighten the failing light.

"Sadly folks, only water to drink, courtesy the ghosties of Lynchburg!" Then he looked at the shadowy trees nearby, "Oh God they're coming!"

The girls squealed in mock horror at the mention of the name and the boys laughed like at their antics. When they quietened down, they all tucked into the food.

After they had feasted they stretched their legs a bit more. The teenagers asked Martin and Ralph several times where they were going, but to no avail. They were all too tired to press the matter further and uncomplainingly got on the coach. After a while they all fell into a gentle sleep courtesy of a mild sleeping powder administered by Martin. It was going to be a very long journey and he wanted no complaints or problems. After five more hours and two driver changes the coach stopped to refuel. The teenagers remained fast asleep. Martin and Ralph took the opportunity to walk around, make a pit stop and drink some strong coffee. It was a remote and lonely one-pump gas station and there were few other vehicles around. A road sign informed them that they were on the outskirts of Nashville.

Martin got behind the wheel. "You look bushed buddy. Get some sleep, I'm okay until about four o'clock. Besides, I like country music." With that he reached down to the radio and tuned into a local Nashville country and western radio station. Ralph didn't need to be told twice and he curled up across the front passenger seats and covered himself with a blanket. Martin really didn't need any rest. He had a lot on his mind. It was really quite fun looking after the teenagers and he needed to get a lot of facts straight in his mind. He had made elaborate preparations for the project and wanted to use the four hours to go over the briefing that he would give the teenagers and run through a checklist of provisions and other things. He was also concerned about Ralph whose erratic behaviour was beginning to worry him. He knew that he had been turning a blind eye to it and knew why he did it. Ralph had helped him out of countless dangerous situations and often put his own life on the line for him. He would never forget that; although Ralph was beginning to stretch his loyalty a little far sometimes.

Ralph took over the driving at four in the morning and although the teenagers stirred no one woke up. Martin commented that either they had wet themselves or they had bladders of steel. He slept lightly and with the sun well over the horizon by eight o'clock found it easy to climb back into the driving seat. Ralph didn't lie down this time and they discussed the next fuel stop, scheduled for about ten o'clock just outside Texarkana.

Ginny lay across the seat with her head in Clem's lap. The others lay in various positions and Ralph's view of JoAnne's cleavage ended when she yawned and turned over, covering herself with the blanket. Walt sat upright with the blanket under his chin making him look like a rather comic child pretending to be asleep. Jon and Matt lounged awkwardly and snored loudly.

As the coach motored across the Texas countryside that was tuning from large forest to rolling plains the sun began to rise higher in the sky. The explosion of light was like an alarm clock and the teenagers reacted to the intrusion, waking in various ways and rubbing their eyes. Martin turned on the air conditioning. Clem yawned and his eyes widened, all too aware of the state of his body early in the morning. Ginny rolled on her back, with her head still in his lap and Clem looked uncomfortable and a little sheepish.

"Mornin' partner, it's a bit lumpy down here!" she said.

Clem blushed bright red.

Ginny laughed and smiled at his discomfort. She kept looking at him. He must be the only guy in the world who was good looking and sexy, and yet so alarmingly innocent. That had a kind of cute appeal to her. She sat up and looked out of the window as he grabbed the blanket. Within a half an hour they were stretching, complaining and passing around water bottles. Martin and Ralph decided to stop a little earlier than planned at another remote and unassuming gas station. The kids complained about the washrooms, but managed to spend longer at their toiletries than Martin and Ralph has wished. They

45

needn't have worried. The gas station attendant was more interested in his breakfast rolls and the morning newspaper; besides, he didn't look too bright.

Once back in the coach the familiar banter struck up again and teenagers found some breakfast sacks put out for them. They were hungry and finished the contents in no time at all. It wasn't surprising after a few more hours that they began to complain of square bottoms and there were signs that they were becoming a little tetchy. But Martin had a plan. Soon he saw that they had reached a point that he had marked on a map. It was a little after one o'clock in the afternoon. He slowed the coach, pulled off the road and followed a track that led through a small copse of trees to a small creek. The coach stopped by the edge of the slow running water and Martin and Ralph busied themselves putting out camping chairs and tables and a small barbecue. Martin put his head inside the coach and shouted, "Good morning campers, here we go, here we go, if you please. Little boy's room is east up the creek and little girl's room is west. Barbecue in forty minutes. Let's go hubba hubba hubba! Oh! By the way, do not pee in the creek I need to fill the water bottle for your coffee. Thank you ladies and gentlemen."

The tired teenagers let out and audible "Ugh!" yawned, scratched and stumbled up and down the path next to the creek, wash bags in hand whilst Martin and Ralph boiled the coffee and prepared barbecue.

Ralph stared at JoAnne as she pulled up her jeans that had slipped below her waistline. Martin grabbed his arm sharply.

"Ralph! For the last time, clear your mind buddy. Get some self control man. We got work to do!" he said.

Ralph pulled away sharply, "Yeah, yeah, man. You're a sour ass today what's gotten into you?"

Martin didn't answer, but his expression said it all. Ralph wandered off in a sulk.

Very soon, the teenagers were tucking into a huge barbecue of bacon, burgers, sausages and beans, and the coffeepot was much in demand.

Everyone was cheerful and even Ralph had come out of his sulk. They relaxed beside the creek in the afternoon sunshine and all was well with the world. It was good to give them all a break from the monotony of coach travel. This was really the only way they could travel to the secret location. If they had chosen to fly or go by rail, they would have been recorded by security CCTV cameras and identified with ease.

Clem walked over to Martin, who was by now standing by the slow flowing creek,

"How much farther Martin?" he said.

"Oh, Clem, it's another overnight stop I'm afraid," Martin replied.

"Overnight? Jeez, man o' man, we'll be on the West Coast at this rate," spluttered Clem.

"Yeah, I'm sorry Clem, it does seem a bit of a trek, but it will be worth it I promise you. Let's see now, you're the video man aren't you?"

Clem smiled. "That's me."

Martin put his hand on his shoulder. "Well, buddy, let me tell you that the video recording gear really is the best I have ever seen. Whatever it is you guys are making, you had better do it justice." He smiled broadly.

Clem was mollified and his heart leapt. He couldn't wait and turned to Martin. "With that description of my equipment, I don't care how long it takes, sir!"

Martin laughed. He thought Clem a little unworldly, in fact they all were. But whatever it was they were going to do he had no real interest. After this baby-sitting job he and Ralph would be back in the field. For now this was not such an unwelcome break – and it was well paid too. He just had to keep Ralph under control.

After a couple of hours eating, relaxing, walking and talking, they were back on the coach and Ginny again sat next to Clem. He didn't mind at all. In fact he rather enjoyed her company.

She turned to him and said, "I guess I'll sit up straight this time!" She cocked and eyebrow and pretended to look prissy.

Clem blushed again and she looked straight ahead, suppressing a giggle.

They were refreshed enough to hear the bad news that they would stop just outside Odessa for fuel at about nine or ten o'clock, but that breakfast would be at the secret location at eight in the morning. They amused themselves as best they could on the way to Odessa. The sleeping draft did its job again once the coach started out on the last leg of the journey; the only purring other than the engine was that of gentle snoring.

Chapter Four

Troy Hammond, Head of the FBI, had just finished briefing his staff for the day, which included organising a replacement for Quantock. He sat back and reflected on the situation that had unfolded around the missing teenagers. Undeniably, Quantock had done a good job. He had been fortunate to follow up on various clues so quickly and his report was very clear and concise - very concise. Now he was running the investigation, answering directly to the president. This troubled Hammond, it was not a good idea at all. He was effectively unsupervised and on such high profile work this was dangerous. If he made errors or took the wrong course of action that left the president horribly exposed. All security investigations had to be checked, verified and discussed in a team environment; this work was effectively now in one man's hands..

Hammond rocked in his chair. He had long since given up being astonished at how his leader circumvented normal protocols and common sense. It was just like the president: patronage was high on his agenda and cut across the workings of the administration in all directions. He was an astute man who knew just who he needed to groom for maximum effect and the tightest control. It was the oldest strategy known to leaders throughout history, and most of the time, it worked – until of course all the acolytes deserted or screwed up big time. Personality driven adventures are fine in business, but not when running the most powerful country in the world.

Things were looking bleak. How long would it take for support to wane completely? Importantly, did he, Troy Hammond care?

He knew the president was running out of friends. It was pretty dumb to take such a chance.

True to Martin's word, after thirty minutes, the coach topped a large ridge and they looked down onto the sub tropical Sonoran desert, now lit by the glow of a yellow-gold sun that now over the horizon. They descended the hill and made their way along a badly made-up road dotted with potholes and littered with boulders, surrounded by small shrubs, trees and cacti of various types. Before them lay a sprawling range of hills that rose gradually on their left before levelling out, taking on the appearance of a light blue-purple brush stroke between sky and ground.

After ten more minutes driving, during which they endured a rough and bumpy ride that shook their bones about, a large open area at the base of the hill came into view. At the far end of this flat gravel space was a group of buildings that looked old and in need of repair. The road continued to the right finally disappearing around a left-hand bend. On the right of the road there were a few lonely trees that seemed out of place and could only mean that water was nearby.

A notice close to the buildings identified the place as a tin mine called San Quiller. It was quite obviously old and out of use. The coach stopped and parked in front of the wooden buildings. There were two other vehicles nearby: a four by four Nissan Prairie and a small black sports car that looked a little incongruous in this setting. Everything looked neat and tidy, but very bleak. Thankfully it was late October and the temperature was only in the seventies Fahrenheit and therefore not as blisteringly unbearable as it would be in the summer.

Although overjoyed to arrive at last, the teenagers were a little apprehensive and Martin and Ralph shepherded them into the main building. Their eyes popped. The building may have been bleak on the outside, but inside it was quite different. It was well decorated with new wooden floors, whitewashed walls and modern leather and stainless steel furniture in the main seating area. To the right was the kitchen and dining area with up to date equipment and two long oblong tables with bench seats. To the left, beyond the main lounge was a large room the door of which was open wide allowing a glimpse of the sound, video recording and lighting equipment that Martin had told Clem about. To one side, boxes of paper, pens, markers were piled on to the tables. The internal wood cladding was new enough to still smell of pine. The teenager's stood and stared – it was very impressive.

There were two toilets and Martin explained that the main sleeping and bathroom block was next door. Girls were to be located at the far end and boys at the opposite end of the building close to the mess hall and breakout area. He was to be the chaperone sleeping in the middle. The teenagers hooted at this. Walt made a comment about being here to work that no one responded too. He was the same during the walk round the accommodation block, complaining about the creaking floors and water flow until Martin sharply reminded him that he was after all in the Arizona desert. Martin made the comment that it was better than the old tin miners had to endure.

Walt retorted dryly, "Well I'm not a tin miner!"

As the group moved on, Ralph went over to Walt and backed him into a corner pushing his knuckles into Walt's flabby chest, staring into his face.

"Well, ain't you the lucky one. Chunky boy like you would've gone down a real treat in the mining community."

He patted Walt's face and the boy winced with pain and surprise. Then he laughed uneasily and walked on. No one noticed a thing.

The girls had spacious quarters and single beds, whereas the boys had bunk bends. No one complained; Walt thought twice about doing so, but sensibly decided not to.

Although it was mid morning they all agreed they needed to eat something, rest, and then get acclimatised following their arduous journey. An hour later Martin was singing and banging pots around in the kitchen and the smell of whatever he was cooking pervaded the air making everyone's mouth water. Every now and then he banged a pot on the kitchen range and started a new song. Ralph was not so relaxed and wanted the whole exercise done and over with. His life was marked out by sleep, food, action, sex and getting a high – usually cocaine, but these days anything would do. Babysitting was not on the agenda. He walked out of the main building and headed for the rocks back down the road where he could smoke and drink some Jim Beam whisky. He would forego supper.

After the meal, Martin was voted 'Chef of the Desert' by the girls. Walt made some comment about the pasta not being quite al dente and Martin tossed a bread roll at him. It bounced off his head and the girls squealed with laughter. Walt stalked off out of the building in a mood.

Martin stood up and addressed them.

"Well now guys, that's the end of chow time. I know that you want to know lots more but you've all had a long day and as we agreed I think that a bit of relaxation and then an early night might not go amiss?"

They nodded, faked yawns and rocked left and right like wooden models. Martin smiled at their antics.

"Okay then. Just a reminder, although it's still kinda mild in the evenings, it gets real cool late at night, so keep your windows shut. The place is temperature controlled anyway and if you leave them open you're either cooling or warming the desert depending on the time of day! Okay, let's get some logs in and light a fire in that enormous grate over there, what do you say?" He pointed to the fireplace and the boys whooped.

The teenagers went for some logs and were quite happy to do as little as possible and laze about after the long drive; they had lost much of their energy and needed a break. Clem, Ginny and JoAnne wanted to investigate the area and asked Martin for permission to do so. Martin felt strange at his new role as

'Daddy'. He wasn't used to it and yet controlling them came easy; he even enjoyed it. He didn't want to dissuade them, but explained that the desert can be an unforgiving place if they strayed and got lost. After thinking for a few seconds he decided to trust Clem with a cell phone and a number to call in emergencies – to be returned immediately at the end of the walk. The three teenagers left and walked past the buildings before turning left and heading along the road and around the corner. It felt good to stretch their legs. JoAnne wanted to turn back after barely twenty minutes, but Clem and Ginny persuaded her to follow them to the entrance to the mine. As they navigated the boulders, JoAnne squealed at the sight of a lizard scuttling across her path; Clem and Ginny laughed at her antics. They gingerly went towards the entrance and were surprised to see that it was open, like a large gaping mouth ready to snap shut on any unsuspecting living creature that went anywhere near it. A sign to the right announced that it was dangerous to enter because of roof falls; it also noted that barriers were placed inside to deter the stupid and adventurous. They sat on a flat saucer-shaped rock and talked about what they thought life would have been like for the miners in such an inhospitable place.

Back at the main buildings, Walt walked passed the entrance to the canteen. Martin noticed that he seemed to have a nosebleed. Moments later Ralph sauntered past. Martin went up to him.

"Ralph, what the hell are you up to?" he said.

"Just a little training in respect Marty old boy. Won't happen again. Promise." Then he gave a mock salute and sauntered away before Martin could give him his usual lecture on self-control.

Martin could smell the whisky on Ralph's breath. He didn't feel easy about Ralph's behaviour – he had been there before. But he had other things to do. He went outside to make a call.

Quantock put the phone down. Senator Randolph Kinz was pleased with the progress and more so with the excellent arrangements made for the teenagers. Quantock had used illegal Mexican labour and materials to fit out the San Quiller tin mine and Adams and Anderson had bought the very best recording equipment. The teenagers had arrived safely and had not been spotted en route.

As agreed, the teenagers' letters had indeed been collected. But, as instructed, Anderson put them in a single large A4 envelope and posted them to a post box number. Quantock had collected them from the postal service and they sat on his desk in front of him. He thought of destroying them, but instead put them in the safe in his office; he may need them again one day; he wasn't sure how all this would turn out. He was leaving nothing to providence. Now it was time to gather the random reports came in, together with comments from the parents and information from agents who visited the teenagers' colleges, apartments and friends. He marvelled at how a story can almost write itself.

Quantock unscrewed the top on his pen and began to write his report, referring occasionally to various papers and files in his trays. For once, this was actually quite enjoyable work. He paused for a moment to gather his thoughts; he couldn't wait to see the president's face and his immediate reaction when he read the report. It was quite a unique experience: writing a report about a situation based on incoming reports, but all along knowing the answers. How easy it was for positions to be taken on the slimmest of information and all kinds of explanations given to provide an answer as to why the teenagers were missing and who was to blame. Human nature hates a void and needs it to be filled.

Clem lay in his bunk running through the plans for the video. He knew that to achieve the goal set by Kinz he had to get the team to form together first of all, to work all the rough edges off each other's personalities before they would start work properly. Then he would outline the time scales and set an achievable objective. No sense in wanting to put together something as big as War and Peace when they had limited time. A tight objective was crucial. They must do this before they even touched the equipment. If they didn't then they would lose their focus. He knew his friends well.

He thought back to his business management classes – what had he learned? There was a quotation that went something like, "If I had to chop down a big tree in two hours I would spend at least one hour sharpening the axe." Who the hell said that? Whoever it was, they were right and he would prepare the group well before work was to begin.

Clem was energised and he knew that he had to divide up the skills and then set tasks for the team to write a particular piece of script so that together they would have a final product. The youth of America speaks. He lay there with his arms behind his head. When the business thoughts were finally laid to rest his mind toured the events of the past day and a half. He thought of Ginny. She was quite lovely.

Then his hands were no longer behind his head.

Ginny had no such luck sleeping. She wanted to think about Clem and his cheeky boy face and young body. But thoughts of her recent argument with her father haunted her. Senator Nick Grivas, of Greek origin, was fiery and outspoken. He put everyone in their place if they deserved it. The trouble was he thought too many people deserved it and it had become a habit. A conversation with him went nowhere these days; all because he couldn't listen. In fact, he couldn't even listen to the fact that people told him he couldn't listen!

Time and time again her mother had said to Ginny, "Turn the other cheek, he doesn't mean it, he's under stress." But Ginny just couldn't hold it inside like her mother could. His tirade against the sexual morals of President Bill Clinton had been right, but he went too far. Ginny had been unwise to pursue this issue and with nostrils flaring she reminded him of President Kennedy's priapic term in office. He had countered badly with Kennedy's courage in the Cuban missile crisis, which let Ginny in with a reference to Marilyn Munroe and a comment that sexual morals are therefore merely an acceptance and interpretation issue: okay some of the time and not on others! By the time their mother had called a truce she had highlighted the defects of almost all past American presidents and a good few senators too. As she saw it, the problem was that unlike her father she accepted human frailty as a reasonable cost of leadership. But dad disagreed.

"Get real dad, do a reality check, nothing's perfect. Each one of our political titans had a moral flaw; we just have to take them for what they are. What makes us American is that we are in control of them and not the other way around. Well, at least until we got this Republican crowd of retards!"

Her mother was always upset when political arguments reigned and she stopped it short of Ginny delivering the coup de grace. At that point her father was beginning to smile.

"Damn," thought Ginny, "I nearly won, I nearly won!"

She turned and buried her head in the pillow. The next few weeks would be different though. Dad couldn't butt in now; when she finished her part of the video he would have to listen. All America would have to listen. The youth of America would have its say. No sham rallies, bright lights, pizzazz or spinning of the facts to suit the politics of the moment or the good ole boys. Just the bald facts would be presented and discussed, as seen by young people who care.

But still she kept repeating, "I nearly won!"

Chapter Five

The teenagers' parents were not that surprised when they were out of touch for twenty-four hours. They had seen it all before. No contact for days then the inevitable call for spending money or a quick visit home with an enormous bag of dirty washing that needed seeing to. But something was not right this time and slowly, one by one, they began to get worried and informed the authorities. Alarm bells rang when they failed to attend school having given various excuses. None of them had been seen for over three days.

Then came a full report from a drug store manager who managed a gas station and store on the outskirts of Lynchburg. It made interesting reading and the facts seemed to fall into place:

- A man of Arab features holding prayer beads had been seen behaving aggressively. He was unaware of the correct use of English language or social customs in a drug store, such as standing in line.
- He substantially overpaid for twelve large bottles of mineral water, indicating a possible lack of understanding of US currency.
- His violent language and the assault on a customer were irrational.
- An abandoned small coach was found and contained a discarded copy of the Koran, maps of several US cities and some blood stains on the upholstery. (The DNA was being checked).
- Witness statements indicate that a second coach was seen driving away from the drug store at high speed. Several customers heard the screams of frightened teenagers.

- Finally, all the teenagers reported missing were children of US senators.

The report was supplemented with details of supposed last sightings of the teenagers and various assumptions, detailed but fanciful notes on the possible routes of entry to the US for terrorists or criminal groups. It's not so much that the facts were important, more that they were woven together in such a way that that the conclusion was all too obvious; precisely what was intended.

Quantock sat back and read the report several times to ensure that he delivered the evidence in such a way that it left the reader in no doubt at all that evil was afoot without actually saying that.

There was a knock at his office door and a young administrator popped her head inside.

"Mr Quantock, sir, it's the DNA you asked for. We got samples from all the parents and a match has been found for a JoAnne Dempster, Senator Dempster's daughter."

Quantock looked at her and took the envelope. "Thank you Miriam. Please keep this to yourself. If it gets out I'll know whom to blame. Right?"

"Right sir, no problem." She turned away and frowned, thinking to herself, "Asshole! Why do men in power think that young women are likely to always give away secrets?" She stomped up the corridor looking neither left nor right.

Quantock smiled and added a late note to his report about the DNA. Good work had been done by the agents; so far so good. Kinz's plan was working well. He sat back in his chair and put his arms behind his head. There was a knock at the door again.

"C'min," he said, "what is it Miriam?"

Miriam half smiled. "Mr Quantock, it seems as though the management of information on this, er, situation, is getting out of control, sir. One of the witnesses in the Lynchburg incident has been selling his story to various local newspapers. It won't be long before it gets to the big guys!"

Quantock feigned dismay and shock and hit the table with his fist.

"For God's sake. Get me the press corps, we need a news blackout and get me an appointment to see the President himself, here," he wrote a name on a piece of paper and gave it to her, "call this woman and tell her it's of national importance!"

Newly inspired because of Quantock's obvious discomfort and pleased that secrets can get shed from sources other than young female administrators Miriam trotted up the corridor to enter the world of national security. Typical man – fancy not trusting her?

She couldn't wait to get home to tell Mom and Dad!

Within two hours Dan Quantock was summoned to the White House and was sitting outside the Oval Office on a long leather bench seat. Various high ranking government officials passed him by without giving him a second glance. He recognised the Chief of Staff, the Chief of the Armed Forces and his boss, Troy Hammond, Head of the FBI; there was also someone who looked suspiciously like a CIA man, as well as several other familiar faces. His boss was walking towards him, his face stern and without expression. Quantock was so out of touch he was surprised he remembered their names. Then he was quite alone in the corridor. He remained calm, rehearsed his lines and breathed deeply.

After about twenty minutes he was summoned by a peon who minced up to him, leaned forward whispering in a strangely high voice, "The President will see you now, sir."

Quantock smiled and followed the man into the Oval Office.

President Brannigan was a big man with a square head that matched his bulky square shoulders. He was built like a quarterback. His dark hair and dark rimmed spectacles gave his countenance a frightening appearance and many a senator had left his presence sweating and palpitating after a verbal assault of tremendous magnitude. Brannigan was not at all intellectual, but he was wily and clever – and as hard as nails.

"Come on in Quantock. I've read your report and frankly I find it reads like a Hollywood script. Give me the facts as you see them. And keep it brief."

Quantock was prepared for this and cleared his throat. Then without a sign of nervousness, he carefully outlined the information as it appeared in the report. He cleverly used the intonation in his voice and the odd expression in his face to convey how much of an insult it was to the American people. He also gently suggested that it could be part of a conspiracy to reduce US global influence at a time of growing military and economic tension in the world, especially the Middle East. He knew what this inferred. Since ancient times any nation that lost the respect of its neighbours, lost its influence and became an easy target for its enemies. That did it. Brannigan scowled clenched his fists.

Quantock wasn't fooled by this show of indignation. This was precisely what Brannigan needed to divert attention from the nation's economic woes and his failing grip on the presidency. It was the oldest trick in the book and Kinz had read his man perfectly and the situation was eagerly grasped.

Brannigan railed against the enemies of the US who would do such a dastardly thing to innocent children. He refused to let the country be held to ransom and pledged revenge. The Chief of Staff tried to intervene but was told to be quiet. Brannigan went on for another five minutes before exhausting himself. He then asked for the views of the others at the table, but it was patently obvious that he was not ready to listen.

"You sonofabitch," thought Quantock, "if you could press the red button for the slightest reason and nuke your enemies and get away with it, you damned well would!"

It never ceased to amaze and amuse him how politicians, in the western world at least, created their own political spin and propaganda, then had the temerity to actually believe it themselves. "The art of selling," he thought idly.

The president turned to his Chief of Staff, Fred Spiker.

"Fred, what do you make of this?"

Spiker squirmed. He was Chief of Staff not because he was particularly brilliant, but because he was clever. He knew that all the president wanted was a stooge and he fought hard against it whenever he could; but sometimes it was simply pointless to disagree or raise a point of order. This situation posed a different kind of problem, but was it worth the aggravation? Besides, the president might not be in power in a month's time. He thought that, all the same he would try the logical approach and appeal to common sense.

"Mr President. We need perhaps a little more time. We are as yet unclear as to the perpetrators of this evil act and it may be precipitous to react too quickly. I believe that…"

Brannigan interjected, "What more evidence do we need. This is an Arab plot if ever there was one. A man of Arab appearance assaults a US citizen, a copy of the Koran, blood on a seat cover of a vehicle in which it is suspected that the teenagers were seen, not to mention screams. What do you want, personal introductions? All this happens at a time when our fortunes in the Middle East are being usurped by terrorists and unstable governments run by crazy Ayatollahs. What's wrong with you? Why shouldn't we at least draw a sword and rattle it against their gate posts?"

The Chief of the Armed Forces General Hal Gottschalk got the president's attention.

"Sir, I believe that Spiker's correct, sir, we should wait and see. Our forces are at readiness sir, and once we have verified the facts we can discuss the next move."

Brannigan seethed openly. Then he exploded and banged his fists on the table.

"Wait, wait, wait? Is this what Americans are made of? When Democrats did that in the past we ended up looking stupid."

Quantock put his hands together and watched the ideological ping pong with interest, realising that this president was writing his memoirs before the conflict, whatever that was supposed to be, had even begun.

"General, put the forces on alert and draw up plans to put a carrier and ships into the Gulf of Arabia. Speak to the Saudi leader and, hell, buy some more oil or something, but get his clearance to send in five thousand more troops as a show of force."

The general paled. "But Mr President, I,......"

Brannigan broke in, "I am losing patience Hal. Six young kids belonging to US senators have been kidnapped by what appear to be Arab extremists. I am in no mood to wait or be patient. Do it!"

The room was deathly silent. The general was already seething at other military initiatives that were being enacted, 'below the line', so to speak. This was almost the last straw. Getting up slowly, he put on his hat, saluted and left the room. He would do as ordered, because he was a good soldier, and he walked away looking neither left nor right. He would do it, even if he was not sure who the hell they were waving the sabre at.

Brannigan turned to Quantock. "Well, what do you think?"

Quantock had prepared himself well and rehearsed what he would say to such a question. He deliberately waited a few seconds then answered.

"Sir. You have decided to get our enemies worried and I think that is the correct decision. Someone is behind this incident and it's better to deal with it right now, and hard. I can only guess at the next move. Before long we will end up on the wrong end of a ransom note or ghastly video and if you react then it will seem as though you have been pushed into taking action. You are choosing to go straight for the throat without delay."

There were several grunts of approval from the Chief of Defence Staff who had remained quite silent so far and one or two acolytes seated at the table. Brannigan smiled and nodded.

Quantock was pleased with his quick response. It was merely a sycophantic summing up of Brannigan's ranting, together with a little encouragement. No one would ever be able to say that it was he who rattled the president's sabre.

Then the president, much calmer now, turned to his aides and said, "Okay guys, contact the Washington Post, CNN and all the other major press players. I want nothing put out on the air until it has been cleared by the Administration Press Office." He turned to the only woman present, "I want every piece of text on this matter cleared by you and me Sadie. Do you understand?"

Sadie Burrows the chief of the US government press corps allowed herself a half smile. She was a tall lady with auburn hair and her whole demeanour screamed confidence. Today she was wearing a red and black suit. Her dark rimmed spectacles made her seem quite severe. Quantock looked at her and she brought to mind the kind of moth that sports a vivid red colour to frighten off predators – it said, you can eat me, but if you do you'll die!

Brannigan smiled broadly straight back at her, "I also want a nation-wide campaign started, you know the kind of thing Sadie, hearts and minds and all that stuff. Yellow ribbons on trees, set up some young friends of the kids to brief on their relationships, likes and dislikes, what they did at High School and so on. I want all the American people behind our action on these bastards. I don't need whining from pinko liberals, so I need tears to fall all over the US – do you think you can do that?"

Sadie Burrows stood up holding a file to her ample bosom. Quantock noticed how voluptuous her figure was in the tight red and black suit.

She raised her head and said, "Mr President, by mid day tomorrow the US will be drowning in lakes of tears!"

The president's eyes stayed on her as she walked out of the Oval Office, he seemed transfixed; Quantock thought that the man might actually dribble at any moment.

Quantock reflected on the rumours that abounded about the pair of them. It was said that the president had bedded her in almost every room and on all the furniture in the White House, but had never ever been caught out. Some said that he had even had her on the table in the Oval Office; Quantock grimaced, looked at the shiny surface and instinctively moved his soft leather briefcase onto the floor beside him.

The president turned to him, and said, "Dan, this is a mighty fine piece of FBI work," he patted the report folder with the back of his left hand, "isn't it Troy?"

The head of FBI, Troy Hammond, mumbled something inaudible and nodded.

Quantock replied, "Thank you Mr President,"

"Anyway, I have a mind to let you run the operation to track down these sonofabitches. What do you say to that?"

"Well, sir, I ..."

Brannigan wasn't listening, "It will mean longer working hours, more responsibility and tight deadlines. More pay naturally. Damn it I will. Quantock, the job's yours. I want your assessment of the staff requirement and your operational plan by the end of the week. Thank you."

Quantock kept a straight face, even put on a slightly strained look, enjoying Hammond's impotence. He wasn't really into Schadenfreude, taking pleasure out of someone else's misfortune; he actually quite liked the man, except that his boss had kept faith with earlier directives to keep Quantock out of the front line.

"Mr President I will do my best, sir," he said and half smiled.

Brannigan's face changed hue slightly and his eyes narrowed. "You'd better Quantock, or I'll fry your ass!"

Quantock left the office and walked slowly down the corridor past the guard on duty. He was amused at the irony. Here he was having put into action someone else's plan to deal with a conundrum, effectively having to bring himself to justice, earning money to boot. Now he had the unenviable job of uncovering his own deeds. This effectively meant that he should organise a nation wide search for six missing teenagers when he already knew exactly where they were. At the same time, he had to make his efforts look good, even when it was obvious to him that they would be unsuccessful. For the finale, he had to co-ordinate an operation that would see them apprehended at some point but without compromising the release of the video to a despairing and hyped up nation. The question was how to do work the two tasks together?

He pursed his lips - this could be fun!

Senator Kinz gazed out of his sitting room French windows and into his rose garden. It had been stunningly beautiful this year. A masterpiece of well tended lawns with a vast array of scented roses set out in various forms. Roses were happy with the extremes of the Washington climate and grew well. His wife Clara had been a particularly good gardener; that was up until her cancer. When she died he had been inconsolable for a long time. During this period of mourning the garden had suffered and he had to hire a team of landscapers to come in and give it a makeover. It was amazing how many men it took to do the work that Clara had done steadily and lovingly, day in day out.

Now it was back to normal and all summer the scent had wafted into the sitting room. He looked at the tidy pruned bushes in the early November sunlight and they seemed to give him some confidence that pruning is what is required of every system, horticultural or even those devised by human beings. It was for the best. That's what he wanted to achieve; a political pruning.

Kinz filled a crystal glass with a large Scotch whisky, drained the contents and tried to recall the scent of the roses in summer.

Then after another swallow he thought he saw Clara coming towards him through the doors and he stared in disbelief. Her laugh and smile filled him with joy. It was sweetness itself. He instinctively raised his arms towards her and she glided towards him smiling and laughing as she used to.

Clara's image came closer, but inexplicably, and to his horror, her smile turned to a twisted frown and her nature became sour. His stomach went cold with shock and his heart beat faster hitting his rib cage like a hammer. Kinz's chest hurt so much at seeing the one he loved behave and look so hurtful. On she came. Then he heard her voice haranguing him for a lack of judgement. When two people are so much in love, insults and rebuke are doubly hurtful and Kinz could not believe what he was seeing and hearing. His lips quivered and his eyes watered.

Clara began to call him stupid and glared at him. She did not approve of his project and said he was pathetic and waved an accusing finger in his face. He was perplexed; she had never behaved like this. Why was this happening? She appeared to even hate him! He was shocked and could not move his feet. Then he became dizzy and everything seemed covered in a kind of red mist. Almost at once he felt a searing pain in his left arm and tightness in his chest. He gasped for breath as the room spun, but was oblivious to everything as he fell heavily to the thickly carpeted floor.

President Brannigan sat in a large leather chair in the Oval Office contemplating his future. He was the son of an Irish Catholic tailor who came to the US shortly after World War One. His father was sickened by the way the Irish revolution had gone horribly wrong ending with the assassination of Michael Collins. When Irishmen turn on Irishmen he said, then all was surely lost? Squabbling, murder and mayhem didn't make for sensible politics and only hardened the English resolve to change nothing unless forced to do so. The famine of the 1920s and lack of any future made his decision to emigrate to America an easy one.

As a young boy Brannigan drank in his father's stories about repression and politics, but above all he learned about the politics of propaganda. His father was a staunch Republican supporter and celebrated St Patrick's Day in New York every year, giving a large donation to the Irish Republican Army. Brannigan heard the stories, the folk songs and music that welded fiction to fact and learned at an early age how conflict could be kept bubbling effectively from thousands of miles away; sentiment and nationalism are powerful factors in manipulative hands.

His father had said, "Son, when people have full bellies, good jobs and money in their pockets they will trust the state to look after them and will avoid politics like the plague. When any one or all of those things are missing they will seek a Messiah. In the case of an Irishman, buy him a glass of porter, sing some songs about the hardships of life and get the wailing bagpipes and the fiddle to play a few mournful tunes and you have the basis for revolution! Besides, the English have been plain stupid, greedy and selfish and deserve all they bloody well get."

The family tailoring business had been building slowly and its garments were respected by many that valued a good bespoke suit. But this did not make really big money. It was President Dwight D Eisenhower's speech on 6 January 1941 to Congress where he pledged to give material support to Great Britain and Europe that provided Brannigan senior with the chance he needed. Spotting an opportunity, his father obtained large pieces of equipment for cutting cloth and stitching. Then he applied for government contracts to make protective clothing and uniforms. To his enormous surprise he was awarded his first contract in the same year and others came long shortly afterwards - his financial success was assured.

By the time the US entered the war Brannigan senior's factories were well geared up for production and expanded even further to provide for US Department of Defence contracts which he was able to bid for and get with ease.

Brannigan grew up in a privileged home and he did not have to struggle for whatever he wanted. He was a good sportsman and a tolerable student. But his key skills lay in his sense of vision and a wily disposition that ensured he was always one step ahead of his peers. He saw college friends leave for Vietnam and never come back. So his father ensured, by giving a few dollars here and there to key political campaigns, that his son never went anywhere near a battle. Brannigan began to appreciate the power of money.

He also saw how even presidents can get themselves into trouble and followed every detail of the woes of Presidents Nixon with Watergate and Reagan with the Contra affair. He was excited by the intrigue of high office and determined to enter politics. After a successful career in the oil industry, during which time he built a reputation for being a bully who, ironically or perhaps craftily, paid the people he bullied very well so, oddly, they stuck with him. He was particularly skilful in his dealings with people, he moved difficult decisions to others to manage and perfected the successful use of 'fall guys' in situations where he needed clean hands to make a name for himself. His reason for running for Congress was also partly based on the influence he would be able to bring to bear on his various business interests.

His great wealth purchased enough PR and votes to ensure an easy victory to state governor. The rest was history. He used the same influence and techniques to win the vice presidency to President Harry Galloway, who was utterly exhausted by the continuing pressures posed by the Iraq conflict. Galloway's untimely retirement due to ill health then plunged the surprised Brannigan into the presidential seat. He revelled in it and held on to it tenaciously for the last two years of the presidential term. Brannigan recognised the bristling resentment of unpaid consultants planning strategy and dispensed with them all; he was his own political strategist. What he wanted was people who did his bidding – he did not like to be told, nor did he need the supporting entourage that so often provided the props needed for high office.

Brannigan then tenaciously reigned as the sitting US president, together with the gentle ex lay preacher Alan Murray who was his vice president. Murray was widely loved because of his deep religious beliefs and his outstanding ability to preach the best sermons in the US. Brannigan bathed in the reflected respect for his vice president who, in turn, frequently showered him with complements. The complements were of course bought at a good price, together with an assurance that surveillance of Murray's activities in rather seedy areas of New York some years back would remain out of bounds to the general public – for as long as it suited Brannigan.

Brannigan lit a Cuban cigar. It always annoyed his staff, many of whom were non-smokers. A nicer man might have agreed to withdraw to a smoking area.

There was a light knock at the door.

"C'min?" he said.

It was Sadie Burrows.

"Mr President, I thought that I might come and update you on the progress of the PR on the missing teenagers since our meeting the other day?"

She slowly closed the door with her rear, wiggling as she did so.

"Sure, Sadie, come on in, why not?" His grin almost separated one half of his face from the other.

Sadie Burrows was in her early fifties, but looked years younger. She dressed in a chic manner, always wearing clothes that flattered and accentuated her voluptuous figure and substantial cleavage. Her high heels clicked across the tile part of the floor. She crossed the thick multi-coloured Chinese rug, pulled out a chair from underneath the oval table and sat in front of Brannigan, slowly crossing her legs with a little less care than she would with anyone else.

It wasn't only her voluptuous physical features that fired Brannigan's libido. Sadie simply had something very sexual about her; a kind of magnetism that was difficult to escape from once she locked onto a man. The way she looked at a man, cocked her eyebrow or said something in a way that set the senses on fire. She had seduced him more by what she didn't say than what she did say.

Their relationship was electric. From the moment he met her at a charity ball he fell under her spell and he wanted her. But what made it a good relationship was that they wanted to remain with their existing partners. In the days of 'kiss and tell' relationships this was unique. This was for a number of reasons. They both enjoyed power and were both aggressive and successful people. Neither felt exploited by the relationship and yet they were honourable as though they were married; Sadie didn't flirt with other men and Brannigan never looked twice at the feckless and fawning female interns. His liaison with Sadie was the only professional relationship that he had ever enjoyed that was based on trust and mutual admiration. She had fallen out of favour with his predecessor, who unwisely sacked her. Brannigan used her forensic and incisive skills whilst she was in the wilderness, to work the PR circuit to bolster his credentials, feeding newspapers with false information to make him look good and discrediting his opponents by evidence or innuendo. He owed her a lot and made her his press secretary within minutes of taking office.

Brannigan's wife Christine was pleasant, plain and homely. She had given him two fine sons and he adored her without question. It was quite a different adoration from his professional and sexual liaison with Sadie. Christine put up with his absences and although there were the odd rumours of affairs nothing was ever proven and he never seemed to display the same traits as men who frequently play around. He also made plenty of time for his home life. Christine worked hard for his political career and was a tireless fundraiser for charity and the Republican Party.

Homely romance had remained, but sexual romance deserted them after the birth of their second son. Christine may have been a picture of kindness, but she was also shrewd. Powerful men have a habit of ditching those they love in favour of younger models and she ensured that she brought up both the boys in a stable and loving home that would make it difficult for Brannigan to walk away from. She need not have worried, her image was perfect and she was an integral part of the Brannigan career plan.

Nevertheless, although Brannigan's libido was not as insatiable as one of his presidential predecessors, a sink of unsatisfied sexual energy had built up. All sex needs some kind of impulse or catalyst and Sadie had moved in to provide just that. At times Sadie only had to breathe on Brannigan and he would explode into a thousand pieces.

Sadie put the files on the desk and placed her hands on top, leaning forward and looking into his eyes. Brannigan covered her hands with his.

"So," he said, "do we have a nation drowning in its own tears yet?"

She smiled back at him seductively and raised her head slightly.

"Mr President, not quite, but almost. I can run through the details but it's all here in the resume. CNN have been given details on various aspects of the, er, situation. The guy who was head-butted in the drug store incident in Lynchburg was reluctant to have himself bandaged all over, but a small cheque helped to convince him of his duty to his fellow Americans. There were also a couple of interviews with pillars of the community who were in the drug store at the time and their description of the screaming kids, the Arab and the coach were out of this world. Since then yellow ribbons have been put up all over the place. Jeez, wish I had shares in the yellow ribbon business! Calls to radio stations are coming in thick and fast. They range from, 'Nuke the Arabs', to, 'What are we gonna do about it?' nice to know they care, huh?"

Brannigan steepled his hands. Popular demand and a president who stepped up to the plate to give the people vengeance; this was what the nation needed. In his mind's eye he could see the battle map and a picture of him cigar in hand directing action against...well, against whom? Did it matter? All Arabs were the same and in any case he had some scores to settle in the Middle East. He only needed the slightest excuse; he was certain he knew who the perpetrators of this horrendous crime were even if the incompetent CIA did not.

It was now pleasing to hear that some of his military staff, initially reluctant to sabre rattle, were now supporting his calls for more direct action. It would be a major coup if he could catch the kidnappers.

Sadie saw his mind wandering and brought him back down to earth and said, "We have various other PR initiatives including a CNN interview with you, sir. That might deflect the awful coverage the administration has been getting following several incidents in New York and other cities due to the economic pressures that have been building up. We need to work out how to deflect these. Do you want to hear more?"

She leaned back and grasped her auburn hair in both hands pulling it behind her head, her bosom sticking out prominently. It had the desired effect and he was transfixed

"Hell no, Sadie. That sounds good enough for me. How about a whisky?"

Sadie smiled and put on a southern accent, "Well, Mr President, sir, you know how vulnerable a woman can be after twelve hours straight if whisky is administered?"

Brannigan returned her smile and picked up the phone and spoke to the security guard along the corridor.

"I don't want to be disturbed for at least another hour, you got that. I have important papers to study with a colleague. Yeah, that's right one hour, no calls, no interruptions at all, got that?"

Then he got up and went to each of the double doors to the Oval Office and flicked small internal locks, fitted courtesy of President Bill Clinton. By the time he had closed the window drapes using the electric switch on the far wall, Sadie had undressed down to her underwear. He quickly took off his jacket and tie without saying a word, almost as though 'show time' was part of the PR briefing process. Then he poured two large glasses of whisky. He gave one to Sadie, who swallowed half the content in one go, then he drank from his own glass, savouring the taste, before easing himself into a large winged armchair.

Sadie got on to the table. Her body was shapely but not perfect, but it wasn't that which seduced him; it was the look she gave him, her complete abandon and the way she easily tuned into his sexual frequency that excited him.

Slowly the undergarments came off and she sashayed around the table laughing. When she came back to where he was sitting she reached down and accepted a glass of whisky. After drinking it she put the glass down and pouted at him. Then in a fit of giggles she removed her dark rimmed spectacles and pushed the arms into the top of her crotch with the lenses resting on her pubic bone.

"Meet my friend?" she laughed.

Brannigan guffawed and leaned forward staring at her midriff.

Then he looked up at her and smiled broadly.

He said, "Damn Sadie, if I had a goatee beard honey, I'd look just like that!"

Quantock sat back in a large cane chair in his study in his Maine Avenue apartment in Washington. Sadie Burrows had done a great job. The shoppers at the drug store just outside Lynchburg were interviewed at length and every detail was pulled out of them. Their views were sought, no matter how wacky they were and conveyed to a concerned and interested nation, by now hyped up to bursting point by newspaper articles, television chat shows and every kind of conjecture on the fate of the teenagers.

The attack on the male shopper turned from a head butt into a severe beating and his photograph in the newspaper showed him heavily bandaged, even though his nose wound had healed. It did not matter. He enjoyed the notoriety and was well paid for his efforts – in the interest of news for the great

American public of course. Almost all of the teenagers' parents and relations shunned publicity, but one grandmother was encouraged to be interviewed and she had no doubts whatsoever that it was an Arab plot to spread fear throughout America and bring down the democratic system of government. She expected her grandson to be ransomed and steadfastly demanded of the parents that they refuse - in the interest of the free world of course.

Within twenty-four hours the nation became hysterical. Several Arab businessmen were beaten up by misguided groups of men in New York and a Sikh restaurant was burned out in Wisconsin. Sadly some Americans didn't know the difference between a Sikh, a Hindu and a Moslem. Yellow ribbons were tied to anything that didn't move and sometimes to things that did. Quantock watched the news programmes and was incredulous as to how something he knew to be untrue could be portrayed in such a positive way as to cause such mayhem.

Quantock had been in the FBI all his life; he had known nothing else since leaving university. He had been a serious college student working hard on politics, geography and economics. Edgar J Hoover had said, "To produce a breed of dedicated men and women you need to catch them young." In Quantock's case this had been true. He was approached by a FBI recruiter and encouraged to "come and meet some folks." Quantock was easily harvested. Hoover believed this was how he had created the most efficient and respected bureau in the world, by recruiting the best, thorough training, good pay and career prospects.

Quantock's early work had been a mixture of research and some stakeouts. The stakeouts were about ninety per cent boredom and ten per cent excitement to catch the prey. It was like fly-fishing. Hours of practising, select your spot, wait and watch the baited hook, don't jump at the first nibble then choose your time to hook and reel in. The adrenaline flowed and there was nothing like it. He loved it.

Quantock was a natural player of the game. He treated each mission as just that – a game. It was a game to be enjoyed and played to the full. Once or twice his colleagues commented on his cold-hearted approach to dealing with criminals who crossed the line and failed to surrender. He would dispatch them without flinching. This behaviour contrasted with his off duty open friendly style. He was dubbed, JH, "Jekyll *and* Hyde".

It wasn't long before the young and ambitious Quantock was promoted to run his own division of the FBI in Washington and that's where his family settled. He was good - invincible in fact. That is until the accident.

His wife Alison was driving their Chevrolet home with their young son in the back seat. They had just been to a school parent and teachers' meeting and the boy was telling his mom all the real secrets about the art teacher and the janitor when a local drug dealer high on cocaine shot traffic lights and ploughed into the side of their car. His wife and boy were killed instantly. The dealer needed to offload some drugs before giving himself up and he ran from the scene of the accident. With an unparalleled lack of judgement, Quantock's grief led him to deploy almost all of his own staff to track down the suspect, despite the fact that the crime was being dealt with by the Washington Police Department.

And find the suspect they did. He was arrested and taken to a local police station, but to everyone's surprise he escaped after being interviewed by Quantock himself. By a perhaps unsurprising coincidence Quantock tracked the man down and shot him several times in various parts of his body. He took ten days to die. The dealer was found to be carrying a pistol, but no one dared ask where it came from although the Police

76

Department was adamant that they had followed procedures and searched the suspect thoroughly.

Everyone felt enormous sympathy for Quantock, but the finger of suspicion was pointed in his direction. Relations between the Washington Police Department and the FBI were severely strained when it was suggested that there had been a lapse in procedures and a conflict of interest.

The district attorney was persuaded to drop potential charges in the light of evidence that the man was armed and a drug dealer, wanted in any case on several other charges. But Quantock's career was effectively over.

The vice president, one Jake Brannigan, had agreed to his removal from all but the most mundane of tasks. In fact, Brannigan's usual casual indifference to anything that smacked of work meant that he only over-signed the directive adding smart words where he thought they were required. That had been just under three years ago. Now Quantock was responsible for the department that provided low level security passes for journalists and other non-government personnel.

Quantock never remarried and he was successfully rehabilitated after a short spell as an alcoholic. Now he never touched a drop.

Then came 9/11 and the horror of the Twin Towers in New York. This enraged him and he applied several times to be put back on security duties. Many of his old bosses had moved on. Eventually, his harassed department heads agreed to consider a move and he was interviewed by doctors and other specialists and passed with flying colours. He was drafted back to homeland security. The work was not that much more exciting than his last job, but at least he was a departmental head again. This time he was responsible for organising security for US senators and their families, working with the White House staff. All he could do was to wait for a chance to shine. But after a while, he settled back into even more routine work and was sure that this would never ever come.

It was during his early period in the job that he met Senator Randolph Kinz. He liked him. He was honest and straightforward and a good 'people person'. After several conversations, Quantock got the uncanny feeling that he was being 'sounded out.' Especially after one chance meeting in a local coffee house where Kinz had explained about the loss of his dear wife Clara and Quantock duly responded with the story about his own loss. Kinz was clever and prised all the other information out of him as well. He had said supportively to Quantock, "I'd have done the same son, believe me I would!"

They shared political views over a few months in different locations around Washington. Quantock found himself being unusually candid and open with Kinz who was easy to talk to.

Senator Kinz nodded sagely throughout their conversations and they enjoyed each other's intelligent and open company. Kinz told him that he would treat Quantock's comments with the confidentiality that they deserved, because they had now become firm acquaintances and thanked him for sharing his views with him.

It was with strange relief that Quantock got so much off his chest in just a few casual meetings with such an eminent man. On the last occasion, he took the rest of the day off and walked around some tourist spots in Washington. Perhaps it was the open discussion with Kinz that acted like a form of counselling that made him feel so much better in himself – better than he had felt for many a year.

Quantock reflected on his past and the situation now presenting itself. Defining moments in life are often no more than casual encounters and these brief meetings were followed up by the surprise telephone call some months later from

Senator Randolph Kinz who wished to speak to him again, this time at his private residence in Washington.

A small group of senators gathered as they always did on a Thursday morning in one of the many common rooms in Congress, getting coffee and gossiping. This was a particularly important group, all of whom held key positions in the Republican Party. They liked to meet and talk about events of the day and make predictions on short-term political outcomes. Two of them broke away from the main group and made their way to some leather chairs nearby, settled in the seats and noisily sipped their hot coffee.

"So, Carl, how was your week, did you attend the Thursday Prayer Breakfast?" said Senator John Radcliffe form Georgia.

"No John, I did not, and neither did you," said Carl Rigby, an elderly and experienced senator from Ohio, "so it's a black mark for you too my friend."

Another senator, John Beardsley from Louisiana, joined the group, laughed out loud and said, "Prayer breakfasts are good for the Baptists and Catholics as well as the rest of us with souls that need redeeming. Hallelujah"

From the coffee point a small wiry man with sharp features, Senator Eugene Caldwell, shouted across to them, "Now that's not good at all gentlemen," he poured his coffee and walked across to them, "that kind of talk is…"

"Treason?" someone added.

"No," he continued irritably, "not treason, but vile talk. We are all of us, God fearing Americans, so why not pray in Congress?"

John Radcliffe, the senator who had started the debate looked annoyed and put his cup down on the saucer, so loud that his colleagues thought it would crack.

He stared at Eugene Caldwell and said, "Look, I know you to be a good man, Eugene, but you know as well as I do that this

Prayer stuff has been going on for about three years now and has nothing to do with religion," he paused and glared at the group, "no, let me finish. The last president claimed to have been guided by God, so what did he do when he stood down half way through his second term, hand the telephone number to Brannigan?"

Some laughed; some did not.

Senator Radcliffe continued.

"Have we learned nothing at all from history? The whole process of 'independence' introduced into our politics a couple of hundred years or so ago, meant cutting ties with the mother country, England, and becoming truly independent. It was about separating the people from the King and, don't you know, religion, focusing on the needs of the people, Eugene, the people."

He emphasised the word 'people' and continued.

"Now it seems that theology is becoming our guiding light and that's wrong Eugene and you damned well know it. Just look at the general picture will you? Liberal main line churches have declined in favour of hard line Southern Baptists and evangelists. On top of that, I think the last I heard was that seventy two per cent of Catholics like you vote for Brannigan because he is a Republican and the Republican message just happens to be tuned into your religious themes. That's outrageous and you know it"

Still not finished, he then leaned aggressively towards Senator Caldwell. "The problem, my friend, is that the road to God stifles debate, because anyone who dissents is seen to be a heretic. What will we do in the next phase of our government Eugene, burn people at the stake?"

"That's an over simplification of the situation and you know it," retorted Caldwell, "we all believe in God don't we?"

The response was swift, "There you go, you see? It doesn't matter what you inject into a debate, a theocracy will always say, 'if you don't do this you are a poor Christian, a bad person, whatever - you lose the debate!"

Comments that trade unions and other interest groups also swayed the vote were met with a muffled response as everyone tried to make sense of the argument. Some of them wanted to be heard and others deliberately avoided the discussion, after all, criticising the values of the founding fathers was almost treasonable. One senator was heard in the background criticising the president and his peers stopped talking, sipped their coffee and looked in the opposite direction, at the same time craning their heads to hear his words.

He was forthright and very angry.

"We need to focus on the economy for Chris'sake. Foreign policy too, India, South Korea and China. Yeah China. Y'know something? China has a massive trade and current account surplus and its foreign exchange reserves are growing like crazy. This means my boys, that they can sell at low prices to the West, keep the foreign currency which they then use to buy US real estate. Hell, they're teaching us about capitalism. And you know what our president said to me recently?"

He was aware that he had attracted attention and lowered his voice just a little. "What's the problem, he said? I ask you. What's the problem? The man doesn't know the difference between foreign exchange and a telephone exchange."

The assembled group laughed, as if they needed a release of tension. If it had not been so serious the laughter would've continued for longer. More discussion on the economy and foreign policy was avoided, this was election time and tensions were high enough. Besides, for the first time in their lives they felt strangely disenfranchised. Their friendships would see them through this spat, but there was a kind of emptiness in their discussion.

After a while one of the senators looked up and said quietly, "Talking of God, here's one of his key disciples."

They looked up and saw Sadie Burrows walking along the corridor. She changed direction and walked towards them.

"Hello boys," she said, knowing the older men hated that label, "plotting insurrection are we?"

Senator Carl Rigby sneered and returned the patronised comment, "Hello, *girl*, and how are we today? No, just taking a well earned coffee break, safe from the tensions of election time."

Sadie Burrows had the thickest skin in the jungle and continued with a smile. Tilting her head to one side like a motherly schoolteacher she said, "Well, can't say that I blame you. Anyway, here we go, the latest press releases on various campaign topics, all done for you. Aren't I kind?"

Nonplussed, the senators reached for the papers as they were handed out. They read them in a stunned silence.

Senator Caldwell, ever the Republican apologist, looked shell-shocked. He broke the silence and spluttered, "What is this Sadie, I would never say that about abortion, I am pro-life, but I would never say that. And look at this, I would never insult an opponent like that." He held the paper in front of him with his left hand and hit it with the fingers of his right hand with a loud smack.

Sadie Burrows regarded him as one would a child in a man's world. She knew only too well that the American people had a rather contrary attitude to negative campaigning – a kind of a love-hate relationship. Whilst most voters, when asked directly about this style of campaigning, claimed to despise it, they found the rough and tumble of politics irresistible, with its salacious trysts, corruption and skeletons in cupboards. It was a bit like the tawdry television shows that put an array of life's unfortunates on the small screen to air their dirty linen in public, unwittingly being gawped at as though they were circus freaks. Voters acted in the same way as television viewers, they were either too lazy or just plain reluctant to turn the set off in case they missed something. Such were the similarities – two horses in the same dirty stable. The current administration had taken mudslinging to even greater heights, as it ramped up campaign spending. Overfed by dollar hungry and unregulated television advertisers, they surfed the societal waves driven by greed, selfishness and decreased civility in public life. Politics had always been dirty, it's the nature of the game; but nobody played that game better than Sadie Burrows.

She gave him a patronising look and said, "Well, sorry about that Eugene, but let's see, that is what you said, er," she looked at her watch, "back in Florida about two hours ago. At least that's what was reported in the Florida State newspapers."

Senator Caldwell was left open-mouthed.

Another senator was equally perplexed. "Sadie, why do you do this. My press release is simply not expressed in the way I would express these issues here in the senate. This doesn't do justice to me or the debate on education."

Sadie Burrows drew herself up to her full five foot ten inches height, and glared at them all. She was a formidable street fighter who took no prisoners. She exuded arrogance and aggression. Her mission was to create power and win elections. News media was her business and she knew what 'popped their toast', and she fed their voracious appetite for copy that was sensational or ladled with innuendo; her sources would often accept anything that they were given without bothering to check the veracity. She practised pure political karate, without mercy on any opponent.

"Look guys, for what it's worth I bust my ass getting the press and television messages right; that is to say to make an impact so that our party can stay in power and you can keep your positions. That's my job, okay? What I wrote is better than what you would've written. It's on message, right? If you disagree with the message then you aren't loyal Republicans. You either want us to win this election or you don't?"

The senators were lost for words. She was good at her job. None of the press releases were ever totally wrong; they were spun out of all recognition, chewed to pieces, left with only a shred of the truth – cuts became 'budget readjustments', stakeholders were hand-picked and the term 'national interest' was used to excuse almost anything unpopular. They wanted so often to argue the toss, but her expertise in debate and ferocious temper invariably won the day. Then she never failed to turn the conversation towards loyalty, to the president and the party. Guiltless, they nevertheless felt ashamed at their impotence.

Without further reply Sadie Burrows, turned, smiled and walked away, saying, "I gotta go now."

A few moments later one of the senators said quietly, "Let's see now, if the previous president supposedly talked with God, I think I now know who was taking all the calls!"

If the situation was not so serious they would all have laughed.

Chapter Six

Martin cooked the group a breakfast of pancakes, bacon and eggs and toast, and pretended to moan like a dad when they all arrived bleary eyed, one by one, at about mid morning. Ralph leaned against the kitchen bar and was regretting eating too many pancakes earlier. He was upset because Martin insisted he smoked his cigarettes and dope outside the building and this put their friendship under stress. He didn't like being pushed around.

The teenagers ate breakfast at breakneck speed that surprised even Martin. He eventually got their attention by telling them that they were going to do the washing up. For one or two this was clearly a new experience.

Ralph sauntered up to Martin and whispered sarcastically in his ear.

"Jeez man, you're quite the daddy-o. I think I'll go outside 'n barf!"

He left by the rear entrance to the kitchen and no one heard the door slam above the hubbub; Martin seethed and knew he was being wound up. He assessed the situation. Realistically, it was true that he was enjoying shepherding the kids around. One or two were a bit dumb, despite their education, but it was different. Then his muscles tensed. He realised that in the kind of work he was in it was unwise to get soft, especially because difficult decisions were sometimes needed and personal feelings get in the way. Perhaps Ralph was right. He resolved that when they moved on from this mission, whenever that would be, they needed to be ready to step up to the plate and act without compassion or second thought whatever the situation. He would guard against softness.

It was approaching eleven o'clock and the sun was high and although the desert was nowhere near its summer heat it was still uncomfortable outside. But inside, the air conditioning worked perfectly and kept the air temperature comfortable for both people and the expensive equipment.

He returned to his avuncular tour guide role.

"Okay, roll up, roll up for a tour guide briefing, hubba hubba, let's do it please, over here and round the table. Let's go!" Martin shouted.

The teenagers responded lazily, feeling the breakfast heavy in their stomachs. The long table had a number of scribble pads, pens and pencils and Martin stood by a flipchart. He hung a map over the top.

"Okay. Let's start. For your information the rules of the game are no contact with the outside world. I am told that this programme is so important that if you are detected you will encourage nation wide, yes, nation wide interest. Then the impact of all your good work will be lost. And we don't want that do we?"

They nodded in mild agreement, still a little confused because they had already given up their cell phones, but by now they were reasonably well settled and content to follow the 'house rules'.

Martin continued his briefing. "Right, next of all, here's a map of the area. You can see where we are, at this old tin mine just here," he pointed to a spot on the map, "and over here is Tucson on Interstate Highway 10. The mine is located south of the highway about twenty miles from Tucson and the same distance from the Mexican border. Oh, and by the way the name of the mine is San Quiller. As you can see on this map, there are a lot of Indian reservations in Arizona. I found out in Tucson that this whole area has traces of people who lived here, hey, over seven thousand years ago, 'n that's a fact. There are twenty-one federally recognised tribes in Arizona, Apaches in the North and Navajo and others I can't even pronounce the name of scattered around the state of Arizona. All in all I am told there are a quarter of a million Indians."

Ginny whispered to Clem, "Jeez, my own country and I didn't even know that. Why the hell did I go to Europe to find history?"

Martin reached for a diagram and opened it up across the flip chart.

"And here my young politicos, is a map of the internal workings of the mine. It was used as an underground mining complex until the nineteen thirties and the depression years, then apparently it changed to open-cut operation in about, oh, about thirty seven. This here's the main entrance, thataway," he said moving his arm to the left in the direction of the road past the buildings, "and as you can see there on the diagram there are a large number of tunnels that go left and right. Left into the loading areas, that is to say onto trucks that were pushed down to the railhead a mile or so away. And to the right, well into the mine, there's the main airshaft and winding gear, which served as the entry down to the underground workings. Rumour has it that the last owner of the mine was so upset that it was closing he hanged himself from a main beam on the winding gear. And even today on a moonlit night some people say you can hear his low moans and see the swaying of his body in the beams of moonlight from the air-shaft. "

The teenagers looked in awe, eyes wide open and when he stopped looking serious they realised that he was, perhaps, half joking and burst out laughing. Martin had to fend off more technical questions. He told them a bit about the desert and surprised himself by being able to outline what life for the tin miners would have been like a hundred years ago. His objective had been to put them at ease and give them a briefing about the area and the mine. It was important not to give them the impression that they were being held against their will. He felt pleased with his work so far. He knew that Ralph didn't understand and as usual yearned for excitement, but he would come around – it wasn't going to be for long.

After his briefing Martin arranged for sandwiches to be made and drinks prepared for a late lunch; he was not cooking again until supper and they would need to snack during this rest day. He walked back to his quarters for a break, leaving his charges to go outside for a couple of hours then to manage their day from then on.

The teenagers scrambled around the rocky area towards the tin mine and Clem showed them the entrance. Matt threw a stone at the sign outside the entrance that read:

Danger NO ENTRY roof unsafe

Jon shouted, "Hey guys, let's go inside?"

The girls shrieked in horror and declined.

Clem said, "C'mon Jon. That would be stupid." Then he turned and shouted to the rest of the group, "come on you guys, let's get back to base and relax we've a long day ahead tomorrow, let's go now."

To his surprise they agreed, accepting his leadership without demur. That pleased him because he didn't want petty squabbles to spoil the project.

So far, the arrangements had gone very well, but Ralph's behaviour made Martin feel even more edgy. He dialled the cell phone to speak to Mr No-Name. It rang, but was not answered. This was strange, very strange. The agreement had been to stay in daily contact, but for over twenty-four hours he had not been able to reach No-Name at all. Ralph had been goading him a lot for accepting the assignment and it made him feel uneasy. It had been too good to be true Ralph had said. Easy money paid up front in cash and lots of it and some nutty senator sending kids off to the desert to put together a political video. What in the name o' Sam Hill was all this about? Ralph thought that it stank and kept telling Martin so.

The real problem lay in the disastrous South American adventure that lay heavily and uncomfortably on their minds, like indigestion that will not go away. They had really screwed up – and badly. Martin seriously thought that they would never work again, or worse, that they may be taken out, so badly was the debacle received by their masters. Ralph got into a fistfight with the CIA debriefer and that only made things worse.

Martin cursed. He would try to call Mr No-Name again before chow time.

After breakfast the next day the teenagers gathered papers and made notes. Clem settled the group down and they formed a circle to look at the papers he had typed the previous evening that sat incongruously against the pile of sandwiches and drinks on the long table.

"Okay you guys, before we even touch any of the equipment and position our video filming we have to sort out a script. That means we need to be sure what we want to achieve, I mean, what our objective is. Okay?"

The group nodded in agreement and they read the notes in silence.

Walt looked up and was the first to speak. His pomposity gone, he was a different person when focussed.

"Firstly, Clem, I think we should regard you as the team leader not just the director or our video shoot."

The others agreed, with shouts of "Yeah, skip!" and other ribald remarks. Clem smiled. The first hurdle was over with, thanks to Walt. Walt continued.

"Next I think it is safe to say that we all have preferences in our view of what is important for the America of tomorrow. I think we should focus our 'State of the Nation' message on the mistakes of the last five years or so, but end up with a list of recommendations for the future."

Jon looked at Matt and they nodded.

Matt said, "That's a good start, Walt. If we take that as our mission objective we then need to sort out who feels strongly about what topic."

Ginny started the ball rolling. "Okay, that's good, we have our process, let's now discuss the issues. For my part you all know me and I major on social justice and medical care. Fairness is what I stand for. Not a country where if you don't have money you don't get medical care."

She playfully turned to Walt and said, "And if you call me Communist again Danberry you're dead!"

Walt smiled weakly and looked at his papers. He was not one for humour at the best of times, and said, "Look here guys, we need to focus on the US style of politics that the American people are coming so close to despising, but that isn't gonna be easy. I've got news for you, this so-called mudslinging and the like, has been around since the end of the Civil War and has been driven by money. I don't like the argument that it's no different in Russia or China, wherever, that's just a pathetic excuse. We should be glad that we can freely and openly debate the way things are. In many areas of the world voters would swap bribery and thuggery that goes on in their countries for just some of our unedifying, but generally unthreatening politics. Well, I for one am homing in on legal and governance issues. You know how I feel about how our courts are becoming a mockery in the federal system. I also feel strongly, very strongly that the House of Representatives has been by-passed too often in recent years. It's not what our constitution is about. Not at all."

There was an uncomfortable silence and everyone new that boring old Walt was right; he might be the odd one out – but he was right.

Matt looked up, "Well, I'm for the environment. I 'er, well, I guess I am kinda supportive to wildlife and conservation. But heck, it's about our environment that I feel strongest – y'know, global warming and all that jazz? I happen to believe the Kyoto Agreement was an impossible dream, but it doesn't mean we can't make products that deal with and reduce the pollution rather than ask the impossible from American industry. And, hey, even the third world, to stop producing pollutant waste. All it takes is a bit of imagination and the will to do it."

Matt's eyes flashed and everyone was impressed by his enthusiasm.

Jon put his hand up like a little schoolboy. "Please teacher?" he said.

Everyone laughed. "I'm training to be a teacher, as you all know. I, er, kinda think that our system stinks. Not a bit, but a lot. Education is the key to our success as a thriving nation and we are continually bringing talent into the country from outside when what we need to do is to increase our wealth of talent from indigenous Americans. I checked before I came here. There's already evidence that unemployment has risen to almost ten per cent, now that's a disaster isn't it guys? Three years ago it was five per cent, or so said the chairman of the Federal Reserve. Sure, we believe that it has a lot to do with the competition from Asia, and lies mainly in the areas of steel and oil production, but people I talk to tell me that the actual picture is a lot different. The original statistics may not have been as accurate as we thought."

He shuffled through his papers and continued. "Around forty per cent, yeah, forty, is made up of men and women in the mid to late fifties. Many younger people got fed up chasing jobs over the years and fell out of the unemployment statistics.

That's been confirmed by several commentators, here I have some notes."

He passed out some sheets.

"I have a question, dear friends. If we don't get our education programmes right and start to teach skills to US citizens instead of buying them from other countries, and we keep on kidding ourselves that the unemployment figure is just fine, we will be in real trouble. We have to ask what happens when people in their mid to late fifties retire and there is no one to fill future skills gaps? We're not only losing jobs to other nations, but we will have unemployment as well. It's crazy guys, just crazy!" He fell back exhausted and his friends gave him some applause and shouts of, "Way to go Jon!"

Clem was pleased with the way things were shaping up, clasped his hands together and looked at JoAnne. She responded by bubbling. "Well, hey, you guys, it's gotta be women's issues for me huh?" She didn't elaborate, but stuttered to a halt. Walt curled a lip and looked bored and Clem glared at him.

Jon leaned across, "It's the women's employment situation too isn't it, Jo'? The forty year trend upwards has simply levelled out."

JoAnne looked grateful. "Yeah. That's right. I guess so too." Then she went quiet and fiddled with her papers.

Clem looked at them all. JoAnne's comments lacked preparation and she needed some one to one support, but it was early days and he didn't want to see her lose confidence. He had to get them going.

"JoAnne, that's just a great theme that we can develop over the next day or so. Say, guys. No one said anything about foreign policy?"

They looked agreeably surprised, now that they had marked their territory they shaped up for some real debate.

"Foreign policy, what foreign policy," said Matt, "American foreign policy is our boys in body bags ain't it?"

Walt looked annoyed. "Don't be so stupid. You need foreign policy to guard your borders, protect your interests in the trade world and, well, to influence the world the way you want it to work for you."

"Bullshit," yelled Ginny, "foreign policy these days means war, nothing else. Is there anyone we actually get on with in the world? If we spent the money we spent on war trying to get on with folks then our country would be a better place."

Jon uncharacteristically stuck with Walt's view. "Not every country is saintly Ginny, we gotta be strong."

"Oh yeah," she replied hotly, "Strong. That's right. The way we always are. Nothing is ever small or medium, it's always big. That's why I'm here. I argued countless times with Senator Randolph Kinz on the subject. He got upset, but it's true. We can't ever do anything in the right proportion."

She leaned forward onto the table. "Think about it. The way big business used immigrants in the early nineteen twenties and thirties, our paranoia about communism in the fifties which was driven by capitalist producers, disdain for the environment and the way we prosecute wars. God, we still fight the way we did in the American Civil War or Okinawa. Annihilate everything in sight. Don't seek accommodation. Shock and awe. Shock and crap guys; shock and crap! Take the burqa off Arab women even if they want to wear it, tell 'em they are hard done by. Shoot the Taliban who were the only ones to ever ban the production of drugs in Afghanistan, bomb Iraq to smithereens so when we win everyone hates us. Boy that's such good sense! Someone here wanna tell me when they saw any good US foreign policy where we didn't lie or dissemble to get our own way?"

Walt looked up with a patronising expression, "Ginny, Ginny please. The world is a complicated place and I am for tinkering with the processes, but you can't just change everything all at once. We are where we are."

Ginny snapped back, "Walt, that's just defeatist crap. The best of all possible worlds huh? Don't rock the boat. Hell I would if I could. The US should aim for the highest standards, not second best." Her face was flushed and her nostrils flared. Clem had never seen her like this before.

That did it. Soon they were all embroiled in fierce discussion, fingers wagged and voices were raised. Clem looked around him and let them verbally scrap with each other. This was just what he wanted, it would liven them up and put some passion into their specialities.

The exchanges went on for a couple of hours well into the afternoon. Eventually, out of sheer exhaustion more than anything else the discussion dried up and they all agreed to let peace reign. Clem had facilitated the group well and he achieved his objective. Each of their specialist areas was now enriched even more with a sense of the here and now and a real bite to the politics. They would now work on scripts that would be the basis of the presentation on the state of the nation. They all knew that they had to be very precise and very right. Otherwise, their work would be laughed off the networks. Keep it simple; keep it based on reality not conjecture. There would be presentations within the group to tighten things up and get the stuff on to the video screen.

The summing up and recommendations would prove interesting but that was the second and last part of the task.

They were enthused and scooped up pens and writing blocks, moving away to gain some privacy.

Clem felt good as he tidied his notes away. The first session had been a success. He was older than his years when it came to understanding people and he was lucky to have a very well developed sense of understanding about human foibles and how to combat them. He was after all the product of a dysfunctional family. The secret was to create an outlet for all the negative feelings, then when they were spent, harness the positive factors. He was running through the day's events again when he felt a hand touch him lightly on his shoulder. It was Ginny.

"Hi, Captain. That was a good session. I got so noisy I feel exhausted. You want some fun?" she said.

He looked at her sheepishly and before he could answer she went on.

"I noticed when we went exploring this morning that there was a large rock pool, right by the trees. Let's take a dip?"

"Ginny, the evening temperatures in the desert at this time of year are about forty degrees, is it wise?" Said Clem.

Ginny smiled, "Aw c'mon Clem. It was quite moderate last night, a bit chilly later on I grant you, but if we catch it early enough it should be all right. Hey the Swedish do it all the time. Let's do it after chow?"

Clem looked at his watch. "Damn your hide, Ginny. Okay. We eat at six thirty, let's sneak away about seven thirty – we gotta let our food go down!"

She smiled at her success, tapped him playfully on the head and went to the accommodation block.

Chow time came and Martin was in good form, despite convincing himself earlier in the day that he should avoid all emotional or friendly attachments. However, the lack of contact with Quantock, as had been originally agreed at the start of the project, began to irk him a lot. He did well not to let his anxiety show. Everyone responded to his cheery attitude and his burgers and fries were given a high five. Ralph ate in silence in the corner of the room attracting a few stares from the diners and Martin smelled the whisky fumes from where he was sitting.

After the meal they broke away to sit and read, or tease each other. Clem and Ginny, with a blanket under her arm, left quietly and unnoticed.

Martin beckoned Ralph to the kitchen. He closed the door.

"Ralph, what gives man? Are you still sore at being on this mission or what?"

Ralph looked irritated. "Yeah, I guess I'm just plain bored. The kids just remind me of all those jackasses I hated at school. Taking the piss. Privileged kids who thought they were better than anyone else. No worries about money or parents who beat you when they got back from drinkin'. 'N what's funny is that we picked up this job so damned easy. Outta the blue. Kinda strange ain't it? Damn good money, no danger; why did we get such a plumb job and not some others who are the golden boys of the CIA? It just doesn't make sense. I smell a rat."

Ralph looked down at his feet. "Look, from now I'll be a good boy, huh! I just need a walk."

Martin felt uneasy at Ralph's repeated assertion that something was wrong with this mission. It was a strange situation, he had to admit that much. Why hadn't No-Name answered his cell phone? If only he could contact him then he could square a few things away in his mind. He walked slowly back to his quarters and turned on his small pocket radio – the only one in the complex – and listened to country music.

He fell asleep quickly, dozing off the effects of the evening supper and musing about how he would spend the substantial sum of money they had been given, with a promise of more to come. A new car was top of the list for sure. Then he would look at his deposit account. When it reached the magic half a million dollars he would quit his work and retire. Colorado was his dream. Nice folk, good properties, low crime rate and his favourite, skiing at Aspen, one of the best ski-slopes in the world. He was a good skier and hadn't done it for an age. He had almost reached his financial target and this job may just take him as close as he would ever get.

As he dozed off he heard one of his favourite country tunes, Silver Threads and Golden Needles, fade out and a radio announcer came on.

"We interrupt this programme to report that the well known elder statesman of the senate, Senator Randolph Kinz has had a heart attack. Doctors have not given any further details as to the extent of the attack or his current state of health, but our best wishes go to him and his relatives. Senator Kinz grew up in Tucson and he remains our most favourite of Senators. He lives up to his adopted title as the 'father of the senate'. We will keep you updated on his progress."

Martin jerked out of bed, his head buzzing from the effect of being dragged across the razor blades that form the barrier between sleep and wakefulness. Kinz – heart attack? Who owns this project whilst he is ill? How did he get so ill so suddenly, he has always been an icon of fitness for a man of his age? Was this suspicious? Where does that put him and Ralph? Why hasn't he been able to contact No-Name?

They had lived in a conspiratorial world for so long that anything out of the ordinary could have a devious or duplicitous meaning to it; it was the price to be paid for the kind of work that he did.

It was against the rules of the project to listen to the news. No-Name said it would serve no purpose for Adams and Anderson, and certainly should not be done by the teenagers who would become instantly worried at the emerging situation. But Adams had sneaked a small radio into his bags and, as Kinz had predicted, but not in this scenario, he was being affected by the news as it was unfolding. Earlier news items that he had been able to listen to were almost hysterical in the coverage of the kidnapping of teenage children belonging to US senators, they supposed, by Arab terrorists. He had never known such anger and for a moment he actually felt vulnerable, isolated and surrounded; he was usually in control and wasn't used to this. Anyone caught with the teenagers was sure to be lynched without question?

He reached for a bottle of Jim Beam and took a large swig, then another. After a few more drinks he had convinced himself that something wasn't right. Maybe Ralph had it right after all. Then he dialled No-Name again.

Ralph sat in a rocky outcrop just to one side of the accommodation quarters just as the evening began to close in. He pulled out his special silver box, which when opened up would allow him to put cocaine on the mirrored inner surface to then be 'cut' into lines with a fancy razor blade, ready for snorting through a dollar bill tube. As he sniffed it he looked up at the now deeply reddening sky and walked on the clouds. Colours became brighter and the silence of the desert evening filled with electric shocks and lights all around him. He closed his eyes and great waves rushed through his body. He was on fire and raring to go. After a while, he focussed again and started to laugh uncontrollably. Cocaine always had this effect on him. If Mike Tyson had challenged him to ten rounds he would have accepted, or he would have offered to stop a bullet with his teeth. He was invincible. He was horny.

It was after about an hour that he noticed a light switched on in the end room of the accommodation block. Ralph's body struggled with the counter effects of too much whisky and the cocaine and he fumbled for his binoculars. It had been a good show last night, perhaps tonight it would be better? He sang some country music to himself whilst he waited. After a while JoAnne came into view. She was dressed in her underwear and carrying a wash bag and was unconcerned at the open curtains, expecting no prying eyes from the desert. Ralph focussed in on her and he began to laugh.

"Go on honey, give me a good show, that's it gal!" he said, as she removed her bra and began to apply body cream to her arms and chest, arching her neck as she did so.

Ralph couldn't contain himself any more and he took several swigs of Jim Beam and slithered down the slight rocky incline towards the block. He had had enough. This gal needed a man, a real man. He, Ralph Adams was just that man.

He slowly and quietly opened the main door, made his way down the corridor slowly past half open doors to the boys' rooms. He needed no directions, the smell of female perfume would have been enough to guide him to his prey.

Ginny led Clem about a quarter of a mile down the road keeping close to the edge of the hill, then as they approached the trees on the opposite side of the road they crossed over and followed a stony path down a short incline. The trees obviously grew there because of a plentiful supply of water and as they rounded a rocky edge there was a large pool. It was just as Ginny had described it. It was small with a gravel edge and the water was as still as could be, giving the impression of a large round glass mirror. It reflected the darkening red evening sky and the rising moon and made it look like an eerie fiery pit; half beautiful and yet a little frightening.

Clem stood on the water's edge, bent down and put his hand into the mirror-like surface, withdrawing it quickly.

"Jeez, it's freezin' Ginny. We must be crazy!" he said.

"Oh, you coward. C'mon be quick," she said and started to remove her clothes.

Clem was a little slower, shyly matching her garment for garment. When she was eventually naked she laughed at his embarrassment and turned and walked into the cold water. He nervously followed suit. As he entered the water his senses sharpened with the sharp drop in temperature.

"Aargh," said Clem, "you go in a man and come out a boy – Jeez that's f-f-freezin'."

Ginny laughed and made similar noises, but her style was to keep moving and keep the circulation going. They splashed around in the shallow water and then came out within a few minutes. Shivering with cold they dried themselves with their underwear and dressed quickly in their clothes. Then they settled into a cleft in the rocks on a blanket that Ginny had the good sense to bring and where roots of a tree spread through.

When she looked up at his face her eyes sparkled and she smiled enticingly. Then they kissed. It was a wonderfully delicate kiss; her warm cheeks surrounded her cold lips and as they opened he sought the inner softness. Clem enjoyed holding her tight and felt the warmth of her body as she nestled into him.

It was the nicest feeling in the world and he wished it could go on forever.

Martin's head was spinning and he was hopping mad. The whisky had given him a sore head, the news programmes were getting angrier and he still couldn't contact Quantock. His nerves were jagged and raw, and he walked around his room swigging more and more whisky. Grabbing his jacket he put it on against the cool evening air and went to look for Ralph. They had to talk and think about this situation. It had to get sorted out; it damned well had to. He walked into the rocky area in front of the buildings with a flashlight in his hand moving it slowly over the ground in front of him, shouting Ralph's name in a low voice.. He scoured the rocky outcrops and at first saw nothing, and then something flashed. When he reached it he saw that it was an empty bottle of Jim Beam. He took stock of the situation and stood and surveyed the area.

Then he caught sight of a light in the female part of the accommodation block.

"Oh no!" he muttered to himself and he ran towards the building.

Martin entered the accommodation block and crept quietly past the boys' rooms. He looked into Ginny's room her light was on, but she wasn't there. Then he stood outside JoAnne's room.

There was no sound. He opened the door slowly. As he did so, he saw Ralph sitting at the foot of the bed. Ralph simply turned slowly and when he saw Martin he gave a crooked smile and shrugged his shoulders.

"It was an accident man, we were sorta, er, rompin' an' she kinda fell and, well..." His voice tailed off as he waved an unsteady arm at the bed.

Martin opened the door wider and saw JoAnne's body lying face up, half-naked, on the bed. Her head lolled to one side and her neck appeared to be broken. He entered and closed the door, snarling at Ralph.

"Jeez, Ralph, you've been drinkin' 'n snortin' that stuff again, haven't you? How did this happen?"

As Ralph began to mumble an explanation of sorts, the door burst open and Matt burst in.

"Hey JoAnne, can I borrow..." his words fell short.

Out of basic instinct, Martin turned, grabbed him by the collar and smacked him across the head with the heavy flashlight. Matt fell heavily to the floor.

Martin looked down at the body as he quietly closed the door. He bent closer and lifted Matt's head, and then put his fingers on the boy's neck to feel a pulse. There wasn't one.

Ralph turned to Martin and half smiled, "We got one each man!"

"Oh God," said Martin, "as if things weren't bad enough already."

Ralph looked perplexed. "Whadya mean buddy?"

Martin explained about Kinz's heart attack, the frenzy on the radio and not being able to get through to No-Name. Ralph's face changed from dumb, 'don't care' and 'coke-head' jerk, to a snarling angry oaf. He jumped up and wheeled around, his eyes bloodshot and bulging and mouth crooked.

"I damned told you. Didn't I?" and he glared at Martin, "There's a plot here that we don't know about and we are the patsies. We're the guys who failed in Chile. We're gonna be set up. Duped. Dumped. I bet our faces will be spread all over the place soon, newspapers, TV, and then we'll be surrounded and taken out. Damn. No Kinz and no Mr No-Name, just us playin' baby sitters and me, the actor with the part of a crazed Arab. Andy hey, I played the best damned part of my life didn't I? Didn't I?" Ralph's eyes were bloodshot with rage and he went to the window with his hands on his head rubbing his scalp hard with his fingers, repeating. "I just knew it?"

Martin was getting wound up now. They sat and spun their thoughts a dozen times, each welding together a better and more plausible explanation to justify their next move. Then they sat in silence for a while and calmed down enough to make plans. Ironically, when they were calm they planned better and when they planned they were dangerous.

They knew what they had to do and both went back to their rooms to get their guns.

The silence of the perfect starry, moonlit night was broken by a sharp sound, like someone banging a metal tray sharply, or perhaps a shot. They heard it again. Clem sat up and Ginny pulled away from his warm body and gave him a lazy gaze.

"What was that?" she said.

"It was a sound, like a shot?" said Clem, "We'd better find out what's going on. Could be an electrical short of something."

Ginny couldn't believe her ears, shrugged and zipped Clem up.

"Okay, okay, whatever you want!" she said frostily.

Together they walked back up the slope and onto the road. They turned to the left taking care where they stepped, because of the darkness on the building side of the ridge and the number of boulders and stones in the road. The lighter side of the ridge, which benefited from the moonlight, was on their right on the way to the mine. They walked for a few minutes, and then as they began to edge round the corner towards the lights of the buildings, Clem stopped in his tracks, putting his hand across Ginny's mouth.

They couldn't believe their eyes. Martin and Ralph were standing over the bodies of Jon and Walt. The guns in their hands were held loosely in their hands and they were looking around anxiously as if looking for somebody: Clem and Ginny perhaps?

Despite the shock of the scene, Clem had the presence of mind to turn to Ginny and put his finger to his lips and steered her slowly backwards down the road. But Ginny was petrified and her eyes bulged with fear. She instinctively let out a kind of small yelp! Martin and Ralph turned instantly and shone a flashlight in their direction. Clem and Ginny found themselves illuminated in the long sharp beam.

At first Ralph tried to reason with them, "It's okay, there's, been a bit of an accident that's all. C'mon over here, 'sokay, c'mon now?"

They were so scared they kept backing away. Ralph lost his temper swore, raised his gun and fired; the shot missed Clem's feet by inches spraying stone splinters everywhere. Clem's adrenaline was flowing like electricity through his veins and he grabbed Ginny's hand and shouted, "Run!"

They turned and ran back down the road towards the mine. They had the initial advantage of running towards the lighter side of the ridge and ran as fast as they could, their legs wobbly like jelly and hearts beating like steam engines. Soon the entrance to the mine came into sight and without changing step or slowing Clem pulled Ginny inside.

After a few yards, feeling their way quickly in the pitch dark, their steps faltered as they came across rocks and debris. Clem fell and cracked his shin against a barrier and he yelled in pain. He rubbed it furiously and prepared to move on.

Ginny had by now regained her wits.

"This must be the safety barrier marked on the map. It's dangerous to go any farther into the mine," she said.

Then they heard Martin and Ralph arrive at the entrance about fifty yards behind them. They had no choice, they would have to go on and quickly.

As they felt their way along the tunnel they came to a shaft to the left. Ginny stopped Clem and said, "No, keep going. I remember the map that Martin showed us. We should cross over the other side of the tunnel and take the third turning on the right to the main winding shaft, the area's a lot bigger and we can hide more easily."

Clem readily agreed and they picked their way along the right hand wall until they counted the third turning. Before they turned into the tunnel they heard Ralph and Martin making their way through the main channel. Their progress was slower because they were checking the entrances to each of the tunnels and didn't know which one Clem and Ginny had taken.

Ralph was getting angry.

"Damn. They could be anywhere. I can't see a damned thing outside this damned torch beam." He flashed the beam all over the place and stopped in his tracks reluctant to search every inch of the complex.

Martin put his hand on Ralph's shoulder and squeezed it; they both listened carefully for a few minutes, but there were no sounds. Then he said loudly, still squeezing Ralph's shoulder, "Let's go back to the main entrance. This is useless even with the torch. If we go too far in and they are in one of the earlier tunnels then they could double back behind us."

They both noisily walked back towards the main entrance, Ralph shouting, "Okay, let's get outta here, I've had enough," hoping that the teenagers would think that they were quitting the area. When they were almost back at the entrance Martin indicated to that Ralph he should bring up the four by four vehicle and they would stake out the entrance. It would get cold tonight and they had to think hard about how to locate the teenagers.

Clem and Ginny heard them leave the area.

"Do you really think they are going?" said Ginny.

"No, I don't, but let's rest here a while," he whispered, and they sat and held each other tightly.

"What the hell is going on?" said Clem, putting his hands to his head. "I just can't believe it. One minute we are all friends and everything is going so well, and the next, two of our friends are laying shot outside and we are running for our lives. This is just crazy."

Ginny held him tighter. "I don't know either. Ralph has always seemed a bit strange, but Martin is such a regular kind of guy?"

After a few moments, Clem said, "Ginny, you remembered the layout of the mine, that's pretty clever."

She replied, "Yes, I'm lucky. I developed a good memory technique at High School and it has repaid itself many times. I guess this has been the biggest bonus of all time!"

After an hour Clem was beginning to feel his muscles contract.

"Ginny," he said, "we'd better move. If they come back then we will be too cold and numb to find our way to the winding room."

Ginny agreed and they stood up. After rubbing each other hard to get their circulation flowing, Ginny led the way along the tunnel following her recalled memory of the directions to the winding room. The rock walls felt sharp and cold against her fingers and she called up as much information from memory that she could.

What was it that Martin had said? The old mine owner had hanged himself from a large beam in the winding room. His body had swung to and fro' in the moonlight that shone down from the airshaft. That was it!

"Clem. There's an airshaft in the winding room. It could be a way out," she said.

"Yeah, could be," said Clem. His voice sounded tired and dispirited and she realised that he was now in a state of shock having been so positive earlier. It was now her turn to be strong and she had to encourage him.

They made their way gingerly down the tunnel, tripping over small boulders and then after about fifty yards came up against a wall of rock and sand. Ginny gripped Clem's hand in fright.

"Oh, God it's blocked," she said.

They felt their way along the base of the rubble from one side of the tunnel to the other, but there were no gaps. Then they started to crawl up the steep incline of bounders, stones and sand feeling around them as they went. After a few moments Clem stopped.

"It's no good, we can't get through," he said dejectedly.

"No, we must keep on. Stop a minute," said Ginny and they both stopped still in the darkness, so total it was intimidating.

"Feel that?" she said.

"Feel what?" said Clem. Then he felt it too. "Yeah, I feel it. A slight waft of air."

They scrambled a little higher and as they did so felt a gap at the top of the rubble. It was about two-foot high and as wide as the tunnel. It wasn't really what she wanted to find.

Ginny's heart beat faster as she realised that Clem would ask her to crawl, in pitch darkness through the flat opening toward what they hoped would be the winding room. But of course it could just be a dead end. She stiffened with fear.

"I can't do it," she said, "I just can't stand enclosed spaces."

Clem knew that he had to pull himself together. Ginny had to cope with the ordeal that was surely their only possible way out.

"I know how you feel, I am claustrophobic too. But we have to do this if we are to survive." He held her hand tightly, "It's different when you are with someone else, especially if we are side by side. It's not like a small tunnel or anything it feels kinda low and wide. What do you say?"

Ginny took a deep breath. After about a minute she said, "Okay. I'll do it. But promise you will stay beside me and that we will talk all the way. 'N if I want to go back we will be able to. Promise me?"

"Promise," said Clem, holding her hand tightly, "let's go?"

Ginny and Clem groped their way into the gap. All went well at first as they clawed gradually up a slight slope in the pitch dark. Ginny felt her heart race and her mouth was dry with fear, then to her horror the tunnel began to significantly narrow and every muscle in her body froze. Clem was afraid that she would back out. But she didn't. She managed to gather her courage and slowly move on. He kept talking to her as they inched forward slowly across the sharp stones. Conversation ranged from school friends, holidays, pop music to when they first met. After about twenty-five feet even Clem was feeling as though he could lose control any minute. The cold confined space and darkness were beginning to take a toll on their confidence. Even Clem wondered if it would ever end. What if it was a dead end? What if a rock fall happened behind them and they were trapped? His mind raced.

"Whatever you're thinking Ginny, don't," he said, sensing that Ginny must be following the same thought process as he was. Then he had a brain wave. He moved his left hand to his face. It was so dark that even the dimmest light from the luminous hands on his watch illuminated a small area. He put it to his face and moved it around.

"Hi gal, it's me," he said and gave her his biggest smile, "just keep talking and no thinking, okay?"

"Okay," she said with a very shaky voice, "no thinking. Let's move or I swear I will never go another inch."

They crawled along the rubble and by now their knees and elbows were scraped and sore. Ginny swore she was bleeding everywhere. Then she put her hands out in front of her to feel the side of the tunnel and realised that it narrowed sharply, turning the wide gap into an even smaller tunnel.

This was the last straw for Ginny and she hyperventilated with the extreme fear and anxiety caused by claustrophobia.

"Okay, that's it, that really is it. I gotta get out of here Clem, I gotta get out," she said hysterically, and began to turn over and push the roof of rock above her as if to move a large imaginary lid, kicking her legs wildly.

Clem grabbed her like a clamp with his arms and legs held her tightly, kissing her and talking tenderly until the fit wore off. It took a long time before she could get her breath back and settle her heartbeat. During her wriggling, he thought something caught his eye. As he held her tightly he focussed on the darkness in front of him, then he said, "Ginny, I can see something," she stopped moving and whimpered a little, "it's a bit of grey, I'm sure it's light, Ginny, it is light, it really is, I'm not joking."

Ginny gulped and looked ahead. She saw it too and became calmer. Now she could go on - the quicker the better.

Crawling the last twenty yards was painful, but their spirits were higher and they kept the grey area in their sights, lest it should snuff out like a candle flame. But it didn't, it got larger and as this happened they crawled slightly faster with spirits rising.

Like a couple of desperate mice they reached the edge of the rubble and looked through the gap that could not have been more than eighteen inches high by about four feet wide. They looked over the edge of the rim and their eyes widened.

The cause of the light was a bright silver beam that looked as though it came from a large search light, shining down from the roof of the mine onto the ground, spreading out as though it were liquid. It lit up what was obviously the old winding room.

Martin's brief to the teenagers had been right. There was a large beam running across the roof of the mine, north to south. It was situated in the middle of the mine and some of the light from the airshaft nudged against its right hand side. Below the beam was an assortment of rubbish, machinery, wooden pallets, poles and bits of metal. The area of the room was about four hundred square feet.

"We did it," said Clem, "we did it," and he held Ginny in his arms

For the first time since they left the pool, Ginny felt safe. She held him tightly and said, "We did too."

After they had rested, they crawled over the lip of rubble and slid down the slope to the floor. Standing up felt strange and they had to find their balance before continuing. They were still bruised and sore. It was still dark, but not that oppressive absolute darkness experienced in the tunnel.

They walked over to the area where the beam of light shone down the air shaft and looked up at it; Clem assessed its height to be about sixty feet from the ceiling edge, which itself was twelve or so feet from the ground. The shaft was about five feet square and seemed to be clad in wooden slats all the way up, although some dark patches indicated that some slats had fallen away. This was confirmed when Clem kicked some rotten wood away from the underside of the shaft.

"We're gonna have to create a pile of rubbish to get up to the airshaft. Then we'll climb to the top," he said in a matter of fact way.

Ginny turned to him and said curtly, "Yeah, easy really. Clem, I need a rest, I really do. And as for climbing that thing, I may not be able to do it."

Clem took her to one side. He found a pile of sacking that was bone dry and although it was a bit smelly, at least it would allow Ginny somewhere to rest. After calming her down he set about building a pile of rubbish, from the floor to the edge of the airshaft in the roof of the chamber. The task was easier than he thought because of the availability of pallets and other heavy items. When he had finished he went over to Ginny.

She was fast asleep. Her face looked beautiful in the dim light and he realised then and there, that he was falling in love with her. He wanted to protect and keep her safe. Clem leaned forward, brushed her left cheek gently with his fingers and she woke up. As she did so, he bent down and kissed her gently, slowly and with a gentle move of his jaws left and right. She moaned and looked up at him when he disengaged.

Smiling she said, "You're not gonna take advantage of a girl in distress now are you Clem Johnson?"

Clem smiled. "If I thought for one moment that I had the energy ma'am, I would do just that. Besides, those sacks are a might smelly – or is it you?"

"Beast," she shrieked grabbing him around the neck, bringing his head towards her. "Get out of this then," she said and she kissed him square on the mouth.

Despite her encouragement Ginny knew that the fear of their circumstances, their aching and scratched limbs and the smelly sacks, would prevent passion from blooming. But nevertheless, the next hour was heaven itself as they rested in each other's arm's, for the moment at least quite safe from harm.

They slept deeply.

Quantock cursed at having to pull together a team that would carry out a search of the country for the missing teenagers. It had been a more difficult job than he had expected. Quite understandably his clever and professional team had their views on the situation. It made it difficult for him to lead them – especially since he already knew the answer to the exam' question.

The Director FBI was angry at Quantock's popularity and his new responsibility. Several blocking manoeuvres had to be overcome before he could be sure that the team was in place and their focus was placed anywhere but Arizona. It had not been a good day.

When he got home he stripped and then showered, totally exhausted from his efforts over the past few days. At least the radio reports where going well and the PR was still pretty effective as the nation pondered on the whereabouts and fate of six young teenagers.

He finished showering and put on a towelling bathrobe, then went to his lounge and poured himself a cranberry juice from a decanter. As he sipped the fruit juice he heard a loud bleep. After searching several coat pockets he found the cell phone that he was reserving for calls to and from the mine location in Arizona.

He cursed. How could he have been so stupid as to leave it in his coat pocket and not put it into his briefcase?

There were a dozen missed calls and several messages. He listened to the first few messages and Martin's anxiety was clearly building. Then his heart sank as he listened to the last one. Martin Adams' voice was slurred and he sounded almost hysterical.

"Okay, man. So this is friggin' it. Kinz is nearly dead and who did that I wonder, eh? You ain't answerin' calls. This is it then. It doesn't matter anyway. It's all gone wrong Mr No-Name and it ain't my fault. See you in hell, man, see you in hell!" Then the call abruptly ended.

Quantock's stomach turned to ice. He quickly called the airport and booked a flight to Tucson and a taxi to the airport. Then he dressed quickly in a denim shirt, leather jacket and light blue jeans. Then he pulled on a pair of boots. After packing he pocketed a pistol and some ammunition. An FBI man would be allowed to carry firearms on an internal flight.

He was in the air to Tucson within the hour. As he flicked through some notes he wondered what the hell he would find.

It was about five in the morning and Martin was snoring loudly in the back of the Nissan four by four, parked about ten yards from the entrance to the San Quiller tin mine. Ralph was hung-over, edgy and angry and hadn't slept at all. He wasn't prepared to wait any longer. The teenagers were in that mine and he was gonna get them out – smoke 'em out in fact. He had seen a pile of wood and brush nearby and got out of the vehicle and began to pile it inside the entrance to the mine. After about forty five minutes he had a substantial amount of combustible debris such as wooden pallets and boxes in place and he took a can of petrol and sprinkled the contents onto it. Minutes later he threw in a match and it burst into flames.

Martin woke up with a start. "What the hell are you doing?"

"Smokin' 'em out buddy, and if they ain't smoked out then they'll end their days chokin' to death."

Martin didn't disagree. He thought it was a wacky idea, but had nothing else to offer as a suggestion. If it didn't work then perhaps the fire would bring down rocks at the entrance and this would trap the teenagers and give them a head start to get away undetected. They didn't just need to get across the border and into Mexico, but had to go deep into the country, avoiding the police so as to hold up with one of their contacts. It would take about a week to organise that.

Ralph watched the flames and realising what could be achieved he quickly grabbed a couple of old tyres lying alongside the road and threw them on too. Then he got some more and added them to the flames. They burned slowly then gave off thick black smoke that swirled and disappeared into the mine – surprisingly quickly he thought. They stood watching the fire, drinking bottled water to quench their thirst. After about forty minutes Martin let out a yell.

"Ralph, look there," he said and pointed to the East Side of the mine and along the ridge, "I'll be damned if that ain't the smoke we're making?"

They looked at each other and their thoughts were as one. There had to be an airshaft and if it was easy to climb, then it was a way out. They walked quickly to the four by four.

Clem led Ginny to the top of the stack of pallets and other rubbish that provided a firm platform for them to get into the airshaft. He left about a four foot gap between the stack and the shaft. Carefully, he put his back against the slats and put his feet against the opposite wall, then he moved upwards using his feet to move up a few inches, and then his back would do the same.

He moved up slowly for a few feet then called to Ginny to follow. It took some encouragement, but she was brave and not being heavy found it fairly easy to get some purchase between her feet and middle back.

Slowly but surely they made their way up the airshaft. When Clem thought he was going too fast he stopped and encouraged Ginny. Every now and then a loose or rotted slat would break away and this caused them to freeze and lock their muscles. It was painful and backbreaking progress.

Clem was about three-quarters of the way up the airshaft when he realised that his nostrils were itching. Then he saw flecks of black material floating up the airshaft towards him. Ginny shouted, "They're trying to smoke us out. God, it's getting thicker, quick Clem, quick!"

Clem looked down and saw that she had unwisely turned round and placed her chest pointing downwards. Whilst this rested her back it put enormous strain on her hands and feet. After a while she had no option but to move flat to the wall of wooden slats reaching out to gain foot and hand holds.

Clem reached up to the top edge of the airshaft and very carefully felt for a firm area on the wood surrounding it. Some of the wood had rotted and would be useless if he put all his weight on to it. He found a thick plank that seemed stable enough. His hands were aching and sore, and his biceps felt as though someone had stuck hot pins into the muscles.

With one supreme effort he grabbed the plank and launched himself upwards and over the edge of the airshaft. He was halfway out and balanced precariously, when two faces came up close to his. He yelped and fell backwards into the blackness.

Before he toppled downwards, four strong arms grabbed him and swung him out of the airshaft and onto the rocks. He lay spread-eagled in the grit and gasped for breath with his heart beating like a steam engine. After a few seconds he looked up at the two faces. They were definitely not Anderson and Adams. They were American Indians. What Indians he did not know; but despite their western dress of jeans, boots and denim shirts, they were Indians for sure!

The older of the two wore a red band around him head. He looked at Clem and was about to speak, but just then a loud sobbing came from the airshaft. It was Ginny.

"What's going on? I can't hear you," she sobbed some more, "I can't hold on, I just can't."

Then Clem heard the sound of some loose planks falling down the airshaft, hitting the sides as they fell. Without a word, the younger of the Indian boys jumped up and went to a couple of backpacks about twenty feet away, returning with a long length of nylon rope.

Clem rushed to the edge of the airshaft and shouted down to Ginny.

"Ginny, hold on for God's sake. There's a couple o' guys here and they are going to help us. Hold on now," he said.

"Just be quick Clem, hurry," she said.

The younger boy tied a few knots a few yards apart in the rope and then took a log and tied it around the middle, making a 'T' junction. He then fixed it between two rocks, checked the strength with the weight of his body and without waiting ran to the airshaft and threw the rope down. To Clem's surprise he almost jumped after it.

He needn't have worried, the boy was muscular and obviously experienced at rope work. In no time he was beside Ginny, whispering reassurances in her ear. Once he had found good footholds for himself, he wound the rope around her middle and secured it. Then, telling her to hold on tight until he said to let go, he grabbed the higher part of the rope and with incredible upper body strength he hauled himself upwards with little effort. As he reached the top of the air shaft his foot caught another loose plank, and dislodged, it fell into the shaft narrowly missing Ginny's shoulder and she squealed in horror.

The boy was soon up and over the edge and indicated to the others that they should start to pull the rope up.

Clem yelled to Ginny, "Let go of the side now Ginny, you'll be okay."

Ginny was frozen with fear and her reply uncompromising, "Are you crazy?"

She had both feet tucked into small holes in the side of the air shaft, one hand holding the only firm piece of wood in the shaft and the other tightly gripping a large rusty nail; her hold was precarious, but tight.

The two Indian boys looked at each other and shrugged. The without further ado, they walked quickly and steadily backwards against the pressure of Ginny's hold on the airshaft and her weight. This surprised her and tugged her off the side of the airshaft. She screamed as the nylon rope dug into her ribs and forced air out of her lungs. She could hardly breathe.

Slowly but surely she was hauled up against the broken and splintered wooden boards, splinters catching her body and rock grazing her hands. It was like being keelhauled!

Sore and exhausted she was pulled up and over the edge and the rope was quickly removed. She lay sobbing in Clem's arms for a full ten minutes before anyone spoke. The two Indians let them have some space and walked over to their backpacks to stow the rope and other items lying around their campsite. After a while, the older Indian came over and offered them both a large unopened bottle of mineral water. They took it gratefully and between them drained the contents in less than a minute.

"I am Christopher and this is Jim. We are Tohono O'odham Indians. That means desert people." He smiled warmly and added, "Before you ask, we both have degrees from US universities and help to run business ventures in our community, namely casinos and tourist goods. We don't carry tomahawks or wear feathered head-dresses, unless it's a party and then it's obligatory! Oh, and we regularly climb up and down these kind of shafts for fun, we abseil our way round these ridges, so we are quite good at ropes."

Ginny laughed, "Frankly, I don't care if you are men from Mars, and as far as your ropes experience is concerned, I am so glad you happened by when you did," she said.

She tried to shake hands but they were sore and limp and opted to raise her hand in a gesture of introduction. It shook lightly as she did so.

"I'm Clem Johnson and this is Ginny Grivas. Guys, we are in real big trouble." He explained the whole situation and left nothing out.

Just then dawn gave way to day and golden fingers of light seemed to flash up into the sky like fingers of gold. It was quite spectacular. As the dim light gave way to increasing sunshine and they saw long shadows cast by Ocotillo, Cholla and Saguaro cacti giving them the appearance of soldiers marching to war across the craggy and barren desert. The light also picked out lonely patches of low Mesquite and Palo Verde trees that seemed to huddle together as if discussing the plight of the two young people. It was beautiful and yet eerie.

"Okay you guys," said Christopher, "if you are in the danger you say you are we had better get going."

They looked round at the airshaft and by now the smoke was billowing thickly out of the top.

He turned to Ginny, "Can you walk?"

She nodded.

"Okay, let's go," he said.

They set off down the rocky side of the mountain and after about twenty minutes the ground levelled and they found themselves in the midst of a patch of tall cactus. A clear path led them to a four by four Toyota pickup truck. After unlocking the cab, Clem and Ginny were helped into the back of the vehicle, where they found some soft tarpaulins to rest on.

"We will now go to San Xavier, our reservation. We can settle down and smoke a peace pipe before having a pow-wow!" said Christopher. Jim laughed at this companion's humour, but Clem and Ginny were now in each other's arms and too tired for humour – or anything else for that matter.

117

The journey north took about ninety minutes. Not that Clem and Ginny noticed; they were soon fast asleep. The vehicle eventually slowed down and Clem awoke. He slowly extricated himself from Ginny's arms and looked over the edge of the pickup truck. Coming into view was a settlement comprising a large number of low adobe style buildings, some with large roofs as if to drain off the rain, and others without. In the middle of the settlement, Clem could just make out a large white painted basilica style church with twin towers with rounded edges, and a mixed white and terracotta brickwork centre.

Christopher saw him looking, leaned out of the window and shouted to him, "The White Dove of the Desert, the mission of San Xavier del Bac. Its restoration is almost finished, you will love it."

Clem settled back on the tarpaulin. He was sure that they would, but what next?

Martin and Ralph had gathered the teenagers' belongings together and stored them with the expensive video equipment - they would sell what they could in Mexico. The bodies of the teenagers were placed in the mess hall. They were ready for a quick getaway – all they needed to do was to catch Clem and Ginny and despatch them without delay.

They drove fast towards the sight of the smoke emerging from the top of the ridge. Their problem was that they had to circumnavigate the ridge using roads that were narrow and strewn with large boulders. Sometimes they even found themselves driving in the opposite direction to the ridge only to cross backwards and get back on course. Ralph cursed as he read a 'hikers' map', spitting insults when roads turned into tracks quite against the indication on the map.

Eventually, they reached an area close to the sight of the smoke that was beginning to thin now. Ralph and Martin almost ran up the hill. When they reached the top of the ridge they looked at the entrance to the airshaft. There were footprints all around it. It didn't take much deduction to see that the teenagers had been helped. Martin walked calmly to the edge of the shaft and saw deep rope marks indented into the end of the wooden surround.

Ralph spoke first. "They got help, but from who?"

Martin looked at the map. "My guess is that is wasn't hikers or tourists. They wouldn't be around so early in the morning. Must be locals. And the only locals around here are Indians or folk living in homesteads. He raised his binoculars to his eyes and scanned the landscape. There was nothing in sight. Then he looked back at the map.

"Okay, buddy, then my guess is that it's Indians from a reservation. And the nearest is San Xavier, right here," and he stabbed the map, "so let's go."

Back in the Nissan four by four Ralph took over the driving. His jaw was fixed and his eyes glared at the road. Martin did the map reading.

They didn't know how to solve this problem and knew they had to think on their feet. When they worked together, they worked in harmony and played hunches; they were good at that. It usually meant that someone would suffer in the end.

Quantock landed at Tucson airport and got himself a hire car. The flight had been uneventful, but he felt ill at ease. There was a kind of foreboding in his mind. He drove quickly to the mine. It was about thirty-five minutes from the airport.

On reaching the San Quiller tin mine he drove carefully into a small cleft in the ridge and went the last mile on foot. If all was well he was to turn around and go home. When he caught sight of the buildings he could only see a sports car parked outside. He used his cell phone to call Adams. When it connected it rang without answer. Before he disconnected he realised that

119

he could hear it ringing in the still air. It was still in the building somewhere – but was Adams with it?

He slowly worked his way around the edge of the parking area past the sports car and to the edge of the building. The curtains were open. He looked inside and he stomach sank. He could see the bodies of four teenagers piled hastily on the floor. The door was unlocked and he went inside slowly, his pistol at the ready. Then he dialled Adams' cell phone again and jumped when it rang loudly; it had been thrown on top of the bodies. He quickly retrieved it and then began to search the buildings carefully, but could find no trace of the other two teenagers who, by a process of elimination remembering the photographs in his briefing notes, he identified as Clem Johnson and Ginny Grivas.

Quantock cursed and wondered what the hell had gone wrong. He retrieved the cell phone and sat down to think. He listened again to Adams' slurred message on his own cell phone. It became clearer. He had been stupid enough not to have the cell phone at the ready to answer any queries that the CIA men might have. Then Kinz's heart attack happened. The operatives panicked and high on alcohol and perhaps drugs too, sore at the failure of their last mission, they had convinced themselves that they had been abandoned to perhaps be set up as the fall guys to make someone, whoever, to be made to look good. He couldn't be sure as to what had been on their mind, but after listening to the call again he realised that they were even more unstable than his contact in the CIA has led him to believe.

He thought some more then dialled a number.

"Hello. This is Arab Blue. The missing teenagers have been located. Send in someone purporting to be a hiker or hill walker, whatever, to the San Quiller tin mine south of Tucson."

He then gave the map reference.

"The news is to break in the next three hours and make sure the candidate you select plays innocent and contacts local newspapers first. Six bodies have been found, you understand? I repeat six bodies. Then send in agents to seal the place off before the local police get to see the scene. No one is to enter the building. There's still more cleaning to be done. Understand?"

The person at the other end concurred and the call ended.

Quantock was a careful and thoughtful man. He drove to the mine entrance and saw the smoking debris, then looked up and saw the thin trail of smoke above the ridge. But instead of chasing his tail, he drove to the top of the highest ridge and parked so that he kept the smoking ridge to the east and a good view to the north and south. Then he took out his binoculars and searched the horizon.

He was rewarded after only five minutes. He trained his powerful Zeiss binoculars on a trail of dust and just made out the outline of a Nissan vehicle heading to the Northwest. He looked at his map. He was confused. The only residential area he could identify was the San Xavier Indian Reservation.

Did they have the teenagers in the vehicle? Where they chasing them? What was happening he did not know? But he would be there to sort things out soon – that was for sure.

But first of all he needed to sort out the situation at the tin mine.

Chapter Seven

Kinz spent two days in hospital and to the surprise the doctors was on the mend. It had been a warning that his stress levels were high and coupled with high cholesterol resulted in a stroke that made him faint and bang his head. He was advised to cease drinking whisky and deal with his diet. He resolved to do just that. It had been an uncomfortable experience.

Despite entreaties for him to stay in hospital he discharged himself and agreed to employ a nurse on his staff. He couldn't wait to get home.

His housekeeper warmly greeted him and fussed him so much that he had to retreat to his study. He glanced at his whisky Tantalus, the crystal decanters nestling neatly in their cherry wood casing, and smiled, wagging a finger at it. Then he made his way to his chair. He sat and thought about the image of his lovely wife Clara and the effect that it had had on him.

He idly turned on the radio beside his chair and settled down to listen to his favourite radio station. As his eyes were beginning to close an announcement came on air. The words tumbled from the radio and he felt the blood drain from his already weak body; his jaw dropped.

News has just been received that the bodies of the six missing teenagers, the sons and daughters of US senators have been found at the derelict San Quiller tin mine near Tucson. They were discovered by a tourist who was hill walking. There was no sign of the perpetrators of the crime. We will bring you more news as the story unfolds.

The music resumed, but Kinz wasn't listening. He stood up shakily and put his hands to his face, which was now wet with tears tumbling from his eyes. Clara's spirit had been right – he had been a fool.

After a while, during which he was rooted to his chair, unable to move or think clearly, he gathered his wits, stood up unsteadily and walked slowly to his desk. Almost in a dream, he took out his writing materials and his prized silver pistol and put them on his desk, then sat down.

There was only one thing he had to do.

The Indian boys drove the Toyota truck to within half a mile of the San Xavier mission and stopped by the wide of the road. Christopher got out, went to the back and said, "Okay you guys. If you are in a lot of trouble then I guess the fewer people who know you are in the reservation the better. So get under the tarpaulin, just for a short while, okay?"

Clem and Ginny obeyed without question and the vehicle then continued on its way into the reservation. Curiosity got the better of Clem and he peeked out from underneath the cover. He saw the mission and was in awe of its beauty. It had two towers over one hundred feet, each was bleach white like the main body of the building. The middle portion was, however, made out of a kind of clay or terracotta material on which there was considerable design work. Each of the towers and the central portion had a black balcony. In front of the Mission was a large wall enclosing a paved area. The hard sand and clay surface around the Mission, dotted with coarse leafed bushes and trees of a small or medium height gave the building a kind of superiority over the landscape. There were many other white buildings as well as a large number of adobe dwellings, some with large roof structures that would provide shelter from the sun or allow heavy rain to flow off easily, whilst others were simple square or oblong structures. It was fascinating - and not a tepee in sight.

Christopher drove on past the Mission for about fifty yards and turned into a large secluded courtyard behind what seemed to be a modern public building. Both Indian boys got out and went to the back of the vehicle.

Clem pulled the tarpaulin to one side and was surprised to see that Ginny was fast asleep. He shook her awake slowly and gently. She awoke and gazed up at him, then took his hand and smiled.

Christopher helped them down and into the rear entrance of the building.

"This is the tourist information centre and gift shop," said Jim, "open every day of the year except Christmas Day and Easter. And we bulk store our gifts on shelves over here." He pointed to the left side of the room they just entered.

They were surrounded by a variety of plates, shallow bowls and square glazed tiles as well as large pots of different designs. Some of the patterns were of butterflies or star shapes, but most of the objects had an interesting circular maze design, with a small wedge shape inserted from top to middle with a human shape in it. Ginny was fascinated by it and wondered about its significance. Most of the pottery and ceramic colours were of a blue tinge. There were some robes and feathered hats, but it was obvious that these were simply tourist items. Not so the blankets and rugs that were obviously hand made and looked as though they were made of heavy woollen material.

Ginny was fascinated and wanted to spend time looking at the items. Clem gave in to her whim and when an old lady came in dressed in a simple fawn coloured shift, Christopher spoke to her in their language and she gave a toothless grin. He talked some more and she looked concerned, very concerned. The she went over to Ginny and put an arm on her shoulder.

Christopher smiled and said, "This is my grandmother and she will look after Ginny, I promise you. Clem, come with me and we can sort out somewhere for you to hide and get some rest."

Then Clem and the two boys left the room and walked away from the tourist centre towards a nearby adobe. They chatted amiably and then, when they had walked only a few yards they stopped suddenly in their tracks. Clem was grabbed and pushed roughly behind a wall just as a Nissan four by four rounded the corner. It cruised past with two men in it who were looking left and right. Then it stopped by the tourist centre.

Martin and Ralph got out of the vehicle and Ralph marched straight into the tourist shop without pausing. Thankfully, the old lady had been looking out of the window and saw Christopher give her a quick wave and worried gaze, which was enough for her to realise that the two men were after Ginny and Clem. Without thinking twice she turned to Ginny and made her lie down by the rugs then she piled two or three over the top of her; then she sat on top of them.

Ralph burst into the centre. "Hi there old squaw," he said with a sickly grin, "I'm looking for two good friends a boy and a girl, you understand me. Huh?"

The old lady beamed at him and showed several gaps in her teeth, but said nothing.

"You understand what I'm sayin'?" Ralph repeated menacingly and he walked towards her.

She just smiled at him, beaming toothlessly. Then without ceremony she raised the left side of her bottom and broke wind noisily. Ralph recoiled.

"Ugh, you miserable old hag. Jeez man, I bet you're a beauty in bed!" Then he turned around and quickly made for the door exiting without shutting it. The old lady heard his footsteps walk back to his vehicle and then saw him stand by the front of it, obviously waiting for his companion.

Martin came around from behind the tourist centre and joined Ralph.

He looked up at the sky and without directing his words to Ralph and said conspiratorially, "The vehicle in the compound at the rear is a Toyota pickup truck. Cream coloured," and he passed Ralph the registration that he had written on a piece of paper, "the engine is warm and it is covered in desert dust. They are here somewhere buddy, but where I do not know."

Christopher and Jim walked up to Martin and Ralph. "Hi there, can we be of any assistance?"

Martin took the lead. "Why yes, sir, thank you both very much. We need to find the whereabouts of two young people. You see, they've run away from their parents who are now very worried about them both. They are causing a lot of distress, but hey buddy, you know what kids are like, eh? Anyway, me and my friend have been taken on to look for them. The last sighting we had was up at the San Quiller tin mine. Have you seen them? The boy is called Clem and he is medium height, a hundred and fifty pounds, fair hair and is dressed in a denim blue shirt and jeans. The girl is called Ginny Grivas, she is about five foot six, slim build, with auburn hair and dressed in a white blouse and blue jeans."

"Are you police?" said Jim.

"No, no, not at all, we are private detectives. Look, if you do get to hear anything call this number eh? We are staying locally." Martin looked left and right. "There is a very good reward for information, you know what I mean. The parents are very wealthy and keen to make sure that their children are safe and sound. You would too if they were your kids wouldn't you?"

Christopher and Jim nodded in agreement and took the piece of paper with the cell phone number on it.

"We'll get some of our folk to look for them sir, and if we find them we will call you straight away, you betcha," said Jim, a little too enthusiastically for Martin's liking.

They shook hands and Martin and Ralph drove off out of the Reservation, past the Mission building and onto the main road back to the desert. Several miles down the road they stopped the vehicle and Martin turned to Ralph.

"We're gonna have to watch the reservation from the ridge over there. There is only one large road out of here and my guess is that they will try and make it out during the night. If they are confident that we have gone on our way then they may be stupid enough to use the same vehicle. That's the one we will follow. So let's hunker up and do what we are good at. If we get no joy in twenty-four hours we must take our chances and run for the border come what may. What do you say?"

Ralph held the wheel tight. "Can't we just tour around the reservation making offers of hard bucks for information?" he said.

Martin shrugged, "We could, but my guess is that these people are highly suspicious of authority and any outsiders and more likely to take sides with those being chased. We've sown the seeds of financial reward, maybe we will get a call maybe we won't. But I reckon our best bet is to be patient."

Ralph agreed and they set about selecting a good spot, where there were a few trees and rocks, from which they could keep watch on the road.

Clem and Ginny were reunited and they hugged thanking their lucky stars for the narrow escape. Christopher went off again to find a place for them to sleep and Clem reluctantly accompanied him. Ginny hugged the old lady and they both laughed at her last minute tactics to avoid Ralph's attentions. Over the next half and hour they both sat on a rug and by dint of sign language and some English words they communicated on things that women can talk about without much complication. They laughed at each other's attempts to be understood. Ginny wanted to thank her and took off a silver ring that her mother had given her for her twentieth birthday. She gave it to the old lady, who smiled and held her hand. Then to Ginny's surprise the old lady went to a large carpetbag, brought it back to where she was sitting and emptied the contents on the blanket. She indicated that Ginny should select something. The contents were a mixture of soaps, necklaces, old coins and small carved models. But Ginny's eyes immediately fell on a small cell phone. Without hesitating she pointed to it and the old lady readily reached for it and then passed it to her with a broad smile.

Ginny pressed the right keys to access the past calls and found that only one number had ever been called on this cell phone, it had 'Christopher' as the contact. It could have been a present from the boy so that they could keep in touch. There were no other details. It had a low charge. She kissed the old lady and after a while she left her. She would call home – she simply had to. Her mother would be worried sick when the news of the massacre was discovered, as indeed it would be soon. She had to call her first.

Ginny leaned against the warm rear wall of the tourist shop. The number rang and she wondered what she would say if it was her father. But it was her mother who answered. For a moment she could say nothing and a big lump formed in her throat.

"Mom, it's me," she said almost gasping the words out.

Her mother was delirious, and choked back a scream. "Oh, honey, my little girl. Oh God. What's happening, we are so worried Ginny. Where are you?" She started crying.

"Mom, I can't talk for long. Listen. We started out on a mission to make a political video, like I said in the letter I wrote you. And...."

Her mother broke in, "What letter, I got no letter, and neither did the other parents?"

Ginny's heart sank. But we all wrote letters to our parents it was a mission, oh God, what a mess. Mom, the important thing is that we are safe and being looked after. Look, there is something terribly wrong with all this and I want you to promise me that you will not, repeat, not tell anyone outside the family of my call. I will call again, I promise Mom. I love you."

Her mother sobbed words that were barely audible, but sounded like 'I understand'. She started to talk again, but the signal started to crackle and then the phone went dead. The battery was out of power. Ginny bit her lip and tears welled in her eyes. Then she rushed back into the tourist shop. The old lady was sitting looking at the ring that Ginny had given her and looked up. Ginny waved the cell phone at her and said, ""Please, cable, er, wire, charging," then she shook it as if it were empty, "please, I need to call my mom....."

Then she burst into tears.

The old lady looked shocked and jumped up. She took Ginny in her arms and cuddled her whilst Ginny cried like a baby. After about five minutes she let her go and went to a box of junk. Then, with a big broad smile on her face she brought out a cell phone charging cable. Ginny squealed with delight and hugged her again. Soon the cell phone was being charged. Ginny would be able to use it again. The old lady left her alone with her thoughts.

Ginny resolved not to tell Clem about the letters. She had respected his resolve and strength to get her through the tunnel and out of the tin mine. But she had seen the signs of stress in his face and they had a lot more work to do yet. For the moment, she would keep the information to herself. Something was terribly wrong. Why were the letters not delivered? Senator Randolph Kinz was such an honourable man, what was he up to? Why were their friends killed? They were obviously being hunted because they were witnesses. The most important question was: who could they trust?

Clem and Ginny met up again in the tourist shop. He walked towards her with his gentle boyish features looking saggy at the edges. Lack of sleep was catching up on him and it was evident that he was having trouble keeping his eyes open. Christopher led them both to an adjacent adobe building and they were soon standing in a room that was furnished with a pine sideboard, an Indian-style stool with three legs and a large bed with a brass head-end. Just the sight of the bed made their bodies sag with tiredness. Christopher didn't even check to see if they were happy to be sleeping in the same bed. Without ceremony Clem and Ginny fell onto the bed, then turned and faced each other, holding on as tight as they could before they drifted into a long sleep.

They slept until early evening without waking once. Then Ginny began to stir. She was having a bad dream. In the dream she was stuck fast in a hole in the ground that was getting smaller and smaller, compressing her body until it pushed the breath out of her. She squealed, sat upright and the blanket fell from her revealing her naked breasts. Although the Indian chaperone, sitting just outside the door to look after their every need was a woman, she averted her head to avoid embarrassment. Ginny covered herself up and put the blanket to her eyes to stop the tears. Clem woke up with a start, saw her distress and took her into his arms.

The chaperone quickly left them alone then returned with hot tea and crispy flat bread leaving the tray beside the bed. Moments later there was a knock at the door and Christopher came in.

"Hi guys. You slept well. We've been talking and reckon that you ought to get out of here pronto. There is only one course of action. I want you to meet a very interesting guy, he's called

Hobo Joe, he's an Apache would you believe, and we can talk about how he can get you out of here. Now up you get and get washed and fed," he said, and then he smiled and left without waiting for an answer.

Clem sipped the hot tea and looked at Ginny. Hobo Joe? It seemed a kind of cliché, but there it was: Hobo Joe. After washing and getting into a change of clean jeans and tops left by the Indian chaperone, they made their way back to the tourist shop. It was now early evening and the orange sky was breathtaking. In the stock room at the back of the tourist shop, Christopher had set up a table and a number of chairs. Christopher came in with some friends and joined them, then later his grandmother also came in and she smiled broadly when she saw Ginny. Ginny returned her smile and gave her a wave. Christopher introduced Hobo Joe. He was a man who travelled the AMTRAK railways, but without paying. He would show them the way out of the desert and away from the attention of the two men chasing them. Joe was about sixty or seventy years old – it was hard to tell, his skin, wrinkled by the continuous attention of the desert sun and wind, resembled cracked mud on a dry river bed floor. He wore his long hair in a greasy ponytail tied with a leather cord. His eyes sparkled and his smile was broad and encouraged even more cracks to appear. He was dressed in a leather top and jeans, and wore cowboy boots. Around his neck he had a leather and silver necklace studded with blue stones that shimmered in the light. It seemed to be quite special to him because he kept touching and stroking it throughout his conversations.

Although his accent was thick and he language was peppered with a lot of slang and Indian expressions, there were no problems communicating with Joe, the only problem they had was stopping him from talking. He talked for some time about his antics on and off the AMTRAK trains that travelled west to east from well beyond San Diego through to San Antonio an on to New Orleans. He described the many trains he had hopped on. His eyes sparkled as he mentioned the locomotives, almost like long lost girl friends, the bulky red Southern Pacific Railroad EMD GP60, the ugly little San Pedro SPSR25, but his favourite was the graceful Union Pacific GE C41-8W with its long nose and sleek livery.

When he finally paused, Clem looked at Ginny and smiled. This guy may be a hobo, but he would gain a master's degree in locomotive identification.

Hobo Joe noticed this and smiled back. "The way outta here for you two is to let me show ya how to get onto a slow moving locomotive, s'easier than you think. Then you only need to hang on until Benson town. It's a very large junction and the loco' will slow down before stoppin'. They stop overnight, or take on fuel and water. From there you can get yourself off and into the town. 'Tain't that big, 'tas a population of p'raps , say four thousand folk. Best of all though, it's situated smack on the interstate highway I-10. Get yourself a hire car and you're goin' places pard." He smiled as though he had planned escapes all his life.

Clem turned to Ginny, but said nothing. She turned to him and raised an eyebrow. "Jeez, Clem. I got you to skinny dip in cold water and you get your own back by getting me to crawl through a hole in the ground, then up a steep shaft. Now you want me to jump on a train. Is this getting your own back or what?"

Clem laughed and turned to Hobo Joe. "I guess that means yes!"

Christopher was good to them and gave them a hundred dollars cash. They should pay it back when they could. Clem shook his hand and thanked him profusely and Ginny gave him a big hug. Luckily Clem still had his wallet with his driver's licence and other documents. Once away from San Xavier, they would hold up for a few days then head home. He hadn't really thought of a plan – he just wanted to get away from the desert and the agents on his tail.

They talked over the plans for a while then as it got darker Hobo Joe explained what would happen. He showed them a map that highlighted a sharp curve in the rail track, which was at a beginning of a short incline and explained that they would jump on a locomotive at that point. Jim brought Clem and Ginny two San Xavier waterproof hiking tops with fold away hoods and lined with wool, from the tourist shop. Each had a small motif on the top right side of the waterproof, of the man who had founded mission in 1783, Father Eusabio Kino dressed in a wide brimmed hat, who rode into a village of Tohono O'odham Indians and set up his home. They would get some more rest and set off in the early hours of the morning.

Most of the Indians left the room, including Hobo Joe who went out for a smoke. Clem sipped some hot tea and said, "Christopher, I really appreciate what you guys are doing for us. It's a far cry from what people think about Indians, you know, I mean, well, sorry but I know my friends would know nothing about you guys. Yet you are the indigenous people of America."

Christopher smiled and tapped his mug with a spoon. "Yes, I learned that at the University of Arizona. Got into a couple of fights too when stupid young men would demand a war dance or magic potion. The fact is that the Tohono O'odham Indians have a strong sense of personal and cultural identity. Traditionally our home has been the Sonoran Desert." He paused and drew a breath before continuing. "I brought my new learning and skills home, as other Indians have done, but nothing shakes my belief in my background and sense of being an Indian. We are Catholics you know? But our religion is flavoured with a lot of cultural themes. You know something, our tribal view of wellbeing revolves around the spiritual harmony between individuals, family, the community and the land. We are family oriented and the individual has never been the main focus. Even today, a lot of our decisions are based on consensus."

Clem found this ironic. For all the early historic American repugnance of European monarchy with its restrictions on the freedom of its citizens and feudal links to the church, the resulting fabric of America's politics never borrowed anything from its indigenous people. The contemporary focus of the American citizen seemed to be as a person to be 'sold' to rather than talked to, it was about what you owned and how important you perceived yourself rather than the kind of life you lived and how you behaved to your fellow man. He shook Christopher's hand, his expression showed his admiration and thanks.

Christopher's grandmother treated Ginny's lacerated body and scratched hands, binding them tightly to avoid them hurting as she boarded the locomotive. Ginny didn't know how it would end and she was confused and scared as hell.

All she wanted to do was to get home safely to her family.

It was approaching four in the morning and Martin was wide awake. Ralph was snoring. He wondered whether or not his plan would work. If it didn't they would have to run for it. But he couldn't be sure that they wouldn't be caught before they made it to their contacts in Mexico. The Mexican and US government had an edgy relationship because of the lack of security on their borders, but when they got their act together, fleeing criminals were easily caught. Of course, money changed hands and this helped the process. Naturally, it depended on the importance of the fugitive. He knew this because he had used the system many times himself. No, the only answer was to catch the kids, dispose of them and buy time to get to their contacts in southern Mexico.

As he mused about days gone by, he noticed vehicle lights coming out of the reservation. He sat bolt upright, shaking Ralph with his right hand. Ralph snorted and woke up. "Wha's up?"

"Lights. Aha, as I hoped buddy," he said, as the cream coloured Toyota drove past them and down the road.

Martin turned on the engine, but not the lights and followed the Toyota. It was a moonlit night and he had to keep well behind the vehicle so as not to be noticed. They had taken the precaution of wetting the Nissan and covering it with dirt to cut down the reflection of their white vehicle. A couple of miles away the Toyota stopped and after a while it turned round and headed back up the road at speed. Martin only just managed to turn down a dirt track and get out of sight before it passed them on its way back to the reservation.

Martin was confused. This was crazy – what were they up to? But as he looked closely at the front seat he noticed that there was only one passenger. This must mean that Clem and Ginny had been dropped off where the Toyota had stopped.

After a few seconds Martin started the engine again and set off slowly down the road to where he thought that the teenagers had been dropped off. He stopped the Nissan in a small lay by as close to the spot. They both got out and listened carefully. The Sonoran Desert was so quiet they could easily hear the faint sound of voices ahead and set off in pursuit.

Ahead of them, Hobo Joe was guiding Clem and Ginny between the various ocotillos and saguaro cacti and small groups of Palo Verde trees. Luckily it made them hard to spot, as the landscape appeared speckled in the moonlight. In the distance they heard the unmistakable sound of an approaching locomotive. Martin looked at Ralph and they instinctively knew what was being planned. They hurried through the rough terrain and made more noise than they should. Ralph grazed his hand on a nearby cactus and yelped.

Hobo Joe stopped dead in his tracks. He put his fingers to his mouth. "People come," he whispered.

"Where?" said Clem.

They waited, but the sound wasn't repeated. Hobo Joe was concerned. Ginny took the cell phone out of her pocket.

"Clem, have you got that telephone number that Martin gave you when we arrived? You know the one he wanted you to use if we got into trouble on our walkabout the tin mine?" she whispered.

Clem said, "Yes, in my wallet, but why?"

"Here's why," said Ginny, waving the cell phone.

Clem looked aghast, but shrugged his shoulders and quickly felt into his shirt pocket and pulled out the paper. Ginny cupped the phone in her hands so that the LED light would not show up and read the number, and then keyed it in. Seconds later the phone rang about one hundred yards away to the left. There was loud swearing and Hobo Joe smiled in the moonlight and deftly guided them in the opposite direction. Ginny quickly switched the cell phone off in case a return call was made and hurried to keep up with Hobo Joe.

Joe enjoyed getting the better of the two chasers and waved the teenagers on, smiling like a schoolboy. Just as he did so, Clem and Ginny caught sight of the locomotive coming around the steep bend to their right. It came slowly as it negotiated the bend and the gradient. Hobo Joe stood by the track and motioned them to watch him and follow his lead.

As the train came past he loped alongside, then as a gap appeared between two trucks he pointed to a ladder with a step at the bottom of one of the cargo carriages, he let this pass, and then he pointed to the next one. He was telling them that each one had such a ladder and foothold. Clem gave him the thumbs up and told Ginny.

Then Hobo Joe waited for the next truck and deftly hopped on, grabbing a rail with one hand and putting his foot on the step. It was easy to haul himself upright.

The train carried on at a slow steady pace.

Clem then got Ginny to go first and to do the same as Joe had done following behind her as she ran alongside the trucks. He needn't have worried. She was fit and negotiated the manoeuvre with ease, although the soreness of her scratched hands proved excruciating. She looked back and he gave her a thumbs-up. Then he did the same.

When they were both safely on the train, holding on as hard as they could, Hobo Joe waved and yelled, and then he hopped off. The train took a few minutes to pass him completely and he watched as it disappeared into the distance. Then he sighed and turned around to go home.

Facing him were Martin and Ralph.

Clem and Ginny hung on tightly to the cold metal ladders as the train gathered speed towards Benson. They wished that they had gloves, but managed to console themselves that they were putting miles between them and Martin and Ralph. The journey was only about thirty minutes, but it seemed like a lifetime. They were overjoyed to see the lights of the Benson rail junction come into view. Just as Hobo Joe had predicted the train slowed to walking pace and Clem shouted ahead to Ginny to get down.

They jumped from the train and despite falling a little awkwardly, Ginny got up and ran to Clem. "Another triumph, Clem. Aren't we the best?"

She kissed him with delight and they held the embrace feeling each other's warm bodies. The nearby Dragoon Mountains looked black against the dim light of the sun trying to crawl up into the morning sky. But they had no time to take in the scenery and made their way towards what looked like a road crossing and the main highway into Benson. It didn't take long for them to walk the two miles or so into town. It was six in the morning, lights were on in some of the houses and shops and folks were just beginning to rise and take breakfast, but all Clem and Ginny wanted to do was to find a bed. They walked into the centre of Benson looking for somewhere suitable to spend the night and get some rest. It wasn't a large town. It was well known for its location near to the famous western town of Tombstone and being located on the rail intersection that received the smelted metals from the local mines to be distributed by rail. It was incorporated as a city in 1924 and named after Judge William B Benson of California a friend of the president of the railroad that was the city's lifeline.

Clem and Ginny were confident that they were out of harm's way. All the same, they decided to book into a small and badly decorated motel, get some rest, then some food and think about their next step. They wanted somewhere low key to spend a day or so.

They entered the small foyer and saw a tired looking reception clerk, a man in his late forties with unkempt hair that concealed a large bald patch. He was wearing wire spectacles that hung loosely on his small nose and dressed in an open necked beach shirt. Somehow coconut trees and surfers on the shirt seemed out of place in good ole Benson town. He looked up languidly, as if preferring not to see to them.

"Can I he'p you, son?" he said with a southern drawl.

"Yes sir, we' like a room," said Clem.

The clerk leaned over the counter and looked around them.

"Travelin' light?" he sneered, as he turned to Ginny looking longer at her body than was absolutely necessary.

Clem was angry and said in a strong voice, "Just a room and can we make it quick, buddy, we're mighty tired. Like, now, please?"

The clerk was taken aback and shrugged. What did he care of morals? He thought "Just pay your dues man. Then move on like most travelling folk do." He pushed the register towards Clem and slapped a cheap biro on top of the blank page.

Clem signed the register and thanked his lucky stars he still had his wallet with Christopher's dollars, his credit cards and driver's license. After signing the register they took the room key and wearily walked to the rear of the hotel where they were directed. He turned to Ginny.

"Not for us the prestigious suite with the Jacuzzi and four poster bed?" he said with a smile. Ginny smiled back and held on to his arm all the way to the room. After a while she had shed her clothes and lay in a hot tub. The feeling was out of this world, relaxing, sensuous and dreamily smooth – even if it had taken all the hotel sachets to get even a minimal level of suds in the water. The scratches and cuts on her hands and body hurt at first, but the irritation soon subsided. She heard Clem yell that he was going out for a while and didn't complain, it meant she could stay longer in the bathtub. She could also make another call to her mom. She lurched out of the bath and without dressing fumbled in her jacket pocket for the cell phone. It took a while to ring and her mother answered.

"Mom?" she said.

"Ginny, oh Ginny, my God, are you all right?"

"Mom, yes of course, look I'm sorry that I got cut off yesterday, but what on earth is the matter, Clem and I are safe, okay?"

"But the news programme honey, the news, it said that all, yes all of you had been found shot at a tin mine called San Quiller near Tucson. Ginny, what's going on? Your father is confused at not being able to shout about your safety and wants to get to the bottom of things. You know dad? He's so happy you called and yet so upset, it means his depression is returning. Oh God this is so stupid, me worrying about depression, what am I saying?"

The sound of her mom crying again made Ginny's heart ache.

"Mom, I'm just as confused as you are. We just need a little more time. Look mom, this is getting so confusing and difficult. I don't know who to trust. Just believe that we are both okay. I promise I will call you when I can. I love you mom."

Ginny was crying and didn't want to press the red disconnect button, but she had to and knew it.

Her mother was distressed, but agreed to end the call and await the next one. Ginny felt the goose bumps on her naked body and quickly hopped back into the hot tub of soapy water. She felt sad but knew that she had to be strong. First she had to get some rest and lots of it.

Clem walked the length of West Fifth Street. He wasn't in a hurry and enjoyed having some time to himself, even though he was tired. The city was coming to life and he smelled the fresh coffee and fast food being prepared. After passing North Huachuca and then North Patagonia Avenue he spotted a car hire office. It took him about thirty minutes to hire a Volvo station wagon giving his driver's licence and a deposit for two day's hire – he knew he wanted it for longer, but what the hell? After checking the vehicle over he drove it to North Huachuca Street and parked it outside the Library. The car radio worked well and he tuned it into the local Benson city radio station KAVV-FM. Life all around him seemed normal, people going to work, the radio playing; but for Clem and Ginny it was anything but normal.

He locked the car and walked back down West Fifth Street towards the Motel. As he passed a shop selling newspapers he saw the headlines for the San Pedro Valley News-Sun.

Missing teenagers sought by the FBI – still no news.

It brought him back to earth.

After nodding off for a long while in the hot tub Ginny awoke to the feel of cooler water around her flanks and cold breasts and feet. She swished the luke warm water over the cold bits and felt instantly better. Then she heard Clem come into the room and thought that it was high time she said 'thank you' properly to her hero. She slid out of the bath, wrapping herself in a medium sized towel.

Hobo Joe held out for as long as he could, but the CIA boys were accustomed to meting out punishment that got results. Hobo Joe's head swam with pain and at its height, he saw the orange sun lighting the prairie all around him. His ancestors were standing some way off shouting encouragement to him, but he couldn't hear what they were saying. Then he could stand the piercing pain no longer. With tears in his eyes he muttered the word Benson. All of a sudden the light dimmed and there was a swirling feeling in his head as the pain stopped. The people in his vision stopped waving and encouraging him. They stood deathly still and slowly lowered their heads. Then they turned their backs on him and began walking into a wide desert. Joe cried out to them to come back, wanted desperately to explain how agonizing it was, but they didn't listen. He felt the pain of humiliation and sorrow.

As he sobbed, Ralph put him out of his misery with a single shot to the back of the head. They dumped his body out of sight of the road and made their way back to their vehicle. As he got in the Nissan, Ralph held Hobo Joe's blue gemstone necklace up to the light. The moonbeams seemed to be attracted to its centre. Then he casually put it into his pants pocket, started the vehicle and headed for Benson.

With luck on their side this should now not take that long to finish the job. Then they would be Mexico bound. He smiled to himself, perhaps his luck was changing after all?

Pure guesswork, good luck and a pliant hotel clerk made the job of locating Clem and Ginny an easy one for Martin and Ralph. Clem answered a quiet knock at the door and, before he could understand what was happening he was quickly overpowered. Now Ginny stood transfixed, holding the towel tightly to her body. She looked at Clem's face, it showed the pain of having his neck tightly held in Martin's iron grip.

"Drop the towel honey, or his neck gets broken," said Ralph, leering at her and nodding towards Clem. He put his pistol into his pants pocket and sat down on the foot of the bed.

Martin had lost his composure by now and was happy to let his friend have some fun.

"Don't waste my time girl!" he barked and she jumped with fear.

Ginny felt that odd mixture of pending humiliation, embarrassment, vulnerability and fear that was strangely sexual. She was powerless. Her stomach was full of a thousand butterflies as the adrenaline drained out. Everything tingled as she reluctantly, slowly let the towel drop to the floor, leaving her naked. She let out a kind of frightened child-like yelp and quickly sat on the bed with her knees up tight against her stomach, covering her breasts with her arms. Ginny wanted to speak, but her throat was paralysed with fright and she felt her heartbeat hard against her chest, making her rock back and forth.

Clem tried to object, his eyes wide with fear and loathing, but Martin only tightened his grip causing him great pain and no words came.

Ralph came closer, smiling and said, "Oeee, gal, aint you the prettiest thing, fair skin and you smell so good?"

He reached out and ran the outside of his left hand down the side of her body towards her bottom. Ginny closed her eyes tight and gripped her knuckles until they were white.

Suddenly, as Ralph moved closer his hands sliding to her thighs, the door was kicked open with a loud crash and a man in jeans and a blue shirt stood their, revolver in hand.

"Freeze!" he shouted, pointing the gun at Ralph.

Ralph was afraid of nothing and was prepared to take his chances. He grabbed Ginny and held her naked body close to his, at the same time discretely reaching for his own pistol in his pants pocket.

They both recognised the man in the doorway and Quantock and a brief silence ensued. Quantock looked around and hesitated for a few seconds.

Ralph noticed this and smiled, but then his smile turned to a twisted curse as he tried to quickly bring his pistol to the firing position in the direction of the man in the doorway.

He tugged and tugged, and as he did so he lessened his grip and Ginny broke free and slid across the bed and onto the floor. Ralph was still trying to raise the pistol, but it would not elevate it more than thirty degrees, because it was held fast by the cord of the hobo's necklace with the blue gemstone that had become inexplicably tangled with the gun whilst in his pocket.

Quantock wasted no time and shot Ralph in the centre of his forehead. His body slumped to the floor. There had been little noise, just a couple of doomph sounds. His pistol was fitted with a silencer. Although there was very little bright light in the room, the blue gem-stone twinkled as it lay on the carpet alongside Ralph's body.

Martin let go of Clem immediately and put his hands up.

"Hey man, steady. Whoa now. Ralph was always a bit unstable, but I wasn't gonna…"

He never finished the sentence. The man stepped forward casually put the gun to Martin's forehead and shot him just once and he crumpled to the floor. The man then closed the door quietly and grabbed a bathrobe.

"Here kid, put this on" he said, throwing it to Ginny.

She grabbed it gratefully with one hand, covering herself with the other and rushed from the room crying. Clem got up slowly stroking his neck.

"By golly sir, am I glad to see you?"

"It's okay Clem. FBI. You're safe now. Relax. My name's Dan Quantock," he said reaching into his shirt and pulling out his identity card, "these boys are real bad, but they won't be hurting anybody any more. I'll explain a lot more to you later, but not right now."

Ginny came into the room, her eyes red with tears and the bathrobe wrapped firmly around her. Quantock explained that he would call up a team to 'clean' the place, but in the mean time he would book another room into which Clem and Ginny to go to relax and while they waited.

Ginny was pleased to be able to get away from the bodies, but her relief was short-lived.

"Can I phone my Mom please sir?" she said.

Quantock looked awkward and quickly, too quickly, replied, "Oh, Ginny, don't do that yet. Your, er Mom, well she knows that you are safe and well, and she will not have known about these guys chasing you. I'm just worried that they may have a tap on your home and that their may be more bad guys around, you know what I mean? Besides, no sense in worrying her. You can call her a little later when I have you both in a real safe place. Let's just get you out of here first, eh?"

With that, he disappeared to make arrangements for the extra room.

Ginny turned to Clem, put her fingers on his lips and said in a low voice.

"Clem, I didn't tell you, but I phoned Mom on the cell phone I got from Christopher's grandmother. I know you didn't want me to do it. It was a short call I promise. She said that she had only just heard the news programme which was full of the fact that we were all dead, shot at the San Quiller tin mine, every one. I actually had to try hard to persuade her it was me calling her. He's lying Clem!"

Clem held her tight and they didn't say anything for a while.

"What does that mean?" she said.

"It means we are still not safe and we both don't know what all this is about. You must not contact your mom again Ginny, the line may be tapped and if we cannot trust Senator Kinz, the FBI, then who the hell can we trust? We need to run again, but how and where?"

He went to the window and could just see where the rental car was parked a block and a half away outside the library on Huachuca Street. Almost obscuring it was a large helter skelter, which was part of the fairground set up in the centre of Benson. Stalls and all manner of food outlets were busy doing trade and country music wailed loudly. He pulled her close.

"Ginny, see over there, it's the car I hired earlier, the blue Volvo station wagon, I got it when I went out for some breakfast. Here are the keys," he passed them to her, "we have to make a break for it and we need to do it separately. The only thing we can do it is to use the fairground over there in any way we can."

Ginny nodded and looked at the floor. "But I don't want to leave you Clem," she said.

Clem put his hand on her neck and brought her head close to his.

"I know. If we can make a break for it, in any way at all, then we should meet behind the helter skelter at the fairground within twenty minutes of the break. You understand that – twenty minutes?"

145

Ginny nodded again.

"If I am not there, or you cannot make it within that time, then make your way straight home. I don't think that's a safe option, but if we get split up it's the only one. In the long run, we need to think of some way to get noticed and maybe then someone will want to hear our story. But whatever, you get the car though. Is that clear?"

Ginny held him tight. "Okay, okay, I don't like it but okay."

Clem went over the details again and they hugged some more.

He had hardly finished whispering in her ear when Quantock returned. The whisper turned into a hurried kiss and they parted as if embarrassed.

"Oh, gee, sorry. Er, the room is just down the hall, number eight." Let's get you outta here?" Said Quantock.

Ginny went to dress and Clem moved across the bed avoiding the bodies. Together they went to room eight. Quantock went to get coffee.

Once outside and well away from the Motel he reached for his cell phone and dialled a memorised number.

"Hi. Yes this is Arab Blue. Code Red. I have an extra job for the cleaners. They are in Tucson at the moment. Send them to, er, The Budget Motel on North San Pedro Street, just off the main West Fifth Street that goes through the centre of Benson town. I want them here within six hours. Two pieces of rubbish to be disposed of, repeat, disposed of. Also, I have, er, two items to be closed down and then disposed of back at the San Quiller Mine without delay. Copy? Good."

The cleaners were good. They were professional and absolutely discrete. Every department could use them, but only through selected contacts; Quantock had kept his old codes and numbers. The feral CIA boys had to be eliminated, but he was not going to sully his hands with the deaths of the two remaining teenagers. He felt bad about that but what had to be done, had to be done. If they got to talk to the authorities or the press then the whole story would come out and he risked being implicated. He turned and headed back into the motel collecting three coffees from a machine near the reception office and took them to room eight. He knocked before he entered, then opened the door and smiled.

"Don't want to catch you two a kissin' now," he said and laughed almost apologetically, "I've phoned for backup and we should be able to take you home in about six hours.

Ginny looked up and smiled. "Oh thank goodness for that sir. Listen, I wanna thank you so much for saving our lives, not to mention my modesty and honour! I was real scared I can tell you."

Quantock noticed that Clem looked more cheerful and relieved. He was sad that things would have to pan out the way they would. But at least they were cheerful and he knew that professionals would do the job quickly and cleanly. If killing could be called clean that is. They would not see it coming and there would be no distress.

"That's okay now. It's all in a day's work," he said, "why don't you guys get some rest now?"

Ginny jumped up. "No sir, no. I am really hungry. I could murder a burger and fries and four quarts of Coke!" she said adding, "Oh don't say no. I need to get out of this motel if only for just an hour or so and I'm starving. You do understand don't you? Please, please can we go, sir?"

Quantock hesitated for a moment then, thinking of the six hours he had to fill, said, "Why not? Forget the coffees, we'll go to a small diner I saw on North Adams Street."

He allowed himself a wry smile. It wouldn't matter. A few hours wouldn't harm anything. Why not give them one last moment of fun. He was quite hungry too. Together they left the motel with Clem and Ginny hand in hand.

Quantock looked at his watch – it was already mid-day.

Clem and Ginny looked at each other.

As they walked out of the hotel and turned right down the main street, Clem and Ginny chatted about nothing in particular, all the time looking at each other with 'knowing' expressions. Quantock seemed lost in a world of his own that was punctuated with wide sweeping gazes around him. The noise of the fun-fair located on a piece of ground to their left made it difficult to concentrate on anything more than shouted directions. Music was playing all around them, including a large organ that accompanied a brightly painted carousel, each melody trying to outdo its neighbour. Stall holders shouted as they tried to purvey their shoddy plastic tourist goods and the smell of food sold from different stalls made the mouth water. Clem squeezed Ginny's hand and nodded towards a large washroom caravan parked to the right and under some trees.

Clem stopped in his tracks and turned to Quantock, "Gee, this is great, I haven't been to a fun fair for ages, kinda like bein' a kid again. Can we mooch around here for a while, get a dog and fries, a Coke maybe?"

He looked appealingly at Quantock as though the man was his great uncle, then Ginny cut in. "Oh, yeah, that would be great, just what I need to take my mind off things. I also need a pee," she said, inclining her head towards the caravan, "see you in a minute."

Before Quantock could speak she skipped over to the fairground area and into to the women's washroom trailer. Quantock looked resigned and waved Clem on, stopping only to hand him a twenty-dollar bill. Clem took the money, feigned hunger and excitement, and went to the nearest food stall. Quantock walked up and down slowly looking around him in the well practised way of a trained FBI agent.

Once inside the trailer Ginny located the closet close at the farthest end. She went inside and then closed the door behind

148

her. Without waiting, she stood on the seat and began to undo the window above the toilet. It was narrow, but she was sure she could squeeze through it to and out to the back of the trailer. As she struggled up onto the window sill, she looked over her left shoulder, half alert and half amused, she saw the face of an Afro-American woman, about thirty five to forty years old, wearing a red print dress looking up at her from where she was sitting. Her eyes were wide and she showed a half smile.

"Hey honey, what you doin' up there, this ain't no 'pay for a pee' palace, so what's your hurry?" she said.

Ginny smiled at the situation more than the remark.

"Well, no, ma'am. It's, well, it's man problems, you know what I mean?"

The woman rolled her eyes. "Yeah I do honey. But if you have one that you don't want right now, you jus' gib him t'me, 'n I'll see him alright, I will that!"

Then she gave a great earthy laugh and Ginny giggled in return, moving momentarily away from the fear in her belly. She grabbed the sides of the frame and squeezed through the window, catching her stomach on the raised piece of metal that held the window latch, and then fell awkwardly to the stony ground. She felt a bit jagged after the fall, but stood up, took a few breaths then looked for the helter skelter. It was easy to see, situated towards the back of the funfair and slightly right. In order to keep out of sight she took the long route to it behind instead of in front of the many stalls.

Clem got to the counter of the hotdog and burger cabin.

A large round man wearing a paper hat and striped blue apron said, "What can I do for you son?"

Clem placed the twenty-dollar bill on the counter and said, "Here we go sir, dogs, burgers, plenty of tomato sauce, really, sir, lots of it and mayonnaise, fries and three large Cokes."

The man patiently gave him a few dollars back and said, "You can get enough for ten dollars son, you don't want to get as big as me now do ya, huh?"

Clem nodded, but wanted to say something like, do you know what I intend to do with them sir? But he kept quiet.

The stallholder gave Clem the order, 'to go', all the packages open and ready to eat, ketchup and mayonnaise almost dripping down the sides. He stood for a moment and contemplated the situation. Then to his joy, he saw a group of elderly ex US Army veterans mixed in with other people, but moving as a single phalanx, coming through the Fun Fare towards where Quantock was standing, right by a low fence. They laughed and joked and were jostling each other in a good-natured sort of way. He walked slowly towards Quantock trying to coincide with the arrival of the veterans.

They arrived at almost the same time. As they did so Quantock looked up at him with surprise, "Goodness, Clem, you feedin' an army or…"

Before he could finish the sentence with "…or what?" Clem pretended to stumble by kicking his rear heel and fell against Quantock. He raised his hands out in front of him in the direction of Quantocks upper body and face and the sticky gooey foodstuffs and Coke spilled all over him and he fell backwards over a low fence. He let out an angry yell.

Just then the veterans came to the rescue.

"Hey, man that's terrible, are you all right sir?" said one old man.

Another veteran said, "Here let me help you up?"

Whilst two others brought out handkerchiefs and began wiping him down. As they did so Quantock was trying to get the Coke and sauce off his face. When it was clear he thanked them profusely and turned down several offers of further help. He looked around to admonish the clumsy Clem.

Clem was gone.

Clem leaned against the side of the helter skelter and panted for breath. He had run like fury from the chaotic scene that he had created, zigzagging, for about fifty yards and hid just behind a trinket stall so that he could still see which direction the Quantock would take in pursuit. He knew that he could have a decision to make regarding his rendezvous with Ginny; he was afraid that if he ran to her and was chased, then Ginny would be compromised. He would stay absolutely still for a few moments. Better for one of them to make it than both to fail. Quantock was helped to his feet by a number of the veterans and wiped down. Clem was well hidden and from his vantage point saw Quantock looking around as he was being fussed over by the vet's. But he didn't cut to the chase. He looked furious, took off his jacket and just stood in the same spot looking around for a long time; then eventually turned and left the fun-fair walking steadily back towards the hotel.

Clem's heart leapt and he turned and headed for the helter skelter.

Ginny caught sight of Clem and she ran towards him and they embraced.

"It's okay," he said with a smile, "he's gone back to the hotel."

Ginny tried to mouth the words, "But how?" but Clem just grabbed her arm and, looking left and right to make absolutely sure Quantock had not doubled back. He steered her through the crowd and together they made their way quickly to the Benson library on North Huachuca Street, where the hire car was parked.

Clem had never been so glad to see an automobile in his life. When they reached it, Ginny gladly gave up the keys. She was too nervous and mentally exhausted to drive. He took them and soon had the car out onto the Interstate highway I-10 and drove out of Benson. He kept his speed within limits, not wanting to attract attention or get arrested for speeding, but it was a strain. All the time his feet itched to hit the floor and get the hell out of Benson, but he kept his composure. They were soon heading east along the highway, which was bordered by arid and dusty land either side with the skyline broken only by the small blue-brown frames of the Dragoon mountain range to the northeast.

Clem looked at Ginny who returned his gaze with a half-smile. They were both elated and yet scared – they got away.

But where to now?

Chapter Eight

Quantock was sore as hell. The teenagers had outsmarted him and that didn't happen often. He arrived at the hotel just as the 'cleaners' were about to sort out the mess. They waited until well into the night to remove Martin and Ralph's bodies and tidied the rooms, checking and putting right obvious signs of trauma and damage. The hotel receptionist deferred to them, giving up the hotel register without demur and Quantock took out a penknife, opened it slowly and then cut out the page with Clem's name on it. He would also arrange a cancellation of the bank card payment so that there was no trace of it having been used. Quantock felt comfortable with his 'cleaning' so far. Luckily the hotel clerk was so lacklustre that he couldn't remember the name the room was booked under. After organising payment for a further clean up for the hotel rooms, Quantock explained that two kids had been part of a minor drugs ring and that they had been apprehended earlier and arrested. The two men who had come and gone the previous day were small town crooks looking to exact revenge for non-payment for the last drug consignment. They too had been arrested. He passed the clerk an envelope containing fifty-dollar bills.

"Now, sir, this is for your co-operation. The FBI is generous to people who help us sort out the bad guys in our country," he smiled broadly and the greasy haired clerk's eyes widened at the sight of the cash, "but, sir, I need to be straight with you now."

His eyes narrowed and he leaned forward and looked directly into the clerk's face.

"If another soul, anyone, should get to hear of what went on here, then we can get very, very angry. You understand what I'm sayin'?"

The clerk paled and nodded.

Quantock reached out and patted his cheek. Then he turned and left the hotel, walking to his car. Once inside his vehicle he dialled a number, 505 248 5290 and waited for a response.

"Ah, hello, this is Dan Quantock FBI, can I speak to John Spielman, yes that's it, Spielman. He's an old buddy of mine. Thank you, yes, I'll wait."

Spielman was the Director of US Security Services in New Mexico. He and Quantock had gone through the FBI academy together and in their young days had described each other as Hoover's young Turks. They had been good friends but drifted apart as each pursued a different career, got married and moved around the country.

Spielman came on the line and greeted his old buddy. "Dan, you son of a gun, great to hear you buddy. First, so sorry to hear about your family tragedy some years back. Catherine and I wanted to call, but hell, what do you say?"

Quantock still grimaced when he was reminded of the past.

"John, it's okay. It was terrible, but life goes on, I'm more or less over it now – well as much as you can be!" he said.

"Sure, buddy, sure. Anyway, what can I do for you?"

Quantock wove a story around the murder of the kids at the tin mine. He made up a story that two local teenagers had come across the bodies and stolen items such as credit cards and the like. It was no big deal but likely to get messy if the cards were used and the parents of the dead teenagers, who were both US senators, kicked up a fuss. Could Spielman contact his pals in Arizona and organised some kind of car watch? He expected them to travel Northeast or east, most likely along the interstate highway I-10, but couldn't be sure. A local car hire company had advised that a teenager who fitted the description of one of the suspects hired a car for cash and he gave Spielman the details. There was a long silence. Quantock continued.

"John, I am working directly to the president on this one. You have heard the news. The shit will hit the fan soon and he just wants to make sure that there are no loose ends. Two mouthy young teenagers spending on stolen credit cards and wearing items of clothing belonging to the victims of a terrible crime is not what he wants at all."

That did the trick.

"Okay, Dan, it's irregular, and all I can do is to promise to do my bit along the New Mexico/Arizona line, and I will, I promise, contact a good friend in the Arizona State Police who I know will do something to help. But it's likely to be very low key. Few if any road blocks, except perhaps one or two on main roads and no mass searches buddy, we most assuredly need more background information in writing before we go that far."

Quantock readily agreed and thanked him profusely. After exchanging idle chat and each agreeing that they really must catch up with each other, he hung up. If the teenagers were caught then he knew he would be called. He might as well go back to Washington.

It was getting dark as he headed out of town towards Tucson airport some forty miles away. The local Benson radio station KAVV-FM played popular music and interrupted to outline details of the teenage murders at the nearby San Quiller tin mine. The information was brief and exactly as Quantock wanted it to be. A little premature perhaps. All he had to do now was to apprehend Clem Johnson and Ginny Grivas - and quickly.

If they were not caught in two days then they never would be. He had to start second-guessing exactly what they were going to do next.

That wouldn't be easy.

The drive from Benson was uneventful and for the most part Clem and Ginny did not talk much. They were both too exhausted and shocked at the events that had unfolded. The inevitable question of 'why?' kept coming to mind and to that there was no reasonable answer. About an hour out of Benson they had travelled about fifty miles and Clem decided to take a chance and buy something to eat at a gas station. There was enough fuel in the car so he didn't need to top up. Ginny gratefully used the toilet facilities. Then they set off again.

Clem was thoughtful and after a while said, "Ginny. If that guy was a FBI man, and I think he was, he could ask for an APB and the state troopers could check vehicles. On the other hand, that would mean he would have to give a reason and he can hardly organise road-blocks for two teenagers without good reason?"

"Yeah, that's sound enough," replied Ginny, "but my bet is that he can fabricate what he wants, so we had better be alert as we leave Arizona and cross into New Mexico on this road, the I-10. That's if we take that route of course?"

She flapped her hands on her lap and looked perplexed. Clem put his hand on hers and said, "I think any route is gonna have its dangers. But even if – I mean when – we cross the state line, this car will eventually be traced. So we need to think ahead," his brow furrowed and he gripped the wheel determinedly, "but we're gonna be okay Ginny, I promise."

Ginny smiled back at him, but was not wholly convinced.

They drove for about forty minutes and Clem decided to turn off the interstate highway for a while and follow a side road. Ginny stirred after taking a nap and was too tired to argue. As they drove through the countryside that by now had patches of thin forest thickening the longer they drove, he began to encourage her with silly comments and stroked her face with his right hand. Then they came over the side of a hill and before them lay a long straight road with telephone poles either side. It was getting slightly grey as misty clouds swirled above them and heavy rain was on the way. As they looked ahead, they saw in the distance a large family saloon with a bulging roof rack, turn onto the road about a half a mile in front of them; Clem slowed the car instinctively so as to maintain some distance between them.

" This is not quite how I imagined we would ever, well, we would ever enjoy each other's company!"

Ginny smiled, "Well, it certainly isn't your fault," and she touched his arm, pinching it for good measure.

Clem huffed, and then said playfully in a mock southern accent, "You and me, and two kids, huh honey-bunch, my little Ginny-Bell?"

"Two kids," she said, playfully holding her hands to her heart.

"Two jobs and two bank loans," he continued.

"Two jobs and two bank loans?" She grimaced.

"Two Homes and two babies," he smiled stupidly.

"Aaaah, two little babies," she cuddled her arms and rocked left and right.

Then they laughed and looked ahead at the laden family vehicle that they were now slowly catching up with. There was a dull second or so as their brains both synchronised and they suddenly looked at each other. Clem braked and the vehicle skidded to a halt.

"Two of everything, yeah, that's it. Two automobiles! Yeah two of 'em! That family is going on vacation and in their garage I bet there is another auto'!" yelled Clem and he quickly turned around on the broad country road and headed for the turning that the family ahead of them had come out of. It was a rough track that was lined with large pine trees for about fifty yards and when they rounded a bend a small homestead with some outbuildings came into view

"What if it's alarmed?" said Ginny.

"What if it isn't?" Clem replied, too excited to be put off by anything so sensible, "besides, this is a long way from other houses by the looks of things, so who will respond?"

They parked the car and walked around the dusty yard. Clem looked into the window of a large shed, but saw only farm implements and a few kids swings and things. Then Ginny called out.

"Clem, you were right, here look, it's a Chevrolet, in this large building here," and she waved her arms, then put her head to the window screening the light with her hands, "it looks in good condition, definitely a second family car. Clever boy!"

It didn't take long for Clem to break the garage lock. The car was a standard family saloon with half a tank of fuel and he had to spend some time siphoning from the hire car to top up the Chevrolet. Then they quickly switched cars, putting the hire car in the garage and leaving the Chevrolet in front.

"I need to clean up. We can get some food too. Besides, I have to leave some money and a note. We're not criminals and I bet these folks are nice people."

Ginny looked admiringly at Clem and his concern for the people who owned the house made her like him more.

Clem soon found a small window at the back of the house and it didn't take long to break and open it sufficiently for Ginny to crawl inside. It took her ages to find a key hook, but once she located it she found spare house and car keys easily. She opened the front door and let Clem inside.

Clem washed his oily hands and cleaned himself up. Then they went to the fridge. It was empty of perishable goods – the family would be away for at least a week. Mom householder had been efficient and nothing was left in the cupboards that would go mouldy. But there was a stock of tinned food in one cupboard and they grabbed tins of sausage and beans, and some tinned fruit. They were ravenous and ate heartily. Then they put some tins into a plastic bag for their journey and a tin opener and some bottles of water and took them out to the Chevrolet. The car keys worked and they felt their spirits lift.

As Clem shut the trunk, Ginny put her arms around his waist.

"Thanks Clem, you're one strong willed guy you know. Without you I just know I would have perished along with the others. You're the best!"

Then he turned and they embraced.

"For what it's worth I am as scared as you Ginny and I only did what came naturally. I'm nothing special."

Ginny moved her hands from his back to the top of his leather belt at the front of his jeans and pulled him towards her, looking up at him. She offered a kiss and he took it. It was warm and sensuous and he felt giddy with the feel and scent of her body and the way she tenderly bit his lip.

"Let's go inside," she said, "we've been close to this twice before Mr Hero and I don't want to let this opportunity pass me by again."

Then she kissed him again and all common sense was lost – he knew that they should go, but the over-powering longing for sex with Ginny made him throw all caution to the wind. He was almost breathless with desire and his heart pounded heavily against his. Ginny stroked his cheeks that by now displayed small pink patches under his eyes.

They didn't run upstairs, it was more a slow walk, punctuated by long kisses. Despite a choice of bedrooms they fell into the first one they came to. It was a comfortable room, obviously for guests because it was so tidy and had that well laundered but 'unlived in' look. Besides, there were no obvious personal items anywhere. Clem and Ginny embraced, kissed and were soon both quite naked, feeling the coolness of the bedcovers on their hot bodies. The tiredness they felt supercharged their bodies and each touch was as if they were connected to an electric charge.

They made love, lovingly yet lustily, and then fell asleep.

Quantock sat in his office and contemplated the action of the last few days. What a mess! The cleaners had taken care of the two renegade CIA men and disposed of their bodies. Clem and Ginny had proved to be clever at evading Quantock, so they had one less task to do, and all he could do was to return to Washington. On his way back he read a copy of the local Benson newspaper the San Pedro News-Sun he had bought late that afternoon. The headline read:

Teenage Killing Outrage – Bodies of Missing Senators' Children Found at Arizona San Quiller Tin Mine.

It never ceased to amaze him that news could so quickly be cascaded when the situation demanded. He was pleased that no reference was made to the number of teenagers murdered, his instructions had been adhered to. His next challenge was to work out how to deal with Clem and Ginny's parents. He had their telephones tapped and waited for the teenagers to contact them. This angle had to be played as it unfolded. If questioned, which was unlikely, then he would not deny that he killed the agents, but had done nothing to threaten the kids, they just took off out of fear of what had happened; it was understandable really.

He looked at his chessboard on the large coffee table beside his armchair and realised that the cleaner, or his cheeky young administrator, had moved a single piece out of sequence. Far from being upset, he enjoyed this interference and saw it as the kind of challenge, one that came from outside the rules of the game. That kind of thing happens in life - a plan is made then a random event derails it. He reached for a black bishop and moved it to the centre of the board in a threatening position to the white king. This was the way to deal with such random events: intervention of the pious kind!

Then he turned to another real time random and unexpected event. He leaned back in his chair and looked at the envelope lying on the table beside his chair. It had Kinz's unmistakable handwriting in black ink on it.

Kinz's suicide had shocked everyone, but none more than Quantock.

He opened the envelope and read the letter slowly taking in every word. When he had finished, he put it to one side, ran his fingers through his hair and closed his eyes. Kinz's conscience was understandable and he should have foreseen it after the mission went horribly wrong ending in the killing of the teenagers. Sadly, in the short time available to him, he had not been able to get to Kinz to persuade him that although terrible things had happened, the end game could and should still be played out for the good of the US people, of course.

True to his word Kinz heaped the blame on himself and he did not implicate Quantock in any way whatsoever. He made it clear in his note that he had contacted him because they were friends and he respected Quantock enough to trust him implicitly. He wished to ensure that the enclosed letter to President Brannigan was delivered personally and without being seen by anyone else. He took his time reading the content of the president's letter.

Kinz told the story to the president exactly as it was and left out nothing. Except that he said that he had worked alone and had made all the necessary arrangements. Things had obviously gone badly wrong and he deeply regretted it. He explained why he did it and pulled no punches, adding that the president's actions had been precisely as he had predicted. Nevertheless, the tragic death of the teenagers meant that he should take full responsibility and nothing would ease the guilt and pain he felt. He was therefore going to take his own life and ensure that the president was fully apprised of the situation so that he could explain it to the media in any way that he wanted. He wished the president well and ended with, "God bless America."

Quantock felt a wave of pity for the old senator and instinctively reached to his chess pieces, the white pieces this time, and castled the king in an effort to protect his position.

He went out to the photocopier and copied the letter, putting the copy into his office safe and the original back into an envelope, which he sealed and addressed to the president. Then he began to assess his own situation. He poured himself a glass of mineral water and sat down again in his armchair. Contemplating the board again he reached to make another move. Life was like a game of chess. It was always the first moves that dictated the game, and then later came the 'events' that turned a winning situation into a losing one and vice versa. But chess was all about planning ahead and Quantock was a good player. He would now need to assess the current situation and look well ahead.

Quantock considered the options open to him and as if to illustrate the fact he moved black king pawn to king pawn three in order to open a route for the queen.

He could advise the president that the two remaining teenagers, Clem and Ginny, should be encouraged to see him and the situation be explained to them with full television coverage. This would ensure openness and may just get the president off the hook. Then he turned the board around and moved a white knight into a well-protected position in front of the white king and thought for a while.

On the other hand, there had been a large measure of over reaction by the president and troops and warships had been despatched to the Gulf of Arabia and, as CNN never failed to point out, this had made a bad situation even worse. The president had been convinced he was right and was unlikely to back down. He wouldn't see this as a good idea at all. He would want something spun so that he could continue to try and take the minds of the American people away from the country's current economic problems. He would definitely not be happy.

Quantock would then be back on Senator Protection in Homeland Security. That is of course if it was possible to assure the teenagers and their parents that he had no designs on killing them in Benson and was merely trying to ensure their safety. There were too many loose ends and this troubled him. He spotted a gaping gap in the white king's defence.

There was another option. He then moved the black queen out to black knight seven, aggressive and ready to attack anything in sight. The two teenagers should be apprehended and moved out of sight – there were ways of doing this. The Kinz letter would then never be made known to anyone else other than the president and Quantock. The heightened state of alert would be maintained and who knows where the game would go from there. With luck another event would, by sheer chance, as is the way with history, come along and muddy the waters. He would keep his new job, or better, be moved to a more powerful position. He dispassionately considered the two options and chose the more attractive and less risky second; less risky, because he was in control.

All he had to do was to convince the president that it was the best and only thing to do to achieve the optimum result for all concerned. Minutes later he put the telephone down after talking to the president's personal assistant and made his way across town to the White House. Eventually, he negotiated the various security stations and as he passed the pictures in the hallway on his way to the Oval office he saw his reflection in the glass, paused, adjusted his tie and straightened his shoulders.

President Brannigan was in a foul mood. Television reports of the Washington diner incident, too close to home for his liking, were being linked to other similar incidents of unrest throughout the country. It was making his electioneering difficult, some said impossible. The presidential press corps was having a hard time keeping the wraps on incidents and was hurriedly but deftly spinning the stories away from criticism of the US administration. Sadie Burrows was doing great work and her PR was first rate; but this still did nothing for his mood. Quantock was announced by the president's personal assistant.

He barked, "C'min, Quantock, Dan, you want to see me urgently. It had better be. I have to deal with all sorts of crap at the moment what with your finding the bodies of those poor kids. That was well done by the way Dan, I look forward seeing your detailed report, you don't have to deliver it now you know? On top of all this mess is Senator Randolph Kinz's suicide, poor man."

He paused for a second and added, "What I really want is for you to tell me is that you've found the killers of the teenagers. So, spit it out."

"Quite the contrary Mr President. I know I have to brief you on the incident, which I was involved in having followed a hunch, and that is being prepared in detail now, sir. But I also have to give you this letter from the late Senator Randolph Kinz. I got it this morning. It was in an open envelope so I read it and resealed it immediately; it explains everything. You will need a few moments to read and digest it, sir."

The president took the letter glaring at Quantock as if insulted by his insistence that he read it. As he read it his forehead furrowed and his fists balled. Then he put the letter down, took off his spectacles and began to clean them without saying a word. He thought for a moment then with some reluctance passed the letter back to Quantock.

After a full five minutes the president spoke.

"Well whadya know? Who would've thought it of fuddy duddy old Kinz?" He paused then continued. "You say you were involved in the incident, somewhere called Benson I believe? I can wait for your report, why don't you just tell me in your own words – and quickly?"

Quantock weighed his words carefully and then explained how he had received a lead about teenagers being seen at a deserted tin mine and had gone down to the Tucson area only to find the mine and the four of the teenagers dead."

"Four?" exploded the president.

"Yes sir, four. I tracked the remaining two through a local Indian reservation called San Xavier. Two men were chasing them. These were the men that killed the four teenagers at the mine. Eventually, a stroke of luck really, I was directed to Benson by the Indians who had hidden the two remaining kids. I decided to tour the motels in the town, there are only eleven, and I started on the East Side. I checked out a small motel that had a Nissan four by four parked outside and, to cut a long story, arrived just as the men were about to kill the kids. I managed to overpower and kill the two men concerned. These men have since been identified as two rogue CIA agents Adams and Anderson – a really weird couple of guys working on the fringes of the CIA. I wondered what their involvement was and now Senator Kinz's letter explains it all. Before I could question the teenagers they escaped, I guess they must've been shit scared. I have to give it to them it was a slick move. They're still on the run. But there is another angle."

Quantock feigned a worried look and balled his hands for good effect.

"Mr President, I believe that despite their terrible plight they were, well, I hate to say it, about to make a subversive video

165

rather than the gentle and innocuous mission that Kinz had given them. That's why they ran out on me. I think, for what it's worth, that they are politically motivated, anarchists perhaps? They saw my presence as dangerous. Initially, I thought they feared for their lives, but after reading this letter from Senator Kinz I guess they knew that their political views could put them in a position to be arrested. Precisely what for I don't know, only they do. Poor Senator Kinz had unleashed more than he bargained for. Anyway, it's my guess that they are intent on making a fuss before the election, sir, to prevent your attaining the next presidency, or worse to bring about revolution or instability. Heaven knows who else is involved"

Brannigan sat quite still looking at Quantock. After about half a minute, which felt like an age, he spoke.

"So what do we do about it, Dan?" he said.

Quantock stiffened and prepared himself for his delivery.

"Sir, I believe that we could try and call the kids in and assure them that they are safe and all is well. But, it would appear that Kinz's mission is complete. The US did send more of its troops and the navy to the Middle East area. It does appear, although I support your action, sir, to have been a tad impulsive," he caught sight of Brannigan's pulsing temple, "although I fully support your action, the American people may sadly be persuaded otherwise."

"Answer my question Quantock," barked the President, "what are we gonna do about this?"

Quantock answered without delay.

"Catch the kids and put them into a secure hospital under sedation – like it or not sir, other administrations have condoned this action in favour of, well, elimination. It's standard practice. Then we spin the story that the kids were killed by Arab terrorists. The original brief remains and, right up to Election Day, you establish the fact that whosoever kills American teenagers will one day pay the price. We find four

Arabs, arrest them and then put them firmly into the frame. Put simply sir, the American people will always give support to a sitting president in a crisis, all we need to do is to tie up the loose ends and show how your administration cleaned up this mess."

Brannigan's composure changed perceptibly. He didn't speak and he sat up straight in his chair. He offered a cigar to Quantock who declined and he went through the lengthy protocol of clipping it, rolling it in his fingers and smelling its quality. Then he lit it and blew the smoke out slowly after letting the taste roll around the inside of his mouth.

"The Cubans may be happy with their failed communist ideals, but they still make one hell of a cigar! I want you to know Quantock that I like you. I think you are a shrewd cookie and you know your business. I take it that only you and I know of the content of this letter?"

"Yes sir," Quantock replied earnestly.

"Then, in the interests of the American people, I suggest that it is of no value whatsoever that political agitators be given the slightest pretext to make mischief. The country has enough problems to deal with. I therefore intend that you should be solely responsible for leading America out of this morass."

Brannigan then lit a match and held it underneath Kinz's letter. It soon caught light and burned quickly. He put the glowing blackened embers into his large ashtray and he fanned away the smoke. The fire alarms had long since been turned off to cater for his cigar smoking.

The president turned to Quantock, "Dan, I will give you full authority to set up a search for the two remaining teenagers. You have your own department already so you need no more resources I'm sure. The mission is to be top secret. When you catch them you are to ensure their safety and at the same time their complete isolation from the outside world. Do you understand that?"

Quantock said, "Yes Mr President, I understand."

President Brannigan wrote a short note to his Chief of Staff to ensure Quantock was given special security clearances and a budget for the mission. Then he buzzed his intercom. A bright young female intern answered and the president said, somewhat dismissively, "Get me Sadie Burrows, tell her it's urgent," and in his customary manner he put off the switch without waiting for a reply. That marked the end of Quantock's audience with the president and without exchanging any further words Quantock left the office and walked down the corridor to the main entrance, his head spinning.

This was getting to be quite a game.

Chapter Nine

Clem lay next to Ginny under a thin cotton bed cover. It felt cool on their warm bodies. He turned and looked at her face and stroked her hair with his right hand. She looked back at him and just smiled, bringing his hand to her mouth to kiss it lightly.

Then they heard a noise and both sat bolt upright. Someone was coming into the house. Then a car door slammed. They were frozen with fear and didn't move an inch; Clem was trying to form some kind of story as to why they were there.

Heavy footsteps came up the stairs and Ginny slowly pulled the sheet up to cover her breasts. She shut her eyes and bit her lip.

The footsteps halted outside their room. Then they heard lighter footsteps coming up the stairs.

"Wait for me will ya! The bedroom. I told you the kid's bedroom. Martha wants their roller blades, knee and arm guards and a couple of other things," yelled a mature elderly female voice.

"I know woman, I just forget which room is which," replied a man's voice.

Just then the door handle to the bedroom where Clem and Ginny lay turned slowly. Ginny nearly fainted.

"No, damn your ass man, you know that's the guest room, we sleep there some times. No, it's that one there," said the lady exasperatedly.

"Oh, yeah, I remember now," said the man and from the sound of footsteps Clem and Ginny knew they had narrowly missed being discovered. But they still kept as still as they could. Any sound of a bedspring or creak on a floorboard could alert the elderly couple, probably grandparents, to their existence. They waited for what seemed an eternity, whilst cupboards and drawers were noisily opened and closed, then a door slammed and there was a sound of two people moving across the landing, then down the stairs.

"Even at the age of fifty nine I've gotta run around after that son of mine. Always forgettin' things. Good job he's got us that's what I say. Damned boy even left front door unlocked and his Chevrolet outside, well I ain't puttin' the damned thing away, that's for sure."

The lady chastised him for being like a bear with a sore head and said she would tell her son when they saw him in a week's time. She saw no reason to get picky when he and his family had worked so hard and looked forward to this holiday.

Then she added, "So you mind your tongue, grand-daddy Daryl Garbut or you'll have me to answer to, understand?"

A loud huffing was the only answer. Clem and Ginny heard the front door close and the sound of it being locked, followed a few minutes later by the sound a car being driven away. Only then did they relax their muscles.

Clem fell back on the sheets.

"Was that an incredible flow of adrenaline or what?" he said.

Ginny breathed a large sigh of relief. Then she smiled and turned to Clem who lay on his back. She quickly sat up and moved astride his stomach and he yelled in surprise. Holding his hands either side of his shoulders she leaned forward and kissed him.

"Yeah, quite a kick, that's for sure. So let's not waste the feeling?"

Clem was in no position to argue.

The evening began to close in and Clem and Ginny lay looking out of the window at the pine trees surrounding the house. They looked like black paper silhouettes, lit as they were, by a large bright moon directly behind them. Most of the clouds that had hung around during the day had dispersed and it was a clear starlit night.

"Clem, it's been so nice. We may as well stay the night now? That was the closest shave we are ever likely to have. The only problem, I suppose, is if the old feller has a conversation with his son and he mentions the door and the Chevrolet. What are the odds?" said Ginny.

Clem thought for a moment or two.

"You're right. We can take this chance, just for tonight, then go well before eight o'clock tomorrow. At least we can have a bath and some more food," he said.

Then Ginny gave out a loud, "Hmmmmmm?"

"Oh yes, and of course ma'am, some more sleep in a comfortable bed," he added quickly.

"Sleep...?" she yelled and hit him with a pillow.

"I give up," he yelled back playfully, "I need food!"

After a wrestle and some energetic rib tickling they dissolved into laughter. They agreed not to put the lights on anywhere in the house. Later after a good bath Ginny looked into one of the cabinets and could just make out some of the directions on the bottles.

"Hey, look at this, its hair dye. Clem, I can colour my hair and if we make it up half strength then so can you. Every little helps, huh?" she said.

The dye was very dark and gave Ginny quite a severe look. After cleaning up after themselves, they had a look around the house. By now their minds were supercharged and they discovered a doll and a cot. Ginny was full of ideas and decided that they could put it into the Chevrolet wrapped up like a baby. This might throw any curious investigator off the scent. To make it look more effective they borrowed some baby products from the cabinet to scatter around the back seat of the car. The wardrobes held a variety of clothes that fitted them both so that they were able to shed their jeans and shirts which by now needed a good wash. Ginny also found a pair of old fashioned spectacles that she couldn't see clearly out of, but considered them to be useful props.

Exhausted again, they had some more tinned hot dogs and beans for supper and went to bed; this time to sleep.

The bed was warm and the room smelled clean and fresh, the events of the past few days had caught up with them. The next day it was difficult to raise their bodies from the warm, comforting embrace of the bedding. They slept in much later than they had meant to and weren't ready until mid-day. It was important to clean up, after all, they were relieving the family of some victuals and their second car. Clem wrote a message to the owners of the house leaving them a small amount of money and pledging to make good any loss. Then they loaded their new 'baby' into the back of the car and set off along the local road towards the Interstate highway. The air was damp and as they drove east they saw dark black clouds forming ahead. It looked grim and angry, quite unlike the bright dry climate of the desert. After only an hour and a half the weather became rainy and misty, and the visibility closed in. Through the mist they could make out the changing terrain as it became hilly and covered in patches of forest. Several times they passed police patrol vehicles parked at the side of the road and Ginny quickly put on the spectacles she had borrowed and grabbed the baby doll cuddling it to her breast. At one stage, some distance ahead a policeman got out of his car and walked to the edge of the road, but perhaps seeing Ginny suckling a baby, thought better of it and got back into his patrol vehicle. But it was getting scary and still the weather was closing in and they hadn't travelled more than ten miles from the homestead.

Clem looked worried and said, "Ginny, if we stay on the interstate I-10 I have this feeling that we will see more policemen and one of them might be inclined to ask some questions despite our new hair do and the presence of a baby.

We still have Wilcox, Bowie and San Simon to go through. The odds are not good."

Ginny agreed and took off the spectacles, blinking as she did so.

"You're right," she grabbed a map from the glove box.

Peering at it for some time she said, "If we take highway 191 towards Douglas we can cut through the Conorado National Forest and pick up highway 80 to Lordsburg in New Mexico. We might be lucky and only encounter one serious check, if at all."

Clem was finding it difficult to concentrate because of the rain on the smeary windscreen. He was getting edgy as he tried to peer through the gloom ahead of them.

"Yeah, yeah, whatever Ginny. But I definitely don't want to stay on this road for long," he said.

They drove very slowly for about another thirty minutes and Ginny saw a road sign giving the distance to Wilcox at twenty miles. She prodded the map.

"In about ten miles you will see the sign for the 191, okay," she said.

Clem was trying hard to concentrate. Despite stopping the vehicle several times and rubbing hard with a variety of rags, he just couldn't get the smear off the windscreen. It was probably something on the wiper blades, but the rain meant that he had to keep using them.

"Yeah, okay, whatever." He said irritably.

Several trucks overtook them and splashed dirty spray on the windscreen and this made visibility worse. Clem cursed. After about fifteen minutes Ginny shouted.

"Clem, you missed it, you missed the turning," she said.

"No, it must be further on we can't have been travelling that long," he replied without taking his eyes off the road.

"Did you check the miles on the clock?" said Ginny.

"No Ginny I'm driving, I am trying to see through this crap on the windscreen I can't do everything. Anyway, I think it's up ahead."

Ginny was used to her stubborn father and said nothing. Besides, Clem was stressed and it did no good whatever, by telling him what was obvious, she would just have to be ready for the inevitable mistake; this took only another ten minutes to be revealed. It was after they had turned right two miles outside Wilcox that they realised they were on highway 186 and headed into the town. Clem said nothing for a long while and they eventually entered and exited southeast on the 186 towards the Conorado National Forest. After about thirty miles he stopped without acknowledging his mistake.

"Here, gimme the map let's see if we can get to highway 80 a little quicker?" He said.

Ginny gave Clem the map and wiped the condensation off the window with her right hand, taking a silent defensive position: if he wants to navigate and drive then so be it. Convinced that in bad weather and with a smeary windscreen he could navigate them towards and through what was called Pinery Canyon Road and a town called Portal to highway 80 Clem set off full of the confidence of youth – well male youth anyway.

The mist got worse, but at least the rain lessened and Clem turned the Chevrolet left off the 186 following a sign to Portal. But then the mist really closed and visibility worsened. After about four and half miles the road began to get windy and steep. Ginny began to get worried. Clem said nothing, but tried to seem unconcerned and even put his foot down on a straight stretch of road. Ginny caught sight of a sign that said, Organ Pipe Formation and they just missed a parking spot on the left of the road where they could have turned around. She had to say something and turned to face him.

"Clem, you're not gonna like this, but this is not going to get us to Portal," she said.

Clem frowned, even he was uncertain.

"So where are we?" he replied.

"I don't know, you're the navigator and driver remember?" she replied tartly, "why not stop and take stock of the situation?"

Suddenly Clem saw a parking place on the left, but was going too fast to negotiate the tight corner properly. He wrenched the wheel and the car yawed left and right eventually obeying the steering wheel turning left. The brakes on the Chevrolet were effective, but not on gravel and the car slid onwards, despite Clem's foot hard down on the brake pedal.

To their horror they were headed towards a woman standing in front of a large old-fashioned station wagon that was up on a car-jack. She threw herself to one side, just in time, as the Chevrolet slid over the gravel, bumping into her car with a dull thud.

Clem leapt out of the car and went to the lady.

"Oh God, ma'am, I'm so sorry are you alright?" He said.

Ginny arrived and helped her up.

The lady got up slowly and brushed the grit from her coat. She stood straight and looked at Clem. She was tall and had a medium build, with dark curly hair that fought to escape from a red bandanna that tried to keep it in check. She wore a thick multi-coloured coat that flapped open at the front revealing a denim dress and rows of beads around her neck. They seemed odd clothes for someone who was probably in her mid to late fifties. She looked imperiously over the top of large spectacles.

"Young man, if you want to drive like you're in the Indianapolis 500 then get a better car. Otherwise cut the speed. Okay?" she said.

Before he could speak she went on.

"Besides, what the hell are you doing up here in this place in early November?"

175

"We, er, want to get to Portal, ma'am, that's all. The weather has been awful," he replied.

The lady looked askance.

"Yes, well it can be in these mountains," she said still brushing herself down with wide sweeps of her hands and added, "anyway, you failed the first test, you should've turned right about four miles back. It's Pinery Canyon Road that you want and it's unpaved. You'll find it difficult to drive along in this wet weather, but as I say, that's your road, not this one," said the lady.

She stood there and watched them both. The sight of a brown stain forming around their necks, encouraged by the misty rain falling, intrigued her and she made them an offer.

"You really shouldn't be travelling in this weather, it is just too unpredictable," and she walked over to the car and looked in, "oh, and a baby. Well that settles it, you must come to my place for the night, I insist."

Ginny started to say something, "Well, I er..."

"I said I insist. My name is Catherine Devine. Devine by name and divine by nature."

Clem looked around him and shrugged, then introduced himself and Ginny by false names: Brad Jones and Susan Rafter. The weather was getting worse and if Pinery Canyon Road was as Catherine Devine said, then their journey would be either pointless or dangerous. He agreed and as compensation for the bump helped her to finish changing the wheel on her station wagon. She was fiercely independent and Clem was allowed only to hump and dump. It reminded Clem of a distant aunt who was a real man-hater and refused to have any help whatsoever until she one day met an ex-marine who had been badly injured during a military training exercise. She looked after him as though he was her brother and then, over time, fell in love with him. After that, he got better and once he was back in shape he was allowed to assume the role of Alpha-male without demur from her. Love conquered all in the end.

Clem wondered about this strange lady. It was perplexing him that she hadn't mentioned car insurance once. But there was nothing for it now. They had to follow her home and think on their feet. They turned left out of the parking lot and did their best to keep her vehicle in view.

Fred Spiker, Chief of Staff sat in his den in his smart New England condominium with his head in his hands. The stress of dealing with President Brannigan had taken its toll of his health and to his enormous sadness his marriage too. Now, at the age of fifty-four, he began to count the cost. Going to bed and waking up alone, distanced from his children and constantly having to act as an apologist for every two-bit failure of the US administration. He winced, even in the privacy of his own home, at the lies that were allowed to just sit there unchallenged by senators who were just plain weary of political wrangling, or worse, in office for the ego and the money. What pained him most was that there had been too many clashes between covert operations and government policy. It was no wonder that the international community had lost confidence in Uncle Sam.

This was not how he had planned his life to be. A loyal and high ranking senior official in the White House with a track record for brokering between parties and a 'can-do' attitude towards seemingly intractable problems, he was quickly identified as a man who could deliver deals in difficult circumstances. When the time came, Spiker was honoured and easily enticed to the appointment to Chief of Staff by the new president. Since that heady day some two year's ago when he and his wife had toasted the appointment with Champagne, life had steadily got intolerable. All those personal qualities that had thus far assured his success in life now worked against him as he became sucked into more and more political problems. He overlooked the issues that really mattered: his home life and integrity. Spiker sacrificed them to the art of compromise and misplaced loyalty. By the time he stopped to think properly about his personal life it had slipped almost unseen through his fingers.

The US had been through a torrid time over the last six years. There was no doubt about that. In particular, the former president's ill advised and ill fated adventure into Iraq, contributed enormously to the country's woes. It was now a widely known fact that the war had been deliberately mis-sold to the American people. The consequences of poor post-invasion planning had led to considerable loss of Arab and American lives and a gradual cavalier attitude to human rights, only marginally better than that practised by Saddam Hussein, sullied American claims for democracy. The most notable failure of all though, was to not fully understand the culture and history of the people they were challenging – history that was five times greater than that of the US. Sunni and Shia Muslims had been at each other's throats for over fifteen hundred years; expectations that this would end in a short space of time were naïve and dangerous. Once the conflict had begun it was always going to be impossible for the US to extract itself without further damaging its reputation. It had approached a stalemate. History had shown that stalemates always ended up in a deadly game of strategy and opportunism.

The resulting political pressures damaged the former president's health and he retired a broken man. Up to the plate stepped Vice-president Jake Brannigan to continue the work of his boss for the remaining two years. Spiker had initially been enthusiastic to get matters back on track, but gradually became disabused of the notion that Brannigan wanted to bring all the conflicts to a halt; quite the opposite in fact. He seemed to relish the discord the more it went on. The Republican majority in the senate had diminished and it was now finely balanced, this led to manufactured headlines and sound bites to gain advantages. Dissenters to public policy were mysteriously outed, citing extra-marital affairs, fraud or alleged homosexual misconduct; Spiker had lost two good friends that way. He wasn't stupid. He knew that they were blameless and this was done, *'pour encourage les autres,'* but of course, whilst fighting to clear their names the troublesome people were out of circulation and no danger to the administration.

For the last year or so the White House had resembled a medieval state where Dukes, princes, bishops or interest groups lobbied for favours in return for support. And so it was as it always was in such situations: weak structures supported by equally weak supports are vulnerable. Hence the dirty tricks. It had to collapse one day. But Spiker had to give Brannigan credit where it was due. The president was never ever implicated – this much he had obviously learned from history. One Italian prime minister was later to describe him as *'mani pulite'* – (clean hands). Spiker got up and walked to the window, opening it with some difficulty and, despite the cold, he breathed in the cool crisp air for a few moments before closely it tight.

Spiker put away several documents dealing with civil disturbances and copies of notes that he had left the president on the subject of the rise of religious fundamentalism in America. There was no chance that he would get a debate on that issue. He sat down again and drummed his fingers against the top of the large maple wood coffee table. The remaining paper on the table was written by Dan Quantock, FBI, the subject of which was the six teenagers, kidnapped by Arab insurgents in the US, who were now all dead.

What was this all about? His heart went out to the parents and families, but something was wrong. No group had claimed responsibility for these terrible actions – no political gain had

179

been made and no conditions had been wrought from the US administration. Terrorists rarely did anything without a clear objective coupled with a blast of propaganda public relations. Also, he was no expert, but the search always seemed more hype than substance. Spiker read the reports again and was still confused. He ran his hands through his hair and sighed loudly.

There was nothing for it but to return to Washington tomorrow. He now faced the fact that he hated his work. He despised many of the senators that clung to office looking for favours and the sight of the low level managers lurking in the corridors of the White House in the hope of hearing gossip about one senator or another. He had never indulged in *schadenfreude* – enjoying the embarrassment or humiliation of others – no matter what they did wrong or got up to. Washington was now a hateful place and a personal nightmare for him.

He took one last look at the Quantock report – he must talk to the Head of the FBI, Troy Hammond, because something was not right. He just knew it - but what?

Catherine Devine's station wagon didn't drive far. After about only a mile and a half they turned left down a rocky path shrouded by trees of all kinds, finally winding round to the right into a large flat area bounded by a wooden ranch style fence with a large open gate in the middle. They drove through the gate and parked outside a wooden cabin, a few feet from the door. Lights were on and smoke curled from a small broad stone built chimney.

Catherine Devine got out of her vehicle and beckoned them with her arm to follow her without even looking round. The door was unlocked and she stomped her wet boots in the porch, took them off and went inside.

"What do we do," said Ginny nervously, "leave the cot and doll here and play for time or what? We should turn around and go Clem, this is stupid."

Clem looked bemused. He knew he had been stupid to agree. Perhaps they could just go in for a cup of coffee and then wish her well? They had to make sure that she didn't report the accident to the police or insurance company. Just then Catherine came to the door, leaned against the frame and half smiled. After a few moments she straightened up and started to walk towards the Chevrolet. They wound the window down.

Clem was just about to speak, but Catherine got there first. She had a kind of exasperated, 'I don't have time to talk this through with you' expression on her face.

"Look, I know your dilemma. I've been there - trust me. You don't want to come in because you're afraid that I will know that all you have is a doll in the cot. If it is a baby then please tell me what you are feeding it to keep it quiet through a car bump and all this noise. Anyway, I saw its eyes and one eye was closed and the other open. I can tell you, it's not a feat that's easy for a baby! Finally, you both look suspicious, act suspicious and need to do a proper job on the hair colouring before the brown stains damage any more of your clothes."

Clem and Ginny were wide-eyed and speechless. They felt stupid.

"So there you go. There's hot water for coffee and I'm just about to cook up bacon. The fire's warm and you can tell me what your problems are – you never know I might be able to help. I'll leave the door and the decision up to you."

Then she turned and went into the cabin.

Ginny turned and looked at Clem. "Stay or go?"

Clem was certain. "We gotta stay Ginny. If she's a whacko she could call the police and if she isn't then we lose nothing. Besides," he looked out at the mist and rain, "we are not going to get far unless we drive back to the interstate highway I-10

181

and onwards into New Mexico. Jeez I'm sorry. We can't be more than a hundred and twenty miles from Benson. What a stupid sucker I am!"

Ginny pinched his arm and kissed his cheek and they both got out of the Chevrolet and walked into the cabin.

Even though it wasn't that cold outside, the warmth of the cabin heated by a large log fire hit them full on. Bacon was already cooking on a griddle that was situated on the left of a large open plan room, at the opposite end there was a large log fire. The smell of burning logs and food cooking were pure heaven to their senses. Several easy chairs were arranged around the fire, each covered with coloured 'throws'. The walls were roughly plastered and covered in all kinds of modern art, including work by Andy Warhol. A large bookcase full of books took up almost all the wall facing them, leaving a little space for three separate doors. One door was half open revealing a bathroom and toilet and the other two rooms were closed and were probably bedrooms.

"Take a seat," said Catherine, "coffee will ready in a minute."

Clem noticed that she had almond shaped eyes. She was quite tall and slim, and wore loose fitting clothing, almost Hippy in design. As she handed them both coffee cups, he saw that her hands were long and thin. He took the coffee and as he did so she caught his eye; he was mesmerised. Catherine was a very attractive lady, difficult to age, but as he had originally thought she was certainly in her mid fifties. The way she looked at Clem was what he found alluring. She had a kind of knowing smile that stripped away all pretence, because when under its spell it would be difficult to be anything but absolutely honest. So the next question put him right on the spot.

"When I was young I was a political agitator and always in trouble. I know the 'in and out' of police cells and only age has dented my enthusiasm for a fight. So that places me in the early sixties, for your interest. Now, you guys wanna tell me about your situation?" She said, turning her gaze on Ginny, who seemed to equally melt under its power.

After sipping his coffee Clem weighed up the odds and elected to tell her all that had happened. He and Ginny needed someone to help plan his way out of this fix and they introduced themselves to Catherine under their correct names. He told her everything, only leaving out Senator Randolph Kinz's name – he couldn't believe badly of him, neither could he betray him. As he spoke, it was like recounting a fairy story, it was almost unbelievable. But as he spoke, he found it odd, really odd that Catherine didn't once express surprise or indignation; she just listened and nodded occasionally. She sipped her coffee and when Clem had finished she looked up.

There was a long pause before Catherine spoke and she had a kind of knowing look on her face.

"That's quite a story. Well, let me see now. The first thing I need to do is to advise you to keep your heads down for a few days. Despite what you say, there's not exactly a hue and cry out there, otherwise your faces would be plastered all over the newspapers and television. But nevertheless, you need to let the world pass you by a little. What's your plan?"

Clem and Ginny fidgeted. Clem said, "Well, we kinda don't have a plan ma'am, er...."

Catherine broke in, "Don't call me ma'am please, I'm not a school teacher and don't run a bordello, it's Catherine if you don't mind."

"Okay, sorry," said Clem, "Catherine. We don't have a plan."

Catherine cocked an eyebrow and swept away to the griddle without a word, returning a few minutes later with a pile of bacon sandwiches.

"Here, some ketchup if you want it," she said, "what have you eaten so far?"

Ginny laughed, "Lots of sausage and beans cold from tins."

Catherine put on a pained expression, "Oh no, what have I done, it's gonna be noisy around here tonight."

That broke the ice and they laughed.

The supper plates were cleared away and Catherine made some more coffee. Then she returned, put down the tray and sat down. She paused for a moment, looking straight at them.

"Look, I meant what I said. You need to hunker down for a few days and by the sound of things you need to rest and think a lot. Don't just go charging around aimlessly or you will make all the wrong decisions. But the choice is yours."

Clem got a nod from Ginny and said, "Catherine that 's good of you. But why are you helping us? I just almost trashed your station wagon."

Catherine laughed. "You should see it in daylight – the bump actually improves its looks." They laughed again and Catherine went on.

"I knew you were in trouble when I saw you. A sixth sense I suppose. Anyway, I remember needing help in my youth and I got it too. It's nice to repay acts of kindness and I am happy to do that now."

For the rest of the evening they talked some more, but Catherine charged them not to mention any more of their problems. She got them talking about all manner of things and they felt better for it. One of the doors did lead to a bedroom and by midnight they had talked themselves out and were ready for bed.

Ginny was the first out of bed in the morning and for some reason felt ill at ease, the kind of feeling brought on by severe anxiety. She smelled the freshly brewed coffee and that cheered her up. In the bathroom she found that Catherine had thought of everything. Spare toothbrushes and cosmetics were laid out ready for use. Afterwards, Ginny sauntered into the large main room at the front of the cabin, looking out of the window she gasped and put her hands to her mouth. The car had gone. She ran to the door, almost tripping over a stool. As she stood on the porch, she heard Catherine come up behind her and turned around.

"A little bit of trust goes a long way' she pointed, "I put it over there." Catherine her arm on Ginny's shoulder, "see, over there just behind the tree line. We don't want any nosy neighbours wondering who owns a Chevrolet now do we?"

Ginny felt embarrassed and tears welled in her eyes. "Catherine, I'm sorry. It's because I'm so scared."

Then she turned and buried her head in Catherine's shoulder. Catherine patted and stroked her head.

"Yeah, it must be scary honey. You are a brave kid. Others would have melted I can tell you. Take some time out here at the cabin to relax and get your mind straight. Tell you what, let's go for a short hike after lunch – what do you say to that?"

Ginny grinned up at her. The weather was clear and bright and the rainstorm had passed. A short hike would indeed be a great idea.

Soon Clem joined them and made no mention of the Chevrolet's absence. Both Ginny and Catherine waited eagerly to see the look on his face. When he failed to notice even after they dragged him to the window, they burst into laughter and swore they were convinced that men were indeed different to women. Clem readily agreed with them.

Thankfully, Catherine had a wide range of trekking clothing and boots. She said she had lots of city friends who came to see her and they always forgot something. They left the cabin and followed a trail at the bottom of the turnoff to the cabin and headed north. Catherine told them they would climb to almost 6,000 feet, but the trail was okay for 'city-slickers' and only about two to three miles all the way around. Close to where they set off a large creek drained down from the hills. Catherine said it was on its way to Shake Spring. They walked through the trees and along trails treading on firm ground, but made soft and springy by decades of pine needles and they heard and saw several small waterfalls. In the wooded areas the air smelled of damp and fungus. The sound of water flowing, falling, gurgling and splashing, has an enormously calming effect and Catherine deliberately walked on, leaving Clem and Ginny to hold each other and to be alone for a moment. At a particularly beautiful waterfall they stopped and kissed and Catherine was quite far ahead of them. Then she turned and looked at them quite deliberately and Clem caught her eye. She looked as though she had something to say – it was a weird look.

The trail curved around to the West and they stopped to admire the outstanding panorama. Catherine pointed out the Chiricahua and Anita peaks to the Northeast then directed their gaze Southwest right down to the desert floor many miles away. A different place, a different climate almost – but scene of their worst nightmares. Already they wanted to stay at the cabin, locked away from the world, forever. Finally they reached the top of the Bonita Canyon and Catherine showed them many rock spires and what were called hoodoos; they laughed when Ginny got it wrong and called them voodoos.

After walking almost around in circle the trail became a dead end, a mixture of rocks and log falls. They stopped for a snack and afterwards set off back home. It was late afternoon and they felt as though their legs were going to drop off. They arrived back at the cabin and were almost too tired to take off their boots and outer clothing. As Catherine set about preparing the evening meal, she looked around and saw that both Clem and Ginny had fallen asleep in the large cushioned chairs by the log fire.

Two hours later Clem's eyes opened and he stretched his weary limbs. Ginny stirred too. The fire had been stoked and

Catherine stood over him, her lovely almond eyes shining and wearing a big smile.

"How about a coffee?" she said.

"Great," he replied, "sorry we fell asleep on you."

"That's okay, what with the fresh air and all that you guys have been through I can't say I'm at all surprised."

It felt good to relax and after coffee came the most marvellous pot roast. When they had finished Clem and Ginny did the dishes.

They sat own and noticed that Catherine had brought out a bottle of Jim Beam whisky and three glasses. She had a kind of resigned look on her face. She poured about two fingers each and they drank each other's health.

"So, tell me more about the video your, er, friend, wanted you to make?" she said.

Ginny became enthusiastic. "It was to be a 'State of the Nation' video, that's what it was about, from the viewpoint of six teenagers whose fathers are US senators. Not from the so-called adult establishment, mired in false politics and self-interest, but from our perspective, the young people of America. You know? We are the people that really count, the future, Catherine. We wanted to do this so much. We needed to have our say."

Catherine drank her whisky and poured another. Clem and Ginny were hardly into their drinks.

"Do your bit. And you really thought that a video would do that?" said Catherine almost too dismissively for Clem's liking.

Clem answered, "Catherine it's better than nothing, isn't it?"

"Better than nothing? Let me tell you guys, a bad strategy is actually worse than nothing," she said it almost bitterly and it surprised them.

Catherine looked wistful and gazed at the ceiling.

"Sometimes, you know, I feel that the wheel has actually turned full circle. I'm gonna lay something really heavy on you guys and you're not gonna like it. Before I do, I want to establish my credentials so to speak."

She took a large mouthful of whisky, held it in her mouth and then swallowed it noisily.

"You know what, in 1965 Time magazine called young American people, and I quote, 'a generation of conformists'. Well what about that? Damn. Only the year before, 1964, three young civil rights workers were murdered in Mississippi. They gave their lives for their cause. All around the country the next ten years were punctuated with race riots, the worst happening between 1966 and 1969, anti-war riots and of course the murder of Martin Luther King in 1968. See now, all that many young American people wanted in those days was an administration that lived up to the promise of civil rights for everyone no matter the colour of their skin, and an end to the Vietnam War. Most of all, they wanted the freedom to express their views. You really think your video would've achieved that?"

Clem heard all she said as though he was receiving a punch to the stomach and Ginny fidgeted. Historical truths, bare of all the waffle and spin that wraps facts and distorts them, inevitably makes for uncomfortable listening. Catherine continued.

"I don't for one moment doubt your resolve to change the world guys, but you live in an age of plenty. But don't forget that this has been achieved on the back of yesterday's youth in the face of blood, sweat and tears." Catherine smiled ironically and looked up at the ceiling, "Mind you, many of them are now in the so-called establishment you hate so much. When they were your age they wore Chairman Mao 'T' shirts, then, guess what? They swapped them for smart pin stripe suits and now they are city bankers and attorneys. I mustn't be sour though. I have to admit that in some ways things have changed for the better."

Catherine stopped and sipped the hot coffee, "But then we Americans are surely the best at 'moving on' aren't we? No one will ever doubt our resolve. Oh no, we put things right when we need to that's for sure. Good old Uncle SAM. But do we ever learn the lessons of history? We can deal with the mega-tragedies and emergencies. When New York's 9/11 horror and the tragedy of hurricane Katrina in New Orleans happened, we just wept, got out our spades and fixed things, then we moved on. We left the devious ones in the US Administration to use the situation to continue to perpetuate all manner of dumb-ass policies. But here's the truth of it guys - real people still suffer."

Clem was watching her mood and expression and said, "So what are you saying Catherine?"

"I'm saying that, me, you, the rest of America, must have a close relationship with the state and federal America. We need to feel that we are being listened to, not being treated like a bunch of patsies. They work for us through our votes, not the other way round! Do you ever look at a presidential election and wonder what all those people with the funny hats at conventions are cheering about? They care more about the candidate's after-shave or perfume than politics. They care more about going home winners after a good day's campaigning than understanding the true nature of the policies being touted by the candidate. They like winning more than losing and that's what is more important to them. The razzmatazz guys. You know something? In England there is a park, called Hyde Park and it has an area called Speaker's Corner. You can stand on a box and say, within reason, just what you want to say, without fear of being thought a lunatic or being locked up."

"And?" said Ginny.

"And I don't believe that we can do that here, in this country I love, I really don't," said Catherine, pouring herself yet another large whisky. Her voice was getting slurred but she continued, "You guys think the sixties was the decade of smoking pot and good sex. Well, the sex was good for sure, but there was more to life than that. We could put a man on the moon in 1969, but we just didn't know how to listen to our own citizens, especially not if they were gay, black or shouting that the Vietnam War was wrong. For the next two years demonstrations at universities led to deaths of our own kids in Berkley California, Jackson State and Kent State. Damn, our own kids! When the Chinese did that in Tiananmen Square Beijing we called them animals!"

"But Catherine, things did get better, remember, Nixon was impeached when he broke the rules wasn't he?" said Clem.

"Yeah, he was, but it was a close run thing Clem. A close run thing where true patriots had to stand up and be counted."

Catherine continued. "Look, I just don't want to see good kids like you believe that your video, whatever, would've changed the world. No way! People don't believe videos, they believe people, especially if you've got bad news to deliver. Trust me that's the way of the world."

Ginny was more perceptive. "You were at one of the universities weren't you? What happened to you Catherine?" she said.

Catherine smiled softly and her eyes watered.

She said, "Yeah, I was there, with my boyfriend, my most precious boy. And we protested like mad. We yelled for free speech and despised all those who took things at face value and allowed over one hundred thousand of our boys to die in Vietnam without questioning what it was all about. We asked why it was that we were there at all and what we were supposed to be aiming for. We screamed about the darkest evil of racism that remained in parts of America. Then one day we were letting off steam in the university campus and the National Guard came. Our own boys! You know what

President Reagan is reported to have said when he was governor or California? He said, 'If there is to be a bloodbath let's get it over with.' The rest is history."

Catherine took a handkerchief from her sleeve and dabbed her eyes. After a few minutes she sniffed and continued.

"My boyfriend wasn't the one killed, but he was hit on the head by a young fresh faced National Guardsman who was probably more scared than he was, and badly injured. He never fully recovered and later took his own life in a fit of depression brought on by the head injury. I campaigned like crazy for a long time afterwards, but my soul was shattered. Civil Rights has been my sword for years now. I dropped out of all that ten years ago and came here to the peace and tranquillity of these canyons. I never regret it."

Clem and Ginny were quiet.

Catherine smiled and continued, "So, you want to change US politics huh? My, my, the innocence of youth. I've been there, honey, I really have. You wanna make a start go to California or Texas you'll be spoilt for choice. I will never, ever, lose my burning passion for Civil Rights; this is something that needs constant attention or it will sneak out of the back door and be lost forever.

Clem felt stupid. Catherine frowned, leaned forward and touched his shoulder.

"Now I need to tell you something. You say you were to make a video in secret at the San Quiller tin mine and then something went wrong and your friends got killed. Did you know that right from the word go the whole country was looking for you?"

Clem looked surprised and said, "No Catherine, what I said was that we had left letters for our parents about what we were doing and saying they weren't to worry. That can't be true."

Ginny shifted uneasily in her seat.

Catherine poured another glass of whisky.

"Clem, the news stations across America reported that you and your friends had been kidnapped. Your parents were on television pleading for your return. Sightings of teenagers in a coach in Lynchburg, where a local redneck was head-butted by a man of Arab appearance, were reported as being positive signs that you guys had been taken under duress. The report of the killings is very recent. I left my computer on over in the corner there," she pointed to the far corner of the room where a screen-saver heralded the work of Amnesty International, "I called up the reports and you can see them for yourself."

Clem was speechless. Ginny turned to him looking guilty.

"Clem. I didn't really get time to tell you. My mom. I called her. I was too busy telling her to keep my call secret and that I would ring her soon to listen properly. She mentioned that none of the guys' parents had received letters. She certainly hadn't. It was when I called her a second time she told me news had been released that six teenagers had been found murdered at the San Quiller tin mine. I just didn't want to believe her and there was no time to pursue the matter further. I guess I was too scared, in denial, call it what you will. I'm sorry Clem."

Clem put his head in his hands and said, "I just don't understand."

Catherine was by now bleary eyed and she stood up unsteadily.

"I'm really sorry. I hope my stories and the plain old truth didn't spoil your evening. But I guess that it has - big time. I'm certain of one thing though, if you are serious about making a stand, make sure you have a plan and you watch your back. Or stay here and walk the hills with me for the rest of your life. Your choice."

She leaned down and kissed them both on the cheek, before going straight to bed.

Her words bounced around Clem's mind and he couldn't resist going to Catherine's personal computer and reading the pages that she had called up for them to read. There were countless newspaper reports and the whole episode had also been subject to several radio and television debates. He was staggered. It was true. As they had begun to make arrangements for the video at the tin mine their parents had been worried sick about their safety. Now everyone thought they were dead. He began to realise that simply going home was not an option. Ginny looked over his shoulder and let out a gasp then held him tight burying her face in his back.

They stayed curled up in a chair in front of the log fire, unable to think straight or talk, with chests tight and thumping, until the pink red embers that glowed in the dark, darkened and, like their enthusiasm, slowly died.

Quantock sat back in his chair with his feet on the coffee table and slowly tapped a pencil against his teeth. The two teenagers had not been apprehended, but then with the slim resources deployed over the last two days so as to keep the matter low key and not to raise attention too much, it wasn't surprising. He knew that the president considered this to be no more than a violent itch. Quantock was under no illusions – it had to be scratched.

His feet dropped to the floor with a thump and he quickly pulled his chair up close to the desk. He had to focus and keep a clear mind. Breathing deeply, he unscrewed the green top on a bottle of sparkling mineral water. A fine mist escaped with a soft whoosh and formed a momentary cloud under the glare of his desk lamp. Then he reached into his desk drawer and brought out some white paper and black felt pens.

Quantock didn't like to be beaten. He was good at his job; in fact he knew that he was very good. Well, he would just have to put it into practice. He drank some mineral water from the bottle and the bubbles went up his nose. It brought back a sudden memory. He heard the voice of his son saying, "Bubbles go up my nose Daddy!" It made his chest tighten and he frowned and almost snapped the top off the felt pen in his right hand. He shook his head and tried to focus.

The wheels on his executive chair squealed as he pushed the chair backward to get up. He walked across the office carpet to another small table in the corner on which the chessboard and pieces sat. They were untouched. In fact they were never dusted or cleaned, under his orders. He looked down on the black and white battleground. They seemed clogged up – congested almost. As he looked at them he experienced a slight pain in his left temple and he raised his hand to rub the spot to increase the blood flow. It was difficult to concentrate. The answer? The answer was not to make a move. It was time to think not act. "Then don't make a move," he thought.

Quantock straightened up and walked back to his desk, sat down and took the top off one of the black felt pens. Mind-mapping, where a shape for a subject or problem is drawn first, then around it are sketched or written other words, shapes or pictures that represent the situation. He wrote '*Clem*' beside a sketch of a matchstick man. He opened a file on Clem in which all his known contacts had been listed. Gradually Quantock enhanced the map by adding Senator Johnson and words such as, school, friends, the names of the other teenagers, and then he added another matchstick man off to one side, labelling it Senator Randolph Kinz. He thought a little more about Clem and his environment, and then started to add more words. He worked feverishly for about an hour and when he had finished the map it had scores of entries. Sitting back he admired his work, but it took more time to try and link relationships and think about them in some depth. After some time, he then took a separate piece of paper and began writing short headings under which he placed actions.

Quantock called in his PA. She came into the office quickly recognising the tone of his voice, it was clear that today was not a day to mess with Mr D Quantock. He didn't even look up.

"Becky, take this envelope to Jim Sparrow and tell him to action all the items listed. Then he is to call me when done. But most important, he is to call me about an entry I circled in red. Be real sure to do it now please." He raised his head slowly and she felt the full glare of his eyes. This man could be so unsettling.

"Yes, sir, Mr Quantock. I'll do that right away," she said as she turned and left. She hurried towards Jim Sparrow's office on the second floor of the building. In the lift she tried to tease the envelope open. But Quantock always used a special variety that once sealed would not yield. The only way entry could be achieved was by the conventional and all too obvious use of a paper knife. That was definitely beyond her courage.

Quantock's frown dropped after she left the office. He noticed for the first time that she had a backside that would have stopped the traffic in his day and smiled. He knew how his staff felt about him and that he was not the man he had been before his wife and son had been killed. But then nothing was the same. Sex was the farthest thing from his mind, he no longer drank alcohol and making friends seemed perfectly pointless. He was in a constant state of mourning that occasionally threatened to bring him to the brink of a nervous breakdown; only work saved his sanity. No matter how boring or even exciting – so long as it was work and it meant lots of overtime. At least this Kinz fiasco had added some spice to his life. Which way would this go?

Jim Sparrow opened the envelope, looked at the list and whistled. He had worked for Quantock for many years and was as loyal as they come. After the kidnapping of the six teenagers

195

he was seconded as Quantock's executive officer. A workaholic like his boss, they gelled easily. The other staff even joked that their idea of a wonderful Christmas was sorting out their stationery cupboards and sharpening their pencils.

Sparrow was fully in the picture about Clem and Ginny having survived the killing at the tin mine and being on the run. He was under the impression that they had to be apprehended to stop enemies of the US capitalising on the situation, to bring down the president and demoralise the country. Apparently, if this happened then many American lives would be lost. No one else knew this. He was privileged to play a part in this action. The agents who had cleared the bodies from the tin mine buildings were told that two more bodies lay somewhere in the labyrinth of tunnels in the mine itself following a massive roof fall. Quantock had discovered on his visit that the heat from the fire started by Martin and Ralph had caused the collapse. Had he 'cleaned' the teenagers in Benson himself, blaming the act on the CIA agents, he would not have needed to use this excuse. But he understood that his boss would not have wanted to do this himself and had left it to the 'cleaners' who would leave a neater picture without any need for his involvement to be made known. However, it hadn't worked out and this was the story that everyone involved in the search had been given and it was credible enough, for the moment at least.

"Ooeee, baby! This is quite a list," he said. Then he set about doing his master's business. After a while he telephoned Quantock.

"Hello, Mr Quantock, it's Jim."

"Jim, please, how many more times, in this new arrangement it's Dan. So what's to do buddy?"

"Well, er, Dan, you know already about the road blocks at the I-10 and at Arizona State exits to the East. Anyway, I also assigned just six 'watchers' only, two to airports at La Guardia New York and Dulles Washington, and three to major rail terminals, one of them is in Atlanta, just as you wanted. Low key stuff, our usual reliable retainers, earning a buck or two to look and listen. We are still working on Kinz's personal computer, but nothing significant so far."

Quantock grunted with relief and Sparrow continued.

"We already wire-tapped all the parents, grand-parents and some other relatives of the missing teenagers, so we removed taps on four sets and left two in place, for the Grivas and Johnson families. We took a chance. The records will show that authorisation was given on the basis that it was felt that contact may be made by terrorists. Now, the list of friends you gave me was more difficult and we are working on that. These two kids were a socially active pair of so and so's, but we've narrowed the list a bit. Whilst we work on that plus some of the other entries you gave me, one appears interesting, what's the beef about the guy, what's his name," he stopped and looked at the list. Before he could finish Quantock interjected. "Jamie, Jamie Cook."

"Yeah, Jamie Cook. So what's to do?" said Sparrow.

"The boy was a close friend of Clem Johnson's. Now young Clem wanted to grow up to be a film producer or director, something like that. Anyway, Jamie is two years older and works at the CNN building in Atlanta. Our young aspiring producer managed to get time included in his media studies for some work experience."

"You mean working with CNN?"

"Yup, you got it. My money is on him returning there to do something on air, something, well, revealing, so that he becomes so visible he can no longer be apprehended. If he hasn't thought about it now then he will - I'll put money on it. He's got quite an ego." Quantock coughed. "Jim, they're up to something, I'll bet."

Sparrow felt surprise, since his brief showed Clem Johnson to be a calm, level headed and moderate soul, who could be shy and sometimes a little too focussed.

"What makes you think that?" he said.

"It was his girlfriend's remark to her mother on the phone. We got a late record, too late as it goes, but anyway, she said to her mom that, '…you'll be hearing about us soon enough…' Well, given that they are notorious and newsworthy already that must mean that they plan something a little more momentous than turning up a the local police precinct and handing themselves over to the loving embrace of the local police. Besides, they ran from me in Benson, because they didn't trust me, or don't want to perhaps? Look Jim, I'll put a hundred big ones on it."

Jim Sparrow sucked his teeth. His boss was smart. Together they had sorted out a number of Homeland Security problems and he admired his style, but never more so than now.

"I'm with you on that one boss. So it's a tap and a watcher on Jamie boy?"

Quantock smiled. Articulating his thoughts to Jim made it all seem so much more credible. It still had to be proved, but that would soon be confirmed one way or the other. They exchanged niceties as colleagues do and Sparrow was left to get on with the mechanics of the job.

Clem awoke early the morning after Catherine Devine's outburst. He threaded himself out of Ginny's grasp and got up off the couch. His body ached with the exertions of the previous day and his knotted position throughout the night. Just then Catherine came into the room holding her head.

"Oh, God, my brain shrank during the night!" she said.

Clem wished he could joke back, but his mind was still numb and he just smiled weakly and nodded.

"Clem, I'm sorry for laying so much on you guys. I have a lot of rocks round my heart and a big chip on my shoulder. But I do know what I'm talking about and it just seemed stupid to let you guys wander off aimlessly and possibly into great danger. Let's get some fresh air shall we?"

Clem nodded. Catherine had been right to tell them about her life to set the scene and give them her assessment of their position. They still had the freedom to come to their own conclusions – but he knew in his heart of hearts that would be useless. Her reading of the situation was spot on.

Clem slipped on a coat and so did Catherine and they opened the door silently and crept outside. After about a hundred yards they sat on a large tree trunk. The early autumn sun was rising slowly and its light was more orange than bright. The whole canyon looked beautiful, with patches of mist like balls of spiders' webs nestling throughout the undergrowth.

They talked for an age and Catherine convinced Clem that he should think of something momentous. The situation demanded it. Safe and yet momentous. He smiled and called her a barnstormer. She retorted that that's what made chicks from the sixties and he should never forget it. It was amusing enough to bring Clem out of his addled state and return to normal. Catherine smiled at him and left him to his thoughts, walking across yard she decided to make them all a good breakfast. When she got to the door, she glanced back and saw Clem still hunched up, sitting on the tree trunk obviously thinking about what to do next.

Ginny and Catherine were just preparing the table and the sausage and pancakes lay invitingly in the centre when Clem burst in. He stood in the doorway and gave them the plan. It was audacious, unique and would surely have enormous impact. He could remember his way around the CNN building in Atlanta and knew that news presenters were hungry for good stories – and this was a good story. He also had a good friend,

Jamie Cook, who he could contact and arrange for them to gain entry to the building.

Ginny and Catherine were awe-struck. Catherine quickly retrieved a copy of the Washington Post and turned to the radio page.

"Larry King?" she said.

Clem looked at Ginny, "No," he said, "he's gonna want to be more politically correct than anyone else. He will want too much due diligence, I can understand that."

"Okay, you can try Aaron Brown's news night, that's damned lively and looks at the day's issues including, let's see what does it say here, oh yes, breaking news and live updates. Or, you can go with, Paula Zahn, her show is great and I used to listen to it. Says here that her show is a cut-to-the-chase interview-driven hour. Now that looks more like it?"

Clem's eyes opened wide.

"Hang on, oh dear, Paula is away for a month and has a rookie stand in called Damien Tasker. That's no good then," she said.

Clem jumped up. "No, that's perfect. You know, this guy Tasker will want to make a name for himself. He will jump at the chance of a good breaking story."

Ginny clasped her hands together and said, "That's a fantastic idea Clem, but I don't want to put a damper on it, won't he want to carry out, what did you call it, 'due diligence' too?"

"Yeah, he will for sure. But if someone who works there, someone they all know and like, can verify who I am – sorry, I mean, verify who we are - through personal contact and state categorically that we are alive and well despite all that has been said by the US administration, then I would think that they would find it difficult to say no."

Catherine and Ginny jumped up and cried out loud. The excitement was electric. They hugged and Ginny cried.

After they had quietened down Clem brought them to order. "I need to make a call or two. But not from your landline Catherine and certainly not to the landline of the guy I am thinking of calling. I'm lucky, I remember his cell phone number. It's so odd it is impossible to forget." He looked at Ginny, you still got that cell phone Ginny?"

She nodded. "Clem, I want to call home."

"No, out of the question," he said hastily.

Ginny's eyes welled with tears. "But Clem, they already know that I am not dead. It's pointless to keep them worried any longer. Why not?"

"I don't care Ginny. The answer's no, definitely no. There must be a tap on the line, we can't risk it."

Ginny reluctantly went to the bedroom and got the cell phone and limply handed it over to Clem. Catherine looked on disapprovingly. Later, she tried to persuade Clem to change his mind, but he was adamant in his view. She explained how difficult it must be for Ginny and that he shouldn't underestimate the shock to both their systems. They had been through a lot together. Her parents must also be suffering as indeed his must. But Clem's views of parents were coloured by his own poor relationship. Having got nowhere, she stood up and went to console Ginny who was outside sobbing softly.

Clem put the cell phone into Catherine's charger and called without waiting for it to fully charge up. He tapped in a number from memory.

Jamie Cook couldn't believe his ears, the reception was very poor but could this really be Clem Johnson? Several times he had told friends of his sadness at the recent news of the callous murder of his young friend who had wanted so much to be a film producer and director. He was stunned to hear what he thought was Clem's voice. Clem reassured him several times and then took him through the scenario of their escape step by

201

step. Repeating it over and over, until he was sure that Jamie fully understood. He told him never to mention their existence to anyone and not to use the landline to talk about the situation. When he was sure that Jamie was fully tuned in to the situation, he used his powers of persuasion to draw his friend into helping. It was easy. Jamie was hooked. They agreed to meet in Atlanta in a cafe just behind the CNN Studio Four building, where Marietta Road crosses International Boulevard, at ten o'clock in the morning.

Jamie agreed. Clem was delighted. It felt good to be in control after being chased, threatened and worried sick about what tomorrow would bring. Ginny came back into the cabin and they embraced. She and Catherine were delighted with the result.

Catherine kissed him on the cheek and said, "Smart boy. But now we must get to Atlanta. My bet is rail is best. It's quicker. I think we should split up?"

"We?"

"Yes, 'we', this is not going to be easy Clem and you need someone who is not known to authority and who can look out for you. Besides, you need cash and moral support. Now tell me if I am wrong?"

Ginny took Clem's arm lightly. "Mary Poppins knows best I think? She's right Clem. We can't do the first part of the mission on our own."

Clem looked at them both. They were right. He smiled and said, "Okay, it doesn't seem right to put you in harm's way Catherine, you've been great so far. But you're right. Okay then, we're a team," and they embraced together.

"Just promise me," he said.

"What?" said Catherine.

"That you won't burn your bra in public, smoke pot or do a protest sit-down in the Centennial Olympic Park Atlanta. We know what you sixties babes are about!"

Catherine grabbed a cushion and playfully hit him several times and they laughed. It was the first real spontaneous laughter Clem and Ginny had experienced for quite some time.

A technician put his head around Jim Sparrow's office door. "Jimbo, buddy, sorry, but we just got the wire tap on that guy Cook. He was just hanging up after speaking to someone. We only caught the goodbye. It was male."

Jim waved a thank you. His boss was always right. They needed more confirmation, but he was confident that it would arrive soon.

Chapter Ten

Catherine and Ginny drove away from the train station in Wilcox leaving Clem looking a little forlorn as he turned, waved and then walked towards the train. It made good sense. If people were watching out for them they would be looking for a couple, but not perhaps a single young man alone. How could they be sure – the situation was so confusing? Nevertheless, he would need to keep his head down. Before that, Catherine had taken them both to a mall on the outskirts of town and paid for some new clothes. She felt really odd doing this, but she enjoyed the warm, almost parental feeling of protecting and providing for two young adults.

The car left the station heading east, through side roads and onto North Haskell Avenue, which was the Interstate I-10 through Wilcox. A glance at Ginny was enough to tell her that the next few days would be awkward without Clem beside her. Ginny was subdued and there was a hint of a tear in her eyes. They had built a tremendous bond between them both and had seen more danger in a few weeks than some people ever see in their whole lives. Catherine reached out and touched her hand lightly. but said nothing. Ginny sniffed slightly and turned to look out of the car window.

As the car gathered speed out of Wilcox Catherine sighed and thought about the two seemingly crazy kids with whom she was now entangled. From the time she first saw them that evening in the misty hills above her home she knew they were in trouble. The failed attempts at hair colouring and the use of a doll as a make-believe baby – she found herself laughing inwardly. But, above all that, she knew they were scared and it showed. Why not simply pack them some food and send them on their way?

Because it brought it all back to her, that's why. The sinister nature of politics worried her; when things happen that you cannot fathom out. Catherine had the feeling that there was more to this than met the eye – all her revolutionary hackles had risen and could not be put back in the box. She reminisced about the old days and the successes and failures as the car cruised gently along the interstate highway.

Although sad that Clem had gone by train to Atlanta, Ginny knew that it made good sense. She settled into the journey and preferred not to talk for a long while, hunching up in the car seat and watching the changing scenery. For a while the interstate I-10 ran parallel with the railway track and several times over the next hour or so it crossed from one side to the other, and then parted company only to link up again south of El Paso. She liked that. It kind of kept her in touch with Clem, although by now the train had made good time and miles ahead of them. It didn't matter. She felt that they were at least going in the same direction and would be together again soon.

She was also feeling guilty. In the middle of the night she had crept out of bed and quietly gone to the main living room. It was easy to locate the charging cell phone, its green light glowing in the darkness as it charged from the mains electricity. With the door shut tight, Ginny put the throw from the settee over her head and dialled home. Her mother had answered sleepily. It was difficult but Ginny stopped her from talking and asking questions and told her not to worry, it would soon be over. This would be her last call, but they would hear about them soon enough. Her parents were to keep their spirits up – the important thing was that she and Clem were alive, but they were not under any circumstances to call Clem's parents. If they did then Clem and Ginny's lives could be in danger. She made her mom swear to this, blew her kisses and ended the call quickly. Then she erased all trace of the call having been made on the cell phone records. She hated cheating on anybody, let alone Clem, but when it came to thinking about her mom going through agonies worrying about her, she simply couldn't hold back.

It was over sixteen hundred miles to Atlanta and if Catherine and Ginny allowed four days to do the trip, exchanging drivers and taking only two short overnight stops at most, they might make it in less than that. She was worried about the ancient station wagon and hoped that it would last the journey, but was resolved to park up and hire a better car if they had to.

As the journey progressed, they both talked more. Ginny learned more about Catherine's life and was in awe of the things she had done. An attractive young woman, Catherine had commanded attention wherever she had gone, but it was her forensic questioning and the way she managed to undress a political situation exposing its most private and embarrassing parts to an unsuspecting world. She was the scourge of governors, congressmen and anyone in authority who tried to hide information or discriminate against others. She never got over the loss of her lover and never would. Later years in her life had seen Catherine writing papers or books on civil liberties and women's issues and this had suited her.

Ginny enjoyed her company and despite her lifelong immersion in academic pursuits Catherine was by no means dull or boring. Her wit was as sharp as a knife and she had a raunchy sense of humour. They stopped for gasoline north of El Paso and as they pulled out of the forecourt Catherine saw some men, stripped to the waist, digging a large drainage ditch. She wound down the window and wolf whistled. When the surprised men looked up and smiled, she shouted, "Nice pec's boys!" They waved and responded with hoots and whistles. Jenny compared Catherine to her mom. They were so different, yet she now desperately needed them both.

They drove throughout the afternoon and much of the evening, eventually unable to go any further they stopped at a small motel over the border into Texas. It didn't do food but a nearby gas station provided hotdogs and waffles. After getting ready for bed they sat and talked about a lot of things, as women do when they need to establish points of reference with a newly made friend. Ginny envied Catherine's independent nature and self confidence and yet she detected there was something deeper that was being hidden and not talked about. Rightly, she guessed it was Catherine's loss of her lover that hovered in the back of her mind and drove her on to be the person she was. Ginny talked about her family and how loving and protective her mother had always been. She loved her father deeply, but he sometimes fitted the all-American image of a busy businessman or congressman: no time for family or fun, just work, work, work. She once accused him of being a closet misogynist, because he always questioned everything she said. That upset him. They argued incessantly, but always seemed to hug there way out of trouble in the nick of time. She just wished that he would listen to her and understand her more, instead of putting her down.

Catherine smiled and said, "I don't know the context Ginny, but have you ever thought about the world that he inhabits, the stresses and strains and his family background? I certainly think from what you say, that he needs some reconstruction, but if he is daily immersed in wrangles with aggressive men in business or politics, then he is going to bring that stuff back home with him, isn't he?"

Ginny nodded.

Catherine continued, "And you may need to ask yourself why you don't like him questioning you; what makes you so special that you can't take a bit of delving into why you say what you say and getting you to justify what you believe in. Do that without throwing a tantrum and I guess he may just, well, kinda look at his young daughter and realise that what she says is right."

Ginny put her arms behind her head and leaned back, "Wise old maid you!"

They had established a good relationship and Ginny felt that she had adopted Catherine as a big sister. She felt good about that.

Frank and Cissy Warburton had been watchers for the FBI for about twenty years. They were both amateur artists and had excellent eyes for detail. Together they were a formidable team. They were both in their late sixties, but their eyesight was as sharp as that of a twenty-year old. The money wasn't great, but it did help to pay the bills and let them work together. It also left time for water colour painting that they both dearly loved.

Darrel Bremner the security guard at the Atlanta train station knew Frank and Cissy very well, they had worked together many times. He operated the CCTV cameras and when they arrived, he knew there was important business to be done and let them both sit at the console. Darrel loved them both. They were real characters. Making coffee and buying doughnuts was a joy for him.

"Okay Frankie, what's to do today buddy, who're ya lookin' for?" he said.

"Oh, Darrel, just a couple of wild cats that need to be watched, that's all," said Frank and he turned to Cissy and winked.

For the remainder of the day they fooled around, but as one joked the other watched the screen, then they would swap positions to give each other a break. This is what made them a formidable team. On twenty such occasions they had spotted fifteen suspects who were watched then later apprehended. They had quite a reputation.

Darrel was joking about baseball and Frank had turned to joke about the poor performance of his team. Just as Cissy was putting the doughnut to her mouth, she noticed on one of the screens that a child was running towards the edge of a platform, she saw the mother turn, but too late. The doughnut hung barely inches below her lips, she let out a squeal and she froze. Frank and Darrel looked up. Just then a young man ran at an angle towards the child and dived to scoop him up barely inches before he fell on to the track. She sighed with relief, bit the doughnut and waved to Darrel to zoom in on the action.

"What a nice boy," she said out loud through a mouthful of dough and jam. Then the boy's baseball hat fell off and he reached down and scooped it from the ground, looking up and smiling at the mother – and also in the direction of the CCTV camera. Cissy reached for the photographs now placed prominently on the console and said, "Bingo!"

Quantock got the call that Clem Johnson had been spotted in the train station in Atlanta. He steepled his hands and revelled in being right.

CNN it was then.

Chapter Eleven

Clem's heart was beating fast. If that darned kid had fallen onto the train line then who knows what would've happened. The fall alone would've cracked a bone or two. Anyway, the little boy was safe and the mother was grateful and that was all that was important. He could've done without it though. The train journey had been long and boring and it was important to get on with his planning. He must get on.

The concourse was not very crowded and Clem walked across it swinging his new sports bag, purchased through Catherine's generosity, and headed for the bus station. It only took a few moments for him to sort out the correct bus to take to the Centennial Olympic Park Drive. He took a ride and alighted at the entrance to the CNN building. He stopped and looked up at the tall building and took several deep breaths to help him gather his wits. Tourists were milling around and talking excitedly. One man, middle aged and slightly balding, stood aimlessly to one side. He was tall, thin and rather scruffy and the sort who would look more at home with a six pack, a couch and a television. He looked up at Clem.

"Hi, buddy! Goin' round CNN?" said Clem.

"Yeah, guess so," said the man and he shrugged almost absentmindedly.

"Damn, I wanted to do the trip round CNN today, but didn't get a ticket."

The man frowned and fidgeted, "I don't have a ticket, but my name's on the Atlanta tour bus list for a guided tour. Came here all the way from Birmingham Alabama. Thing is I'm bored with the whole danged thing. My sister thought I could do with a day out."

Clem pretended to look thoughtful and then said, "Why sir, if you don't mind me saying, we can work something out. I could buy your place on the tour round CNN. That would make me happy, you can have some cash and, well, everyone' happy."

The man started to shuffle left and right.

"How much?" he said.

"How about twenty five dollars," said Clem, "cash, of course."

The man needed no further persuasion and accepted the cash. Clem understood that his name was Al Dandridge. For good measure Clem talked him into giving him a letter with his name and address on it, just in case there was a security check. They shook hands and Clem joined the throng from the two coaches from Birmingham Alabama as they entered the CNN building.

The tour guide assigned to the group was attentive and answered all the questions. Some of which bordered on the ridiculous, but that was always the way. When the tourists crowded around the newsroom, looking in at the presenters as they delivered their programmes, Clem put up his hand.

"Excuse me ma'am," he said to the petite tour guide, an attractive lady with a slim figure, brown hair and large serious eyes.

She nodded towards him, "Yes, sir."

"Ma'am, isn't it a little dangerous for complete strangers to get so close to the presenters, I mean terrorism and all that?"

The tour guide smiled and tilted her head in a patronising sort of way.

"Well sir you can rest assured that the presenters are quite safe. The glass you see before you is reinforced and will stop bullets and a significant blast. The only way into the studio is through a door at either end and this has security guards and screening of bags and visitors. So Larry King and others are quite safe I can assure you."

Clem gave her a smile in return. Things had changed significantly since he was last here doing his work placement from university. As the tour guide spoke about the news handling process Clem watched the interaction between the people in the newsroom. They all had security badges and control was evidently very tight. To one side of the centre of the newsroom he could see a glass partition and behind this was where the guests to the programme sat. He knew this because as he was about to leave he saw a woman escorted out of the room, and shown to the desk with the presenter. Others in the room were getting last minute touches to makeup and lapel microphones.

There was no way round it. He and Ginny could not burst into the studio, they would have to persuade the rookie presenter standing in for Paula Zahn that their story was kosher and a blockbuster. If on the other hand the rookie wanted to take it through his producer they may face problems. They had to take that chance.

The tour ended and as he left the CNN building he saw Al Dandridge, the tourist from Birmingham Alabama. He was looking very pleased with himself, having enjoyed a quiet beer or two in one or more of the many local bars. They gave each other a wave, each happy with their end of the deal.

Clem swung his bag over his shoulder and walked a few blocks down Centennial Olympic Park Drive and turned into a small street and found what he was looking for. It was a large apartment block dating back to the fifties. He approached a gray door with numerous bell pushes on the frame. Would anyone be in? He pushed a bell that had a blue dymo tape label underneath it that read: Flat 23c Merric Grabowski.

"Ello?" said a voice with an Eastern European accent.

"Ello," Clem mimicked, "I come for some borsch, the best borsch in the world." Then he returned to his normal accent, "Hi Merric, it's me Clem, open the door, damn your ass!"

"Oh, Clem, but I thought? I come, now," said the unsteady voice.

The door opened and a dishevelled old man peered around. "It's you, it really is!" he said. "Come in my boy, come in."

They both went slowly up the stairs and Clem followed him into his apartment. It was just as he remembered it. Full of mementoes from the man's past. The one that always fascinated Clem was of an old man in his youth, in Polish Cavalry Officer uniform sat on a magnificent black horse. Underneath was the inscription. *"Dla Pukwownika Grabowski od 25-go Pku Oficerow Krolewskej Kawalerii, 23-go sierpnia, 1938"* (To Colonel Grabowski from the officers of 25th Kings Cavalry Regiment, 23rd August 1938). It was Merric's father and he was immensely proud of him. He listened to countless stories of daring escapades and resistance work against the Nazis. Then after his father died, he learned about soviet oppression.

They embraced warmly like father and son.

Clem stayed with Merric when he was doing some work experience with CNN and they had remained firm friends over the last few years, corresponding frequently. He explained the situation, without leaving anything out. When he finished Merric squinted at him. After a while he spoke.

"This is like communist Poland, yes?"

Clem felt awkward, his rational nature wanted to agree and yet his patriotic heart encourage him to demur, and he blurted, "Not quite Merric, I believe that there has to be an answer, but I just don't believe that Uncle Sam has gone as far as that. For now I need your help. Two ladies will join me the day after tomorrow and we have a plan. I will need to use both your spare rooms and am quite happy to pay you something."

Merric looked offended and his eyes opened wide, "Certainly not, no, no, no. You are my friend and now so are they." He raised his chin in defiance and Clem knew that it was stupid to argue.

Clem was pleased when Merric started to prepare a Polish stew and not borsch soup which he hated. Merric poured two large glasses of vodka and after they had toasted each other's health. Clem sat in a big worn leather chair and became sleepy as the effect of the vodka and the long train trip got the better of him. He drifted off to sleep thinking only of his planned meeting with Jamie Cook in the morning.

The stew was served with some ceremony and Merric clapped his hands and almost shouted, *smacznego*! It was a delicious meal and more vodka followed. Clem answered most of Merric's questions, but confessed that he was completely confused as to why his friends had been killed. Merric put his hands on the table.

"So, you are to meet young Jamie, I think I remember him. He's a nice boy. But can you trust him?"

"Completely, Merric, I just know that."

"And what if he is being watched?" said Merric.

"Well, maybe he is, but if that is the case then there's nothing I can do about it. I'll be arrested straight away." Clem frowned at Merric's common sense.

Merric thought for a moment and then said, "When times were bad in Poland during the war we used intermediaries. It sounds terrible, but they were expendable and less of a loss than perhaps a trained agent. I am ashamed to say that children were often used. This is not quite the same thing, but I could get a boy who does errands for me to meet your friend and deliver a note or verbal message. You should not expose yourself to danger. What do you say?"

Clem thought for a moment. It was a good idea. Merric could watch the cafe from a distance and see the response.

"Okay, that makes sense. Let's do it. I'll write the note and you contact your friend." He then sat down and started to write describing succinctly to his friend the situation that he found himself in. He pleaded with him not to tell the rookie presenter anything at all. Just that he had a news scoop that would shock Americans. He should tell the presenter to list an interview with two college students about some obscure subject or another. It would be worth it. Then he sealed the envelope and gave it to Merric. They drank two more vodkas to loud proclamations of *na zdrowie!*

As Clem made his way to bed, his head a little light from the effect of the vodka, he began to feel an uncertain about the plan. Would it really work?

Ginny and Catherine bonded like the best of adhesives. Ginny had never met anyone so liberated, so intelligent and so witty as Catherine. As feisty as she was, she realised only too well that compared to the students of yesteryear she and her companions came in a very poor second place. Thanks to Catherine she resolved to talk more to her parents, especially her Dad. He was a good man, but as Catherine said, that was the problem: he was a man!

They took a short stopover in a cheap motel and that recharged their batteries and set them up ready to finish the journey. Clem called and gave them directions on how to get to Merric's apartment where they would stay. They would come in to Atlanta from the West and needed to take the interstate I-20 East to Spring Street exit 56B turning into Spring Street itself. Head to Marietta Street, turn left then up Centennial Olympic Park Drive, then take the second small turning into Dale Avenue, the apartment number is 23c. It all seemed so surreal, like a spy movie and very sinister. The closer Ginny got the more scared she felt. She couldn't wait to see Clem.

Ginny and Catherine soon found a parking space outside the apartment block. They rang the bell repeatedly and eventually, to Ginny's joy, she and Clem were in each other's arms. After introductions, they hugged the air out of each other. It was such a long embrace that Catherine and Merric decided to move away and get to know each other. Later they ate some supper and watched the presidential election progress. The president was currently campaigning in Ohio, a state that often held the key to presidential success, and Clem didn't know whether to believe in him or hate him. Was he responsible for their situation and if so why? He was confused and angry.

After supper he explained his plan to Ginny and she was enthusiastic about it. Catherine was less so, but had no better ideas and so she went along with it.

"Let's do it. But we'll need to script what we are going to say because you can bet that after the initial shock, say twenty seconds, the plug may be pulled," she said "so get the message across quickly."

They all agreed and Clem set about his script. He also read the letter that he wanted to be given to Jamie again. It was slightly odd thinking about getting a letter delivered in case he was being watched, but he would go along with it.

The note read:

Jamie,

I know this is crazy, but as you can see I am alive and well and so is a girl called Ginny Grivas. Don't believe what you hear on the news programmes or read in the newspapers. Something terrible is happening. We have been nearly murdered by government agents and I don't know why. For this reason alone we cannot give ourselves up – we don't know whom to trust. That's why I am not turning up in person today. I need you to do something really important for me. I want you to get us both onto CNN Television to be interviewed on the Paula Zahn show. The theme is to be "Student's Rights," the sweetener should be that two students, Al McClusky and Jeanette Brown, UCLA, have uncovered serious student unrest in their college, it's topical what with recent incidents and all.

I know that it seems kind of zany, but can arrange this for tomorrow night's programme? I'm just going to assume that it will happen Jamie – I have no time to check – I have to trust you and it's got to be done quickly.

Trust me, this is important buddy. Please help me. It's for old time's sake and a hell of a lot more. I promise you – your rookie presenter will gain more notoriety in this brief interview than he will for a year's worth of work!

Thanks,

Clem

That night they all slept peacefully.
Clem and Ginny got to sleep a little later than the others.

Kristoff Kalescha was a bright, athletic eleven-year old and wanted to own his own roller blades. Today he smiled more broadly than usual. He imagined himself moving gracefully on new blades, hands behind his back, between the people on the sidewalk, swish, swish…..woosh! Adoring girls from second grade watching his every move. The money that Uncle Merric gave him would help him towards his target. He felt very grown up working for his favourite Uncle. Well, he wasn't a blood uncle, it was just a handle that his mother insisted he used out of respect for the old family friend.

His mission was to deliver a letter to a man that would be sitting at a table at the café on the corner of Marietta Street he could hail him if he wanted. The man's name was Jamie Cook.

Kristoff was to say that a man asked him to come to the café and deliver the envelope to a Mr Cook. He smiled to himself: perhaps there would be another tip?

He arrived at the café with a swish of his skates as he carved a wide semi-circle and quickly noticed a young man with dark curly hair sitting alone near the door. It was him. He was obviously expected and the envelope was delivered without a hitch. Although the young man looked a little surprised, this didn't stop him giving Kristoff a dollar. As directed, he skated on past the café and did not head anywhere near Uncle Merric's apartment, making a very wide circuit using a number of buses, before finally returning home.

From a window opposite the cafe a FBI operative picked up the telephone and explained the situation to Quantock. He held the telephone away from his ears for a few seconds then replaced it, saying, "Yes, sir, Mr Quantock. A young boy delivered a note to this Jamie Cook guy at the cafe. What? Oh jeez, that will be tough, an we'll have to be quick, but we'll try."

The agent had minutes to explain the situation to his co-worker. They then slipped into black hooded tops, quickly made their way down to street level and jogged in the direction that Jamie Cook had just taken. Approaching pedestrians made them slow their pace for a second or two but then they crossed the road and passed by on the other side; otherwise there was a reasonably large gap between their quarry and the now distant bystanders. The success of their action depended on audacity and speed; these boys were good.

Before Jamie knew it he was bundled against the wall by two hooded men who told him to stand still or else. Then he received a punch in the nose and it bled profusely and made his eyes water. This would hamper recognition and ensure instant compliance. One man went through his pockets and the other held him fast. They took his loose change and dollar bills and his wallet. The note was retrieved and one agent read it several times before throwing it on the ground with several other items. For good measure Jamie was punched in the body several times and the agents ran across the road and away from the scene. Some people ran along the street to help Jamie who was by now curled up holding his nose.

The whole incident had taken less than a minute.

Within twenty minutes Quantock was reading the transcript of the note passed to Jamie Cook and smiled.

The next day, Merric and Catherine went to the same cafe on the corner of junction of Merrieta Street and International Boulevard and sat close in a corner seat convenient for a good view of the television set on a pedestal above the counter. In view of the cafe's location and the clientele it was continuously programmed to CNN. They ordered coffee and doughnuts and settled back to watch the Paula Zahn hour.

Clem and Ginny took a separate route to the CNN building, avoiding association with Merric and Catherine, just to be safe. They went up the stone steps and into the foyer and approached the reception desk. Two large security men stood either side of the glass door entrance into the studios.

"Hi, Al McClusky and Jeanette Brown, UCLA, we are here for an interview on the Paula Zahn show," said Clem confidently.

The receptionist smiled and looked at a list on her desk. It took an age for her to run her finger up and down the list. Clem's heart beat fast and he felt impatient and nervy, and tried to control his anxiety and stay calm.

"Can I have some ID, sir?"

"ID, we, er, well we kinda dashed here real quick 'n don't have any." Clem looked crestfallen and Ginny clutched his arm. The receptionist's brow furrowed. She reached for the telephone and spoke to the producer. After a few seconds, during which Clem and Ginny's hearts beat like steam hammers, she frowned even more and then turned to them both.

"He cleared yo," she said with a surprised look, "You have an internal docket for introductions so I guess that will be okay." The look on her face was one that displayed a need for process and procedures and her world had been clearly dented. She was obviously the sort of person who didn't like exceptions to the rules.

"Okay, put these passes on. You have access only to the corridors, bathrooms, and the main canteen in the building and as you can see on the pass, to studio three. You are expected there fifteen minutes before the broadcast and looking at the time now, you had better hot foot it there without delay."

Clem and Ginny smiled at the receptionist and she managed just a slight tilt of the lips. Elated, they made their way between the two security guards and into the corridor. Passing studios one and two they heard the sound of interviews and music coming from speakers in the corridor. They slowed as they reached studio three, their hearts beating and chests tightening. Clem looked at Ginny and they gave each other a silent high five, kissed and knocked lightly on the door.

The door opened and a short squat woman with teardrop shaped spectacles peered through the opening. She looked at her clipboard.

"McClusky and Brown?"

They nodded. This was rewarded with a jerk of the head to the left. No introduction or guidance just a silent gesture. As they went through the door they entered a cluttered, behind-the-scenes area, with equipment all over the place and various helpers and professionals sorting out everything from sound and picture quality on the cameras, to changes to scripts involving intense concentration and frantic scribbling onto script sheets.

"Over here," said the woman, "I'm Irma Glendale, executive producer for the Paula Zahn hour. If you go into this side room here," she opened a glass door to a room alongside the main broadcasting area, "Jenny our makeup specialist will get you ready for the show. It's almost a quarter to five and you should be with the presenter at about a quarter past five, okay?" She left them quickly and without waiting for an answer.

Clem and Ginny nodded and then both went into the allotted room and sat in chairs to have face makeup applied to prepare their looks for the glare of the lights and the intrusion of television cameras into every crevice in their faces.

The clock on the wall clicked passed the seconds and minutes with small dull sounds and with each small 'clump' of the mechanism they both felt more nervous. The show had started and they were the second guests to appear. The third guest, a diminutive preacher, arrived and stood to one side waiting to be allocated a seat to be made up.

Then it was time to go. Irma with the tear-drop spectacles opened the door and they stood up to leave the dressing room. Strangely, Irma stepped back into the dimness of the outer broadcasting area without saying a word, as if backing off. Clem and Ginny walked through the door, Clem leading the way. They had gone no more than a few paces into the gloom when shadowy, strong hands reached out and grabbed Clem by the arms. A voice said, "Don't struggle Clem Johnson, we have you under arrest son, it's useless to resist."

Clem's head was ringing as the stress of the moment came upon him in a sudden rush. He couldn't believe it. He struggled, but to no avail, as strong arms held him fast. Ginny

221

was not so constrained. The space in the studio was limited because of the haphazard storage of equipment and files. She was behind and to the side of Clem as he was apprehended, with no one to hold onto her. Wasting no time she skipped past Clem and his captors and screamed as loud as she could.

Skipping over equipment and hotly pursued by a number of burly men in suits, she headed for the presenter's console. The rookie presenter heard the scream and stopped talking; his guest looked around, quite shocked at the sudden scream, his mouth open wide with surprise.

"Stop, I'm Ginny Grivas I'm still alive..." She said. But she wasn't close enough for her words to be heard above a muffle.

"Ladies and gentlemen, I think we have, as they say, been penetrated," the rookie's voice was sarcastic and his guest smiled wanly, "and we are going to have to take a break."

As the presenter finished this announcement, Ginny realised that she was not going to make the console and let out another terrifying scream. Then she was grabbed and wrestled to the ground an iron hand clamped around her mouth to prevent further disruption.

Without delay a soft drinks advertisement was screened, followed by several others in quick succession.

Merric and Catherine were watching the CNN programme and were speechless. The audible screams were recognisable as Ginny's. Merric's coffee spilled from a cup held at an angle and Catherine's hands went to her mouth.

They were shocked and suddenly very afraid.

Chapter Twelve

Quantock didn't have much time to spare. Clem and Ginny were both safely in custody and he was desperate to track down anyone who had been associated with them both. They had to be isolated. He was pacing up and down the FBI office in Atlanta when Jim Sparrow came in.

"We've picked up young Jamie Cook. He's pretty scared and shaking like a leaf. If we formally arrest him then there will have to be charges and that's going to be difficult. What shall we do now?" He said.

"I don't know," said Quantock, "if we act too quickly then he will gain strength and plead the Fifth Amendment, call his brief and defend what he did. We have to break that defence."

Quantock paced up and down more quickly with his right hand to the side of his head. Then he stopped, lowered his hand and clicked his fingers.

"Yazoo! That's it Jim. We make him think that he's been duped."

Jim looked askance, "But how?"

Quantock smiled, "Let's cool him first. Usual stuff Jim, lower the temperature in the interview room, give him a few cups of very strong coffee so that the caffeine kicks in and keep him awake and on his own for a long while. Do that first then come back and see me – quick now!"

Jim Sparrow shrugged his shoulders, but found it easy to respond quickly to a good leader – there weren't too many around these days. He walked quickly down several corridors to the interview room where Jamie Cook was being held, collected a cup of black coffee from a coffee machine, and then unlocked and entered the interview room noisily. Jamie sat on a light metal and plastic chair at an equally lightly constructed table, his head in his hands.

"Hey, man! What's goin' on? I asked for a lawyer ages ago where is he? Someone speak to me, talk to me, but do something for Chrissake." He sounded nervy and agitated.

"Jamie. So sorry. You must be worried out of your mind – well, I know I would be." Jim put the coffee down in front of Jamie, "Here, drink this it's hot and strong and will do you a power of good."

Jamie gratefully took the coffee and sipped it loudly.

Jim picked up on Quantock's theme and gently led Jamie into its mesh. He put his hands on his hips and said, "Jamie, I gotta say that you seem such a straight kind of guy. I'm, well, just so surprised. This is just so damned serious. Words like treason are being used."

"Treason!" said Jamie, almost spitting out his coffee, "free speech yes, treason no. My God this is stupid."

Jim was satisfied with this response and backed off, "Jamie, I have to go now, I'll be back soon I promise," he said.

"No, don't go," pleaded Jamie, who wanted to talk rather than be left alone with his fears. But Jim left the room and locked the door leaving Jamie with his agitation. He began to walk down the corridor, then doubled back and turned down the heating to the interview room.

Back in the temporary office Jim entered the room just as Quantock was putting down the telephone. He was smiling. Then he looked at his watch; it was eleven in the evening. He explained what he was going to do and Jim grinned broadly and called him a 'son of a gun'. But they would wait until three in the morning. It was a slim chance, but might just work. Jim couldn't wait to see this one through – a master at work!

Quantock smiled and turned his attention to the other possible contact, Merric Grabowski a Polish immigrant from the fifties. He had been the person who had provided Clem with accommodation a couple of years ago while he underwent work placement at the CNN Television Station. How much did he know? What was his role in this 'sting'?

It did not matter. They would soon find out.

Merric and Catherine almost crashed through the door to the flat. They slammed the door behind them and breathlessly held each other.

"Oh my God, oh my God!" gasped Catherine.

Merric was calm and cool. After a few minutes he slowly pushed Catherine away. "Catherine, gather your things we must go!" he said.

"What do you mean? No one knows we are involved and Clem won't inform on you," she said.

"It's never that simple. The state has enormous resources at its disposal. I've been through this in my homeland and I know what I am talking about. So let's go shall we?" He went to a cupboard and took out a large old fashioned carpet bag then went around his flat selecting clothes, valuables and money that he wanted to take with him. Catherine had fewer items and it was quicker for her to pack.

"Are you sure this is necessary?" she said.

Merric smiled. "Okay. Where is your car?" he said.

"A block away."

"Here take this," he said throwing a small car blanket to Catherine, "we'll go to your car and hunker down for a while. Let's see what unfolds."

Then he led Catherine down the back stairway, around the parking lot and through a dark alleyway to the main street where Catherine had parked the car. They located the car and after putting their bags in the trunk, Merric guided Catherine into the back seat where they both lay low in the seat leaving a slim view of the road outside the apartment.

They were almost asleep when several cars stopped in the road outside the apartment at about half past midnight. The occupants of the cars got out slowly, there were no sirens or fuss, just quiet efficiency, a dozen or so men fanning out with half that number entering the apartment block entrance and the rest just standing, looking around. After finding the occupants gone, the men left the apartment block stood looking around for a while then decided to go back from where they came.

Catherine was shocked. "Oh God. Okay, then, you were right. I am so ashamed! Let's go."

Merric pulled her down below the seat line. "Wait," he said quickly.

They waited for about five minutes. Then from about four cars down the street they saw it. A flash of orange light as a cigarette was lit. Merric marked the car in his mind and they both sat back to play a waiting game. The night passed and as dawn broke the street grew lighter and traffic along the road gradually increased as people went to work. Catherine awoke, rubbed her eyes and realised she desperately needed a pee. The diner on the corner was just opening up and she eased out of the car slowly. Merric was asleep. She knew that she must be the unknown quantity to any possible 'watchers' and it was a low risk to take. She stretched herself behind a lamp-post then casually walked down the sidewalk towards the diner. After visiting the ladies' room, she bought two coffees 'to go' and a bag of bagels, then paid and left the shop to walk back up the street. As she briskly passed the car that she thought held the 'watcher', she looked inside. To her joy she saw that the man was asleep. It had been a long night.

Quickly, she made her way back to the car, stowed the breakfast in the front passenger seat, then after retrieving the keys from Merric's coat started the engine and slowly pulled out to join the queue of traffic. Merric stirred.

"What...?" he murmured.

"Relax. Our 'watcher' is fast asleep and I have our breakfast. Where shall we go now?" said Catherine in a calm voice.

"Oh," he said through dry lips, "head out of town to Washington. I have a friend who lives on the East side of Washington. We can stay there until we sort out what to do next. But when you can, please stop. I am an old man and need my breakfast, I have had enough excitement already!"

Catherine didn't smile at his attempt at humour. She was worried sick. Clem and Ginny had been arrested and she didn't know what would happen to them. Was this really happening? Was this her America?

What the hell was going on?

Jim broke the news to Quantock that Merric Grabowski had not been apprehended. To his surprise he simply shrugged his shoulders and said, "Well, you can't win 'em all. My guess is that with his background he will want to avoid all trouble with the state and he will keep his head down until he passes away. He's long gone that's for sure. Anyway," he said, "looking at his watch, "it's show-time!"

Jim smiled. This he must see. Everything was arranged and he knew what he had to do. Together they walked down the corridors that led to the interview room. Jim went to the area behind the two-way glass and Quantock entered the interview room.

Jamie looked terrible. Several plastic cups, some a third filled with coffee, lay in a pile in front of him. His nerves were jangling and ragged through too much caffeine and with hair that was dishevelled and face shiny with grease he looked like a tramp. Quantock almost winced at the sight of his dark shadowed eyes that clearly wanted to close but weren't being allowed to.

"Jamie. My name is Dan Quantock. I want to ask you some questions."

Jamie looked up, "Mr Quantock. I have been here for hours, what the hell is going on?"

"Okay. I will tell you. I'll give it to you straight Jamie. I have to decide whether or not you are part of a major plot to drive the president out of office by threat and blackmail. Are you the kind of person to propound the merits of an ultra right wing, anti-negro, anti-Catholic, anti-Jewish political party that, frankly, should never be allowed to see the light of day let alone get coverage on CNN Television?"

Quantock was by now leaning towards the shocked face of Jamie Cook.

"What? Clem? All that. Oh no, I just don't believe it," said Jamie, and he began shaking.

Quantock gently put his hand on Jamie's shoulder.

"Look son, did you speak to Clem Johnson?" he said.

Jamie looked at him nervously, then down at the table.

"Why yes Mr Quantock, I did."

"How?"

"Well, he was on a cell phone, it wasn't that clear I grant you, but hey, it was Clem – I mean I was sure it was."

"Did you meet him face to face?"

Jamie hesitated, "No. No, I guess I didn't. He sent me a note saying that he had to keep out of sight." Then he rallied his strength. "With all this going on I can't say that I am surprised." He was breathing heavily and Quantock knew that the caffeine was reacting with his tired body. His heart would be pounding and he would feel as though he were hyperventilating. This added to the general anxiety and made him susceptible to suggestion or threat. Now was the time to strike.

"I understand your loyalty for your dead friend..."

Jamie broke in, "But he's not dead!"

Quantock continued like a patient parent, "...as I say, to your dead friend. Look, why don't you come with me?"

Jamie was confused and stood up unsteadily; Quantock took his arm.

228

From behind the viewing screen, Jim quickly scrambled out of the side door and made his way down to Interview Room Number Three, joining another man at the table. Quantock followed moments later with Jamie who was by now breathing heavily and shuffling along beside him. Instead of going into the interview room they went into the viewing area. Quantock turned to Jamie as they got inside.

"Quiet now. If you make a noise Jamie I'll get very angry, okay?" he said, planting both hands on the table and looking directly into Jamie's eyes.

Jamie paled and replied, "Yes sir, but what...?" he stopped talking and stared at the window in front of him. A slim young man sat with his back to him. He was medium build, say a hundred and fifty pounds, dressed in jeans and a sweatshirt. His fair hair was curly and covered his ears but it was not overly long.

"Clem!" said Jamie softly, and Quantock put his finger to his mouth. He turned up the speaker knob and the sound of voices filled the small area.

Jim was saying, "...come on now, be a man and sign up to your game. You stepped up to the plate and failed buddy, there's no sense in denying it. But what the hell did you do it for?"

The fair haired man answered brusquely, "You stupid son of a bitch. Lickspittle agent of the state. How can you be so ignorant of what is going on in America? Blacks, Catholics and Jews controlling our everyday lives. No freekin' jobs, our boys dead in Iraq and the rest of the Arabian rat hole." Suddenly he stood up and threw his chair across the room. An armed guard grabbed him around the middle and Jim raised his hands. The boy carried on shouting, "You can do what you like to me buddy, but when bombs go off and blast your Washington ass to heaven you won't be laughin' then. We, my party, have a hundred Timothy McVeigh's out there."

Before he could continue, the guard turned the boy around and Jamie's jaw dropped.

It wasn't Clem.

Quantock led Jamie back to the interview room. When he got back there the heating was adjusted to a warmer level and a plate of sandwiches was waiting on the table along with some orange juice. After one hour, Quantock had the boy eating out of his hand. Jamie accepted that he had been duped and felt stupid. He would resign his job that morning and move on. There was nothing else to be done. Quantock stopped him and offered to mediate with CNN bosses. He would say that it was a government sting to catch a particularly vicious group of individuals bent on mayhem and that Jamie had no option but to comply and, under threat of prison, keep it all a secret. The rookie CNN presenter would also be exonerated. Jamie was relieved and thanked him profusely. Quantock let him leave the building and Jamie waved as he crossed the road, happy to be an American and so well looked after by agents like Quantock!

It didn't take long to talk to the key players in CNN and explain the situation. The story for popular new consumption was to be that some kids tried to get up to political mischief, but they were moved on. Everyone agreed to move on and Quantock put the telephone down, pleased to close down the incident.

Then he called the president's office. After ending the brief, he added, "Sir, they will be held securely. Yes sir. Yes. It will be years before they emerge to the outside world." Then he slowly put the telephone down.

Clem didn't like to swallow the tablet and he coughed when the water was poured down his throat. But then he liked the injections even less. It was impossible to prevent the medication being administered and over the next few days he would move in and out of sleep and feel that nothing mattered whatsoever. He tried to focus on his surroundings, but it was difficult. His vision constantly swirled like the ebb and flow of a tide; each time he wanted to crawl onto a tempting calm shoreline the scene tilted and wouldn't stay still long enough for him to gain some balance. The lighting was low and the sheer net curtains covering the windows billowed in the wind allowing an occasional glimpse of green grass and clumps of shrubs with autumn colours. As he moved his head a middle-aged woman in white uniform came over to his side.

"You okay honey?" she said.

"Where am I?" he said.

"Now never you mind that. You're in hospital and the best thing for you is to get some rest. Don't do any thinkin'. Don't do any moving around, you'll only fall over. It is in your own interest to just stay quiet and calm. If you don't then I'm gonna have to give you some more medication," she said with a warm and yet stern tone.

"Are you a nurse or a prison warder?" said Clem.

"Now honey, you're doin' the thinkin' I told you not to do!" she then reached into a tray and took out a syringe. Clem paled and knew what was coming. Then he felt a slight prick and his ears heard the sound of rushing like a subway train and he was suddenly elated and transported to unconsciousness.

David Weinburger Head of the CIA and Troy Hammond Head of the Federal Bureau of Investigation met at a neutral location in Washington DC, each accompanied by an aide they could trust. The location was a small residential hotel used as a front for clandestine meetings of all kinds. An unseen hand closed the large oak door to the dining room where they were seated at a glass table. There were several bottles of mineral water, a small icebox and six tall glasses on the table. The room was decorated in bottle green wallpaper and was dimly lit by several cylinder-shaped wall lights. The scene resembled a Mafia meeting between two clan bosses together with their minders. The air was electric and tense.

Weinburger started the discussion.

"I don't get it. Six teenagers, each a son or daughter of a prominent US senator, are kidnapped by two of our agents, CIA that is, and killed; why? Your man, what's his name? Quantock, that's it. Your man catches up with them following an unspecified hunch and despatches them both without mercy. It seems we are to believe that our boys, CIA that is, could have been in the pay of Arab terrorists seeking to hold the nation to ransom." He paused and took a deep breath before continuing.

"I know that the two boys concerned could be, er, how shall we say, a little feral at times, but there is nothing to connect them at all with any Middle Eastern country. They never worked anywhere near there for Chris'sake!" His voice had increased in tone and strength and he gripped his hands tight.

Hammond sat impassively listening to the opening remarks. He frowned and responded. "Okay. Try this for size: one of the girls had been sexually assaulted, raped in fact, and the report said, let me see I have it here." He flicked through the pages of a report in front of him, "Ah yes, here it is, Ralph Andersen was known to have a voracious sexual appetite and a drug habit, as well as a record for being erratic and violent. After recovering the bodies, Anderson's DNA was matched to that in the girl's body and his blood showed heavy traces of cocaine. So what makes you love the guy so much?"

Weinburger bristled and fidgeted. "Because we should've caught and interrogated them, that's why. For the record we didn't assign them to any tasks, they were on a sabbatical, gardening holiday, whatever. It just doesn't make sense. They had no time since the end of their last mission to get involved with Arabs or anybody for that matter. What about it all?

Unlimited cash, fancy hideaway decorated and air conditioned and video equipment. This simply doesn't smack of Arab terrorists. They would've captured the kids and slit their throats after videoing them in orange suits and under Arabic banners. Then they would have sent copies to every dumb ass organisation willing to show the film on prime time television news channels. Wouldn't they?"

Hammond inwardly agreed and thought this the most obvious modus operandi for Arab terrorists. Weinburger was in full flow, and continued his assessment.

"This doesn't smack of Arab involvement, Troy, it smacks of insider connection. I tell you this. My people are fed up to the back teeth and mad as hell with getting the blame for everything that goes wrong in the security world. First it was 9/11 and the failure of intelligence; then it was the quality of the information on the weapons of mass destruction supposedly held by Saddam Hussein in Iraq. You know as well as me that if the administration spent less time telling us what they want to find, spinning information to get votes and creating headlines for disastrous policies we would all be better off. I know it and what's more Troy, you damned well know it too!"

Weinburger sat back exhausted, breathing heavily almost as though he had gone ten rounds heavyweight boxing with Mike Tyson. There was silence. Too much for the CIA aide who, exasperated, blurted out, "I think we've wasted our time Sir?"

The FBI aide smiled sarcastically, causing the CIA boy to bark, "What the hell are you smilin' at Hoover boy, I ought to bust your ass…!"

"Cut it out the pair of you," said Hammond, "if this is the way that two agencies act towards each other then America's in a worse state than I thought." He turned to Weinburger, "I hear what you say David, it just takes my 'Hoover' brain a little longer to figure out what's going on, that's all. Now I suggest we send these two boys out of the room to sort out their differences, whilst you and I continue?"

Weinburger readily agreed and the aides left the room after being made to shake hands. When the door closed both men took off their jackets. Weinburger went to light a cigar and Hammond stopped him. "I would be grateful if you wouldn't smoke, if you don't mind?"

Weinburger smiled and couldn't resist making a barbed remark, "Ah yes, the president thinks it good sport to smoke his cigars at meetings to annoy the anti-smoking brigade. Doesn't seem to respect anyone does he? Except of course his Head of Communications, Sadie Burrows. But then she can moisten my cigar any day!"

Hammond ignored the coarse remark. "Look David. I don't like this any more than you do. I have my own suspicions. We should work together on this or we'll end up pitching each organisation against the other and that's counter productive. I can see by your expression that you know more – so tell me."

The atmosphere softened and Weinburger poured some water into a tall glass and helped himself to some ice.

"You're right. I do have some more information. We both know that the organisation termed, 'The Cleaners' went to clean up a mess in Arizona. You know as well as I do that this organisation does a job, but never takes sides or reveals what it found. It cleans up. Period."

"Sure, so what?"

Weinburger continued, "Well one of the cleaners was in Vietnam with Martin Adams, the other CIA agent. In his day, Adams was a first class Army officer, but he got himself into trouble when he beat up a non-comm', a sergeant I believe, who was boasting about his part in the Me Lai massacre in Cambodia. He was busted, but was so good that wherever he went he was regarded as the leader of the platoon. Anyway, they went their separate ways and then, bang, this guy ends up 'cleaning' up Adams' body in Arizona. Well, he told us that the bodies were recovered from a small hotel in the town of Benson. We followed this up. One of our agents, a pretty girl, very persuasive and likeable, visited the hotel and spoke to the clerk. She failed to get anything out of him. In fact he was so uncommunicative that she was convinced his life had been threatened. Undeterred, she carried out exhaustive checks and guess what? Two teenagers were seen in the company of a man resembling Mr Dan Quantock, your man Troy. She also checked out all the automobile rental agencies and, strike two, she found that Clem Johnson had used his credit card to hire a vehicle and that the FBI had been informed of this."

He put his hands together and stared at Hammond.

Hammond frowned, "David, the kid's belongings were left open to the world at the tin mine for quite a period and it is just possible that someone stole Johnson's wallet and used the credit card?"

"Yes, it is just possible. Trouble is Troy, you don't believe that, do you?"

"I don't know what to believe David. We have to be frank with each other. This is not easy. The man you speak of, Quantock, is now quite highly placed and has the ear of the president. All work involving the investigation into the whereabouts of the missing teenagers has been undertaken by him and he has answered directly to the president himself."

"You mean….."

"I mean nothing David, nothing until I can put together all that you have given me and followed up on my own investigations," said Hammond.

The two men talked on and off for another hour. Eventually, they stood up and Hammond handed Weinburger a sheet of notes that were his thoughts on the situation so far. Weinburger felt guilty at laying into his opposite number so loudly; the notes had been written before the meeting and it was clear that the Head of the FBI was already feeling uneasy about the relationship between Quantock, the president and the deaths of the teenagers.

He skim read the notes and said, "I misunderstood you Troy, I'm sorry," then turning back to the notes again he gazed at the recommendations, added, "and I agree with your assessment. We'll follow up as you indicate here. Thanks for the tip and the opportunity."

Chapter Thirteen

Merric and Catherine sat in his friend's apartment in George Town Washington. It had been a long drive, going round in circles to shake off anyone who might be following, although they checked several times and knew they weren't. The traffic was heavier than usual and in a funny sort of way they felt safer because of this. There had been nothing, absolutely nothing on any of the news channels about Clem and Ginny's antics on CNN except for brief cheerful laughs from presenters about teenagers gaining access to play a prank on a rookie presenter. Some laugh.

Merric's friend, Christine, left them to talk. She owned a small cake shop in the local area and had laid out some cakes. A plate was laid with *babka,* or grandmother cakes, small, rich and bread-like, formed in a 'bundt' or skirt shape, reminiscent of a woman's skirt, and *szarlotka*, apple and cinnamon cake. Despite the wonderful aroma of the pastries and coffee Catherine didn't have much of an appetite and just picked at them. Merric on the other hand still remembered the poor times in Poland and distraught or not, held to the notion that the body must be fed.

"What on earth has happened to the kids?" said Catherine.

Merric chewed the remainder of a *babka* cake and swallowed some coffee. After a while he answered.

"*Kto wie?* Who knows? They will be somewhere. Somewhere out of sight. No news on the television, Catherine, means that no one really knows about their situation and that they are, how would you say? Non-people." He looked glum.

Catherine's eyes welled with tears and she felt her throat closing with anger and frustration. There really was nothing that she could do. She descended into a depressive state, put her elbows on the table and her head in her hands. Merric finished the other *babka.*

Christine went out the next day to the bakery and left them to spend the day resting from their journey and the disappointment they felt. She knew nothing about their situation and asked no questions, happy to help for the sake of friendship. Her background was like Merric's and she would give help and assistance without asking for any information or payment in return. Not asking questions and keeping things to herself was etched into her personality.

Merric was drinking coffee and scouring the Washington Post for anything that referred to the two teenagers. Then he sat bolt upright as he heard a small shriek. Catherine came running into the room with a very small towel wrapped round her.

"Merric. We are missing our duty, our definite duty. We have to tell Ginny and Clem's parents that they are still alive. Ginny's mother does know that she was not killed and must be beside herself with worry."

Merric clucked his teeth. It was true. They did have a duty to advise a worried mother. But there were dangers and for a start both parents' houses would be bugged and watched. He looked at Catherine standing in the doorway holding the small towel around her body and smiled as his seventy-five years melted and a strange and familiar feeling made his blood flow faster. He smiled slowly and just sat there looking at her with a stupid grin on his face.

"Merric, what the hell's wrong with you, why are you just staring at me? Answer my question will you?" she blurted impatiently.

Merric jerked himself back to reality, but couldn't surpress a smile.

"Catherine, we must discuss this for sure. But, *O Boze,* I am sorry I stared, it's just that," then he stopped and smiled even wider.

"Oh, Merric, just what?"

"It's just that, well it's just that your towel doesn't quite join at the bottom!"

Catherine looked down at the wide triangular opening at the base of the two ends of the towel, then shrieked with embarrassment and rushed out of the room.

He teased her when she joined him again and she pretended to be haughty, but smiled impishly. For his part he congratulated her for making him feel young again and this earned him a cuff on his head for his troubles. Then after a while he grew serious.

"Catherine," he said, "we should contact Ginny's mother first. I know of Clem's father and he is a dumb guy, really dumb. The boy told me much of his life and relationship with his father. This man will make instant trouble and this will do us no good. He will consider himself to be a distressed father approached by two charlatans who want to get money out of a grieving family. No, from what I hear, Ginny's mother is the best bet. She has at least been contacted already and knows that her daughter didn't perish in the tin mine in Arizona. But if we do this Catherine, we have to plan it carefully. No contact by telephone at all you understand? Although I am, to all intents, a fugitive and how would you say, am in the frame now, the authorities probably do not know anything about you. But I must repeat, no telephone under any circumstances, please."

Merric paused for a second and Catherine interjected.

"Merric you are so right. I have to get to talk to Ginny's mother, somehow. And I will need to start," she looked sideways towards a personal computer on a sideboard near the window, "on the net."

"I agree with you. Research as much as you can and find out what she does and where she goes. You will then be able to get to speak to her. I am sure that she will not be watched that closely. The danger is mostly over except for me."

Merric thought some more then added, "I think I should give myself up."

Catherine gulped and held his hand, "No, Merric, no. If you do there is no way that you can be let back into the outside world. You will simply disappear like Clem and Ginny. That's not a good idea at all."

Merric reluctantly agreed and Catherine set about surfing the net to find out more about Angela Grivas, wife of US Senator Nick Grivas.

John Zirl had been in the CIA for three decades. The Head of CIA included him in the discussions on the situation regarding the deaths of senator's children. He was left in no doubt about the bad feeling between the CIA and FBI. There was a terrible atmosphere between them and it had to be fixed. His mission was to contact US Senator Grivas – somehow. The CIA knew that only four bodies had been found, the other two, it was claimed, were buried deep in the San Quiller tin mine following a roof fall; they had learned that much from the 'cleaners'. They also knew that two US senators were being watched; it seemed ludicrous that the FBI might not have known that this would have been leaked out within the security fraternity. Then a mysterious leak had alerted the CIA to the fact that two teenagers had not been murdered at all and were being held in a secure hospital between Montrose Park and Oak Hill Cemetery, close to Rock Creek and Potomac Parkway, Northeast Washington.

Zirl stood outside the Senate building and watched the senators arriving and leaving the building. He knew that Senator Grivas was chairing a committee on transport matters and that it was due to end at about mid-day. He also knew that the Senator was famous for talking well beyond the finish time for meetings. Patience was a quality all CIA operatives had in abundance.

After waiting no more than an hour he spotted Senator Grivas at the door to the Senate. He looked around and took in those who were obviously in his entourage. It wasn't difficult to spot a man standing alone some way off looking in the Senator's direction. It was to this man that he was to play his drama to maximum effect.

Senator Grivas walked down the steps with a man and woman at his side. Zirl made it look for the entire world as though he was passing by, then animated, he stopped and looked up in the senator's direction. The senator spotted this.

"Senator Grivas, Nick, well my God, how are you sir," said Zirl loudly.

Grivas was nonplussed, but Zirl was quickly upon him grabbing his hand and shaking it vigorously.

"Ron Grainger, you remember we sat on the same committee to discuss South American imports recently. It's good to see you and can I say how sad I was to hear of the terrible situation, well, with your daughter and all…" as he was talking, he pressed a square of paper into the senator's hand that he now clasped with both of his. Then he leant forward and looking concerned and friendly he was able to whisper in his ear.

"Ginny is alive. Don't acknowledge what I am saying. Read this note and respond. Make a fuss and you will never see her again."

Zirl disengaged slowly and picked up the briefcase that he had put down saying loudly, "I want you to know that if you ever want to come and stay with me and my folks in Long Island, you just give us a call now. Don't you forget?" He pointed a finger at Senator Grivas, who, despite initial surprise and reservation did not change his expression one bit, played the game well.

"Thank you, er, Ron. I will and regards to your lovely family too," he said.

As Zirl walked away the senator casually put his hand in his pocket and deposited the folded paper inside. Then he walked casually to his waiting vehicle. The driver stopped reading his newspaper and called out.

"Home Senator?"

"Yeah, home. Straight away and no diversions," he replied.

Once in the car he took out the carefully folded paper, flattened it carefully on his briefcase and read it.

Senator,

This is not a note from a criminal fraternity, but from friends in the Administration. Ginny is not dead. But it is important that you do not tell anyone other than your wife about this note. We need to talk urgently. Call the cell phone number below and use only your cell phone and not your landline.

A friend.

Grivas' throat thickened. He had been hard on his wife when she said she had been called by Ginny. He accused her of hallucinating or to have talked to con-merchants. They had a terrible argument with the both of them ending in tears – not something that came easily to the tough Senator Grivas. But Ginny's disappearance and reported murder had shaken them both to the core. They agreed to never argue on this subject again. But he was certain that she had been contacted again, because she had that faraway look in her eyes and wouldn't share her thoughts with him.

They had both been kept busy. Fellow politicians nominated him for various committees to keep his mind off things and his wife was overwhelmed with offers to run charity events.

Perhaps she had been right after all?

Catherine had spent all the previous day researching on the net and printed off the list of engagements for Mrs Angela Grivas. She stuffed the papers in her handbag and made her way across Washington to St Luke's Children's Hospital on the Jefferson Davis Highway. Occasionally she looked at the faded digital photograph of Angela Grivas and hoped that she would be able to recognise her.

The journey was not long and she got the taxi to stop a couple of blocks away from the hospital. After walking along the sidewalk with others on their way to the charity sale she turned into the courtyard. All the stalls selling a variety of goods were inside the main hall and out of the chill autumn air. She walked around the stalls and bought a few items. Then she looked up and saw a woman dressed in a beige woollen suit, cream blouse and with matching crocodile shoes and handbag that was unmistakably Angela Grivas. She stood slightly to one side of a group of women, occasionally responding to a remark, but otherwise remaining sealed up in her own company, looking slightly aloof and detached. But then she had a lot on her mind, thought Catherine. She walked towards her and stopped several feet away. Perhaps she could do this without saying a word?

Catherine looked steadily at Angela Grivas and after a while, Angela returned her gaze. At first she looked away. Then, on seeing Catherine's persistent gaze she turned her head back in her direction. Catherine raised an eyebrow. Angela Grivas tilted her head slightly, but continued staring. Then she slowly started to walk towards Catherine; bingo!

"Do I know you?" said Angela Grivas.

Surprisingly Angela Grivas maintained a frozen expression, completely without emotion.

Catherine put out her hand and Angela took it, "No, but I do need to talk to you," she looked around her, "about Ginny."

Catherine was impressed by her fortitude. She lifted her head slightly and replied, "What about Ginny?"

"She called you twice, once from Benson and once from my place. Does that mean we can talk some more?"

This time Angela put her hand to her mouth.

Her voice faltered slightly and eyes welled, and she said falteringly, "Yes, I think we should….."

Catherine was gentle with Angela. She touched her hands frequently as they sat drinking coffee at one of the several untidy tables in the school hall, and she explained exactly everything that Ginny and Clem had told her and what she saw in Atlanta. Angela Grivas' eyes widened and big tears fell down her cheeks. After five agonising minutes she composed herself. She needed to stay calm and understand that Catherine had seen Ginny and she was alive. She was alive!

It was a complicated scenario and Angela was uncertain as to what to do next. It was confusing and she felt impotent, but she had to control her emotions, stay calm and be responsible. Catherine told her that no undue fuss should be made without thinking the situation through. Angela agreed. They hugged and exchanged cell phone numbers. When they parted Catherine looked back over her shoulder and caught sight of Angela walking towards a taxi. She looked up and smiled back at her, her eyes glistening with tears.

Catherine knew she had done the right thing; but what next?

Senator Nick Grivas was waiting for his wife when she came in. The script resembled a tragic comedy as they both tried to get each other's attention. Nick dragged her unwilling and angry into the garden sun lounge at the bottom of the garden saying they needed secrecy and he had heard something he didn't quite know whether to believe. He was so wound up he wouldn't let his wife get a word in edgeways. But Angela won the day, because she burst into floods of tears and she recounted her meeting with Catherine Devine; when this double confirmation sunk in, Nick Grivas broke down. They wept and clung to each other. When they were calmer, they focussed on their situation and the need for secrecy even in their own house. Double confirmation, their daughter was, after all, safe and well, surely now they could believe that everything was going to be all right?

Grivas reached for his cell phone and keyed in the number that was written on the bottom of the paper given to him by the man he met outside the Senate. A voice answered and they arranged to meet the following day.

He hugged his wife and said, "Let's get our daughter back. And I tell you this for nothing - somebody will pay for this. I swear it."

The next day, Senator Grivas was in no mood for anything other than straight talking. He was met by the man purporting to be Ron Grainger at a selected rendezvous and allowed himself to be driven to another location. They both got out of the car when it stopped in a small courtyard at a townhouse south of the city. The door opened into a main corridor and they followed it until they reached a small conference room. Another man was there and he shook the senator's hand introducing himself with a smile as John Smith. They were both CIA agents.

"Senator, sit down please. I know that you are worried sick regarding the whereabouts of your daughter, so I'll waste no further time." He then switched on a video player and said, "Watch this."

A clear film played on a nearby screen and showed the surrounding area of Oak Hill Cemetery. Then it slowly moved towards a wooden area. The camera moved through the wood and stopped short of some railings. Slowly some leaves were moved and what appeared to be a large white building came into view. Then there was a short cut in the film and when it resumed it was focussing on some French windows. The telescopic lens was of a very high quality, because it zoomed in a long way and still provided a crystal clear picture. As it did so it focussed on a female form in a dressing gown sitting in a chair. Senator Grivas instinctively leaned forward and said out loud, "It's Ginny, I know it."

The video was freeze-framed.

The man named John Smith confirmed that it was her.

Senator Grivas quickly stood up. "Okay, that's it, I want my daughter out of there, now. Let's go, what are we waiting for?"

"I'll tell you Senator. We just do not know what the dangers are of alerting those who are holding her. We may get her out without harming her, but we will lose the opportunity to surprise those who organised this terrible thing. We also need to flush out the source of all this trouble. Relationships between Capitol Hill, the FBI and the CIA are at breaking point. This situation is bigger than your daughter sir. It is of national importance. If we don't sort out our differences it will lead to trouble, big trouble. We all have to work together on this. Trust me."

Senator Grivas sat down again and said, "Okay. As long as this does not put my daughter in any more danger than she has been put in already. I can't put her through any more. But I am also madder than hell. There is an implication that my house and phone may be bugged – me, a senator! How does this happen? Who breaks rules like this?"

The two men sitting across from him looked at each other before responding, "Senator, no one broke the rules, they simply brushed them to one side. It's the style of today's administration. The House of Representatives is treated with contempt, the culture of public relations spin is so well established that even when members of the Senate know there is bad news they simply wait for the screen version to see whether or not they should make an issue out of it. Senator, even you have been guilty of the sin of indifference. Sir, I'm real sorry to have said that, but it's true"

Senator Grivas stared at them and then spoke.

"You're right. I know it and my fellows know it too. But we put up with the status quo, putting our faith in the next presidential election and staying focussed on our own backyard issues I guess."

Grivas thought how strange it was that the mind focuses more clearly when a critical situation emerges, but just wished he was not in the situation he was in to recognise that phenomena. He remembered several of his friends had been alarmed at the hostile attitude towards dissent at party debates and committees. One senator was sure that he was being followed and that his telephone was bugged. Another talked of being hassled by large men in dark suits when he was preparing to ask awkward questions about the war in Iraq or foreign relations. The two of them got a ribald response when they voiced their fears, but one or two of Grivas' friends had taken it seriously. Grivas had pondered that it was a little like an English Elizabethan court in the sixteenth century – do as the queen bid or off with your head! Was it so comical?

He stood up again and continued, "Can we just get down to a plan of action? I just want to get my daughter out of there and then set about changing my life and my politics."

Coffee arrived and a plan was meticulously developed. The agents had been watching the hospital for some time and noticed that the nursing staff changed every two days. An agent on the inside working as a cleaning assistant would smuggle a drug into the hospital. It would have a devastating effect on Ginny's facial skin, turning it into a flaky and spotty mass. This would be distressing for her, but it would allow a substitute to be put in her place at just the time of the change of nursing staff. She would then be smuggled out and back home. After a while the effect would wear off and she would be free to be put in front of the American public. This time there would be no hitches. They would go back for Clem when it was all over and they had achieved the element of surprise. Then and only then would they get to the bottom of the situation. They also had to work quickly to meet a deadline that was closing.

The presidential election was due on 5 November.

Chapter Fourteen

Angela Grivas contacted Catherine Devine on her cell phone. It was noisy in the local diner but she was happy with that because, oddly, the sounds of people and coffee machines made her feel more anonymous and secluded. She explained slowly and clearly that she and her husband have been contacted by the CIA about Ginny and Clem and Catherine had been right, her lovely daughter and Clem Johnson were alive. Angela explained to her that the agents understood that Merric and Catherine would be suspicious, but if they could meet with them, in Catherine's company then together they could focus on a plan to release the teenagers. The agents wanted it known that they fully understood how the pair felt about authority, but that they should be reassured because Senator Grivas and Angela were acting as trusted third parties.

Catherine and Merric had no other option and wanted to be part of the plan to free the teenagers. They reluctantly agreed to meet with Angela and agents Zirl and Grainger. The men were masters at reassuring witnesses and after ordering more coffee settled down to hear Catherine describe what the teenagers had told her, then the situation at the CNN building in Atlanta.

The agents' mouths hung open in disbelief. Zirl spoke.

"Miss Devine, Mr Grabowski. You have both been enormously brave. I commend you both, I really do. But the story's not over yet. We need to form a plan, in fact we have some ideas already. Can we call on you to help if need be?"

Merric banged the table and several customers sat upright shocked at the sudden noise. He continued unabashed. "Yes, yes, of course. I want these kids safe, you understand me, safe I tell you." His eyes were moist and they understood his upset.

Zirl continued, first putting his hand firmly on Merric's. "Merric, let's work together. Now before we proceed, we need to get you folks together and we must go over the facts as you presented them to us Catherine, without leaving out any detail whatsoever. We have a safe house organised. Okay then, let's go – we've got work to do."

Grainger sat back and admired his colleague for the way he balanced his delivery and guidance with a mixture of empathy and firmness. However, it would take more than emotion to win the day.

John Zirl bonded well with Senator Grivas, but then it wasn't difficult. The man was feeling the pain of separation from his daughter in dangerous circumstances and was at his wit's end with worry. Zirl had a daughter too and knew that if it were him in this position, he wouldn't be able to even think straight. It had to be made better – it now seemed personal. He assembled an experienced team of CIA agents and they discussed the plan that the agents had put together earlier. Time was short. A change of shift for the nurse-come warders was due the next day.

A medium sized cleaning truck drove along an avenue of tall chestnut trees, the remaining leaves were different kinds of red brown and wet with the morning mist. Then it slowed down in front of the gates to the hospital just outside Oak Hill Cemetery, outside Washington DC. The driver showed the correct papers and was waved on by the security guard. The cleaning company often used different staff and so it was no surprise to see new faces. The truck went to the rear of the hospital and three people, two men and a woman, dressed in green cleaning fatigues and the driver got out. They unloaded two lockable boxes on wheels, about five by three by three feet. The tallest of the men tapped lightly on the side of one box and got a light tap from inside in return. They looked at their watches; it was nine in the morning.

"Hi, you guys new here?" said a voice from the direction of the rear door. They jumped at the unexpected intervention.

"Oh, jeez, sorry you made me jump," said the woman, "yeah, we're a new team. I'm the supervisor, Marjorie."

"Okay, for what it's worth your friends usually stay for coffee and doughnuts afterwards, but don't tell your administration – they pay for the extra time. See you later?" said the male nurse.

The woman supervisor winced inwardly and thought, "Ooh, great..!" But she smiled and said, "Sure that would be great, thank you. We'd better get on with the job. See you."

The team had been briefed meticulously, today the West Wing where Ginny Grivas was housed was scheduled for a cleanup. This happened every third day and supplemented the general tidy up carried out by the in-house hospital staff. They pushed their wheeled boxes and equipment to the West Wing, then worked their way through several administrative offices, slowly moving closer to a number of wards at the far end of the building. By now it was almost mid-day. As they entered a long corridor that formed a 'T' junction to the main thoroughfare a couple of nurses bustled past. The shorter of the two and the prettiest was sarcastic.

"Hey guys look where you're going. For Chris'sake, why do they organise the cleaning day when we have a major shift change? Sorry guys, gotta bad temper and all that – I just wanna get home!"

The team pretended to clean everything in sight and put on that, 'Sorry not our fault,' expression. Then Marjorie the female cleaning supervisor went quickly down the corridor to the left and stopped about halfway then turned back and put her thumb up. One of the male cleaners then broke away and pushed one of the metal storage boxes back down the main corridor. The other man quickly pushed his steel storage box on wheels towards the supervisor.

As the first cleaner almost reached the reception desk, he saw two nurses approaching. They were the replacement shift. When they were almost six feet away he pulled a pin at the base of the box and the doors flew open. All manner of equipment fell out including several containers of cleaning fluid. The floor was deluged with different colour liquids, brushes and containers, right in the path of the nurses. The diversion was a real jackpot.

One of the nurses lost her temper, "Oh man, my damned shoes, these are just clean on today, you horses' ass you. My God look at the mess!"

The cleaner knew his script. "Well, ma'am," he said in a slow drawl, "no need shoutin' at me, this ain't my fault. I don't make the damned boxes." His voice grew shrill and angry. "You try livin' on a dollar a day using this crap and see how you like it. You ain't got no call shoutin' at me like that."

Then the shouting match started with each accusing the other of being unreasonable. The noise could be heard back down the corridor and the female supervisor wasted no time at all. She rushed into Ginny's ward, and then slowed as she approached the armchair in which Ginny had been placed for the day. Ginny looked in a terrible state. The drug smuggled into the hospital and placed in her drinking water by another operative a few days earlier had done the trick and her face was a mass of flaky skin and red wheals – she was hardly recognisable. The woman bent down and whispered in her ear.

"Don't worry. You are gonna be quite safe soon."

But Ginny couldn't really take anything in. The drugs being administered to keep her docile were very strong. The supervisor reached for a syringe from the storage box that had just arrived and calmly emptied the contents into Ginny's arm. It was a mild sedative to put her into a shallow sleep. The tall man opened the main body of the steel box and out sprang a young woman of Ginny's build and hair colouring, her own face covered in flaky skin and red wheals. It was so bad she could only mumble. She waved her hand in front of her face indicating that she had found it hot in the box. They removed Ginny's dressing gown and night shift and the girl put them on, handing her own garments to be put on Ginny.

The tall man then reached down and with one hand lifted Ginny's small body gently off her chair and placed her into the padded interior of the steel box on wheels. After making sure the drug had worked and that she was quite asleep and her body was in a comfortable position, the box was locked. The supervisor looked at her male companion. The CIA operative had survived because she was able to breathe through a tube, but Ginny was unconscious and would not be able to do so effectively.

"No more than thirty minutes at the outset. After that she runs out of clean air!"

They both touched the shoulder of their companion to be left behind then made for the scene of chaos at the main desk area. When the second male cleaner heard the squeaking of the wheels on the first steel box and the tap, tap of the shoes of his comrades coming down the corridor he stopped yelling. When the supervisor and the other cleaner arrived at the scene of chaos, she squared her shoulders lifted her head and looked at the operative saying, "Malcolm, what the hell have you been doing and why are you yelling at these nurses?"

"Those boxes are lethal," said the younger of the two nurses, "I'm calling the health and safety supervisor and both of them will be impounded, right now, that's what. I'm not having this crap again."

The situation was now getting serious and Marjorie had to think quickly. At first she said nothing and glared at everyone. That silenced them all. Then she walked towards the metal box on wheels and knelt down. She went straight to the pin that had been used to eject the material and theatrically got down on her knees to inspect its housing. Standing up she turned towards the male cleaner who had been pushing the box and frowned at him.

"How many more times do I tell you Malcolm? This pin is a safety pin. It is used just in case little children get inside the box and cannot get out. You pull it and everything flips apart. Good for the kid whose life it saves, bad for a pair of nurse's shoes. The pin should be secure, Malcolm, secure. Not hanging like a donkey dick ready to be pulled by some fool like you!"

Her voice rose and the nurses physically recoiled at the admonition. They almost felt sorry for the male cleaner. He sheepishly looked down and said, "Yeah, I remember now. I'm sorry. Can I pay for the shoes?"

The atmosphere changed now that the nurses gained support from someone of their own gender. Then, pleased that they had been vindicated, they thanked her, waived the cleaning bill for the shoes and moved on, leaving the two men to clean up the mess. This took about ten minutes because they had ensured a plentiful supply of paper towels and waste bags. They finished and made their way quickly back to their truck.

The chastised male cleaner nudged his female companion and said, in a fake southern drawl, "Golly gosh Marje, you know what? You're quite frightening when you get one on. I'll give you damned donkey dick when we get back to base."

She smiled and knew she'd take some joshing for that bit of quick thinking.

The truck was loaded quickly and watches checked it had taken sixteen minutes; Ginny had been in the box about twenty one minutes. Just as they were about to get in the truck a voice called out, "Hey, you guys, what about coffee and doughnuts?"

They turned around, surprised and Marjorie said, "Oh heck, we want to, but, well, see, we got into trouble today with some of the nurses and on top of that we're late. Real sorry, next time perhaps?"

The voice persisted. "Look, that's a shame. Wait here, I'll see you all right, that I will."

Marje heard footsteps receding and shouted, "No, really, it's okay….." But it was too late. They were forced to wait, hoping it would not be for too long.

The minutes ticked by. The box grew hotter.

When it seemed as though they were going to have to run for it, Marjorie told one of the men to open the steel box that housed Ginny and let some air in, but to keep the rear truck door closed. After ten minutes the friendly hospital administrator waddled around the corner with a big bag of coffee and doughnuts, 'to go'.

"Here y'all are. We have high standards of hospitality here. Have a real nice day," he said.

Marjorie took the package and smiled her thanks. Then they all got in the truck and drove to the gate. As they slowed a stern looking guard stepped out in front of the truck and waved them down. He walked to the passenger window, tapped on it with his hand.

"Okay, vehicle search!" he said loudly.

They all let out an audible groan. Then the guard then smiled and let out a loud guffaw.

"Golly Moses, I love doin' that to new cleaners. Never fails! Off you go now boys and girls," and he waved the truck on laughing wildly like a maniac, "see yo'all next week".

A little way down the road the driver looked at Marje and said, "Well at least somebody got some kicks out of today!"

There was silence. He looked around and saw the answer – they were busy demolishing the bags of doughnuts.

Ginny was beginning to regain consciousness and the mixture of drugs in her body left her confused and unfocused. The team bathed her body with cool flannels and gave her plenty of water to drink. After a short journey to a safe house on the East

Side of Washington DC, she was unloaded carefully from the truck and taken inside. As she was helped into a sitting room, she could just about make out two figures. Then she heard their voices. Even through the mist and with hearing that was dull and full of echoes she recognised them as her mother and father. Tears flowed and wet her cheeks. Then her parents were with her hugging her tightly, all three of them crying and trying to talk.

The CIA agents moved out of the room slowly as John Zirl waved at them and the Grivas family was left to their emotional reunion.

Later that day Ginny asked to see Merric and Catherine and more hugs and tears followed. It was decided to let Ginny sleep off the effect of all the drugs whilst they worked out the next move.

When Ginny had been settled in bed, Zirl, Nick and Angela Grivas, Merric and Catherine made small talk. The senator then put his hands on his knees and started the serious discussion.

"Look, we've gotta do something soon. I have an idea. I'm expected to chair a group in the Senate a couple of days before the election. It's a run down on the exit poll results and has a mixture of senators from different states and is evenly balanced between Republican and Democrats; kind of special really. We have Judy Woodruff, you know her? She does the CNN television programme, 'Inside Politics'. It's quite a coup to have such a televised debate on the pre-election polls. Well, why can't we bring Ginny in and then I can make a speech on, well, the situation? You know what I mean?"

John Zirl put his hands together and frowned. "Our problem Senator is that we suspect that the rogue FBI agent, Dan Quantock, will be watching everything. You will be expected to bring your daughter into the Senate and I don't believe that you will get the chance to make any statement, televised or otherwise. Unless…" His voices trailed off, and then he added, "Unless we can create a diversion."

There was a long pause.

Merric clapped his hands and they all looked at him. "Aha!" he shouted, "My thoughts exactly. The FBI could not find me. They searched my apartment, but we were gone, poof, gone! So, they must believe that I know something. In which case, I go to a hotel and organise a press briefing. It is that special time is it not? When foreign journalists are looking for stories, especially those that relate to the presidential election."

Merric sat, with hands outstretched, eyes wide open and appealing.

The senator looked at John Zirl and they said nothing.

Catherine spoke up. "I could help too. Ginny and I are about the same size. If I wear a wig of Ginny's hair colour and then enter whatever space is being used for the briefing that Merric suggests, some time after Merric and sat there, well wherever he sits, ready to speak. Then perhaps the FBI will be expecting some kind of statement and focus on the Hotel at the expense of the Senate. Merric and I will spin it out as much as we can right over the schedule of your televised committee-meeting, senator. This might buy you time."

John Zirl smiled. "Merric, Catherine, I do think you have it, I really do.

The girl in Ginny's bed space in the hospital waited twelve hours before making herself known to the staff. She produced papers to prove that she was not Ginny Grivas and advised all those she spoke to, to release her as soon as possible because her location was known to a wide variety of government and newspaper agencies. She was interviewed and reluctantly it was agreed that she should be released under caution six hours later.

The matron had the unenviable task of breaking the news to the FBI chief, Dan Quantock.

Chapter Fifteen

Dan Quantock was incandescent with rage; his heart was racing and his fingers tingled. Ginny Grivas had been sprung with such ease it had to have been done with help from people on the inside and he strongly suspected the involvement of the CIA. To make matters worse, Merric Grabowski, Clem Johnson's Polish friend was determined to have his day at a press interview to be hosted in a Washington hotel, the Quo Vadis, and Quantock did not know what he would reveal. It occurred to him that this was probably the best time and place for Ginny to be brought out of hiding, into the press glare. But he suspected that Senator Grivas was now in contact with his daughter and most worryingly of all, it meant he would soon be identified as the key player in the whole episode. The question was, should he disregard the televising of the Senate Committee debate on the state of the pre-election polls so far? Or should he concentrate on the ad hoc press briefing? Clem and Ginny had after all already tried the CNN route already and failed. For a moment he stopped and scratched his chin. He would think on it.

He then walked head up, down the long corridor to the President's Oval Office, having advised him of the situation earlier during an edgy telephone conversation. Confidence was his stock in trade, but he was going to have to call on every ounce of this if he was to survive the week. He reached the door to the office and was met by one of the president's executive officers who announced him. This was followed by a shout from the president, "Get in here Quantock!"

Quantock closed the door behind him, it felt heavy in his hands and the atmosphere of the room was warm and cloying.

"Mr President," he began, "I have to say...."

"You have nothing to say, nothing, Quantock. For the record, I know nothing, you understand me, nothing? I don't know of the Kinz scam, the existence of the remaining two teenagers from the tin mine fiasco. I...know...Goddamned...nothing. Do you really understand what I am saying to you?"

The president's face was red and his eyes bulged. There was sweat on his brow.

Quantock paled and nodded, not with fear or fright, but with the sick feeling of failure and humiliation. At least he was suffering this in private. He chose silence. The president continued.

"I want you to fix this situation, which is getting out of hand, within the next three days. The last day of the Presidential Election is five days away and I hold you personally responsible for the outcome."

By now Brannigan was leaning over the edge of the table and pointing a nicotine-stained right forefinger at Quantock's face. He was shaking with rage. Without ceremony or waiting for an answer from Quantock President Brannigan waved his hand unceremoniously towards the door.

Quantock left the room. He was determined to beat this setback. He had always come out on top and nothing was going to stop him this time.

On reaching his office Quantock called Jim Sparrow.

"Hi, Jim, it's Dan. Look, there has been a threat assessment that indicates some kind of action against the president. We're not too sure about the level, but we can't be too careful. For the last week of the election I want the highest level of security. Bring in the National Guard to stake out Capitol Hill, the Senate and especially the foreign press centres covering the election. When you've done that come and see me at three this afternoon and let's talk surveillance, okay?"

"Yeah, Dan, that's all fairly straightforward, but, er, well, the National Guard thing is going to need the President's authority first isn't it?" said Jim slightly bemused.

"No, no, not at all Jim. Just make all the necessary arrangements, I've briefed the President and he's happy. He's is in a ferocious mood so tell those who feel they have any semblance of a career to think carefully about how they question his decision. I for one will not get involved other than to pass on the president's direction and follow the progress. Say just that to whoever wants to know, eh, Jim?" Quantock was masterful at dissembling and moving the moral responsibility everywhere but in his own direction.

"Yes, boss," said Jim. He put the phone down with a click and Quantock was left listening to the mesmerising dial tone that mixed with the thump of his heartbeat. He lowered the telephone onto the cradle, held it there for a few moments, and then quickly dialled a number.

"Robert, Hi, long time no speak. Yeah, just fine, listen, I need a medium sized tape recorder that can be used to record a few things at a public meeting. You know the type, robust, decent carrying case with lots of pockets and of course easy to use. "He paused as he listened to the response, then continued. "Thanks buddy, I'll collect it from the store today, just put my name on the label. I'll sign for it. Yeah man, see you when I see you."

Quantock drummed his fingers on the desk. Then he reached for his cell phone rather than using the internal landline and whilst thumbing through his Filofax he dialled a number. It was answered after a few minutes.

"Morgan. It's me Quantock. Morgan, listen, don't let's exchange pleasantries I'm in a hurry. I need something from you. When you've delivered it you forget that you gave it to me, right? You forget – completely! If you don't then you will never see daylight again, that is if you manage to swing by a death sentence. The murder case is still open........"

Quantock continued and the man on the other end of the line agreed to do as he was told and keep quiet. The familiar zest that such power over people gives a human being in full control made Quantock feel a lot better and the pain of President Brannigan's fierce admonition receded slightly.

He walked to the chessboard on the coffee table in the corner of his office and reached down for the black queen, lifting it up and hovering over the centre of the action on the board. He carefully checked all the angles several times, and then firmly put the chess piece in place – right in the middle of the battle. He had one more call to make, and then this would be 'the last chance disco'."

Hotel Quo Vadis it was then!

Foreign journalists packed the foyer of the Hotel Quo Vadis in Washington DC, bustling and talking, hoping for some excitement. They were all junior journalists, the more senior press officers were taking the tastier trips organised by the Foreign Press Centres throughout the States. Many had camped out in the 'swing states' otherwise known as the 'Battleground States'. A few were lucky enough to be attending the Senate Committee/CNN television extravaganza that day; many wished they were there and not stuck in a hotel waiting to listen to an old Polish guy.

There was a queue for coffee. None of those present knew what to expect. This old Polish chap had called for the World's Press to be available to listen to something that would be of special interest to voters in the Presidential Election. He might be a nutcase, or he might have something interesting, what was it to be?

Three newspaper reporters from Eastern Europe laughed and joked with some of the other reporters and were clearly not taking things too seriously. Several English television and newspaper men had a strange way of sitting together and yet appearing totally separate, conferring with craned heads, then springing apart like repelling magnets.

Gunter Weismann from Austria turned to Christina Markel who worked for Der Deutsche Dagblad, based in Cologne and said, "After this, shall we take some time out for a good American cocktail. I know a good bar quite close by?"

Christina blanched. Gunter was amusing but he was also over forty years old and married. She was twenty-eight years of age and ambitious for her first big break. The last thing that she wanted was to get involved with an over-sexed married man intent on doing anything but report properly on the American Presidential Election. She looked at him and shook her head. Then she took out a business card and held it tightly in her hand. Maybe this crazy Polish chap had more to offer than her dubious colleagues realised. It was worth a try. She shook her fair hair loose and settled back in her seat to wait.

Salim Kennedy, looked around him. It felt strange to be in a room with so many foreigners, Russians, English, Germans, Chinese and others. He enjoyed taking in the differences of the characters. Although he thought there were times when he himself felt foreign. America was a culturally mixed country, but the events of 9/11 had left people suspicious of cultures that they did not understand. His mother was Iranian and father Irish American, but Salim's looks were distinctly Middle Eastern. That probably accounted for the occasional nods he received from the Arab journalists.

He was annoyed. What a stupid assignment this was. His orders were to sit close to the front, near whatever dais or table was in position. But then came the odd part. He wasn't to record the words of the Polish chap, what's his name? Ah, yes, Merric Grabowski. But he was told to hold the recording until a girl, about five feet six inches tall, with blonde hair, joined

Grabowski. This was the important conversation. It was likely that she would emerge suddenly, but it was not known where from. It was necessary because the tape recorder had proved temperamental and was preset to record at the press of a button. It was simple really, even for a young rookie FBI agent like Salim. He held the tape recorder on his lap and sipped a cup of black sugarless coffee. This was exceptionally boring work. He sighed deeply.

Catherine and Merric peeked from behind a dark curtain. Merric smiled broadly causing his face to look even more lined, like cracked mud on the bed of a dried river creek.

"There are lots of people. It was a good turnout. They all want some blood to take to their editors. We shall give them some excitement, eh, Catherine."

.He reached for her hand and she took it.

"Yes, we shall Merric, we shall. Now let's run through this again. You go and make your statement about being a proud American especially what it means to be free in a democracy. Give some of your past history, your experience of rotten state organised policing and rigged government administration. Your belief in democracy needs to come out too. Then you make some comments about your childhood, Poland under the Nazis then the Russians, then move on to observations of America and how you feel about the politics of 'spin doctoring' information cloaking it with deceit and manufacturing issues, you know the sort of thing better than I do. Then go on to say you have some fears for the future if ever that evil is allowed to manifest itself into American political life."

Catherine was gentle and crafted each sentence slowly so that the old man would understand what needed to be done. He fiddled with his notes, pretending not to be nervous.

"You then move on to say that you have evidence of something rotten. At this point I come out to join you wearing this wig," Catherine twirled the wig around her right hand, "and a scarf and dark sunglasses. You don't introduce me, but you go on to talk about Ginny Grivas, and, well, you know the rest. This diversion should be enough for attention to be focussed away from the debating chamber in the Senate and Ginny and her father make their first televised appearance. Do you copy, Merric Grabowski?"

Merric smiled, "Yes, young lady, I copy. I understand what needs to be done. We're almost there. I must confess to being a little excited myself. It beats playing chess with my Greek friend Constantine Keriokas at the local bar. Besides he cheats. Today, Catherine, we don't cheat."

Catherine looked around the curtain again, and then at her watch, "We'd better move it's full and almost two o'clock. I'm going for a quick pee, but will join you in a few minutes as planned. Now off you go, Merric, quickly!"

Merric looked at her a little nervously and said, *"Duzo sczescia piekna pani, uwarzaj!* That is Polish for good luck beautiful lady and be careful. I wish I were twenty years younger Catherine!"

She smiled and touched his face with her left hand.

He got up, turned on his heel, gathering some papers that he intended to put in front of him on the desk to make the scene look more businesslike. The papers included innocuous information on holidays to Greece, some sports reports and the latest results of the World Chess Championships; that made him chuckle. Then Merric stopped, stood up straight, took several deep breaths, composed himself and walked out from behind the curtain, which flapped dramatically around him. There was a hush as he moved towards the small dais at the front of the room. As he passed Salim, Merric dropped some papers and bent down to pick them up. Salim caught his eyes, old, gray and yet very bright and alert.

Just then Christina Markel saw her chance and she darted out of her chair two rows behind Salim and thrust her business card in Merric's jacket pocket. She smiled at him. Merric thought her quite beautiful and he returned her smile, taking her soft hand in his. As she bent forward to whisper in his ear, Salim panicked.

He dropped his hot coffee over his right trouser leg, but didn't feel it in his excitement and haste, and was relieved to quickly find the on/off switch for the recorder. Salim angled the microphone in their direction and he pressed the button.

The explosion was deafening. A bright flash and a rush of hot air spun around the crowded room.

Debris from broken glass, furniture and mangled flesh flew everywhere. For a few moments afterwards there was an eerie silence, punctuated only by the sound of small particles falling to the ground and the ring of the hotel fire alarm system. Then came the moans and soon, the cries of pain and anguish from those injured, but still alive.

Catherine was on her knees and bleeding from a dozen cuts on her face and hands. Her face was ashen and tears were forming in her eyes. She stared through the smoky gloom, but couldn't even see where the dais had been. She had been blown sideways as she stood behind the curtain and the blonde wig lay beside her.

Where was Merric? Who had done this? Why?

Unusually, the American news media quickly received a detailed report on the bomb explosion at the Hotel Quo Vadis. It was reported that fifty-three people had been killed or wounded and the area had been evacuated in case of secondary explosions from other devices. The speaker, Merric Grabowski, was killed along with many foreign journalists and the final death toll and identities of the victims had not yet been confirmed. A contact telephone number was given to foreign embassies. The identity of the bomber who was also killed was known to the security services; he was Salim Kennedy a newcomer to the FBI. Documents found in the pocket of a leather tape recorder bag in which the Semtex bomb had been housed linked him with a Middle Eastern terrorist group based in Iran. The man had not been searched because he had shown his FBI security pass. It was said that his actions were a complete surprise to his contacts and that he had been security cleared to the highest level.

The city was placed on high alert.

Even Quantock shuddered at his handiwork. He hadn't been squeamish before, but even though his situation was precarious he regretted having to do this. But in the face of exposure, his courage rallied, as often happens to people under stress, and he took refuge in this unreasoning attack on his fellow beings to save his skin.

Just as he thought that it was now almost over and all he had to do was to see out the election, Jim Sparrow came rushing into the office.

"Senator Grivas is in the Senate and he has a girl with him answering to the description you gave us. Jesus Dan, it's his daughter. But she was supposed to be killed at a tin mine out West wasn't she? What's going on?" he said.

Quantock was nearly sick. "What? Are you sure?"

"Sure I'm sure, the CCTV security people do this for a living for Chris'sake!"

"Right, yeah, well. Listen. Er, Jim. I'll level with you, we've got another Pattie Hurst situation here. Things are not what they seem. Trust me. Let's just apprehend them and get to the bottom of all this. Maybe she had a hand in the explosion at the Hotel Quo Vadis? I don't know any more than you do." He stood up and made for the door, "C'mon buddy let's go and sort things out."

Quantock walked out of the office and down the corridor. Jim was surprised and for a moment looked at the departing Quantock, but then followed on without asking any more questions. Then Quantock stopped in his tracks and threw him his car keys.

"Here, go get the car, white Mercedes, the registration is on the key ring. I'll see you out front. I forgot something."

Then he turned and ran back to his office.

When he was sure that Jim had moved out of sight, he closed the office door slowly and went to a metal cabinet. The cabinet opened easily when he turned the key and he went straight to a cigar box at the back of the top shelf. He took down the box and opened it. Inside was a bundle wrapped in a blue silk scarf. He untied it quickly and took out a small point twenty-two-millimetre calibre handgun. Without carrying out any further checks he put it in his pocket and walked quickly out of the office and down to the front of the building where Jim would be waiting with his car.

Senator Grivas' car stopped outside the Senate building. Several people with press badges converged on him; they didn't even notice Ginny in the back of the vehicle. A small dark haired woman with a prominent nose clutched her clipboard and got to the senator first. Her shrill voice grated on his ears.

"Senator, there are lots of mixed messages coming out of the states. Do you see this as another close race with Florida, Ohio and Pennsylvania as the big prizes?"

Although his nerves were shredded, Grivas had to remember that this was his day job and he gathered his strength for an answer. He patiently addressed the question.

"Well, ma'am, yes, that's always the case with these three states; these guys never fail to entertain do they?" The reporters chuckled at his remark and made notes. "But listen, you can be

267

sure that three others, Iowa, Minnesota and Wisconsin can go either way and have a recent history of fooling everybody. A combination of all three in either direction could force the election either way. Overall, well, the tracking polls look reasonably good for us, but it's gonna be a tight call."

He made to move away, but a tall gangly man with large spectacles blocked his path. Normally, he would push him aside, but not today.

"Senator, the President's predecessor was doing badly in the mid term elections in 2006. He was thought of as a lame duck and many thought that James MacBain would be a likely successor either when he stood down or at this election. There were hints that promises were made and broken. Then to everyone's surprise Vice President Jake Brannigan steps into the limelight, grabs the baton and holds onto it firmly. Do you think that Brannigan is the right man for the job?"

Grivas looked aghast. As a Democrat he was expected to say 'no', but any answer he was likely to give would be tainted by recent personal events. Instead he gathered himself and avoided the question.

"My friend, the Democratic Party is fielding a strong woman candidate – one of the very best – we are confident in her abilities and proud of her. On the other hand, the President is the sitting Republican for the upcoming term and has to be judged on his record, that is to say his ability to consult with the American people and his judgement as a leader. It's not for me to say, sir, it's for the people to do so. Now it's time for democracy to do its job. So let's now let the people speak rather than..." then Grivas paused for a few seconds and swallowed hard, "...rather than a cantankerous old fool like me who perhaps has a habit of not listening when he should."

The journalists almost dropped their recorders, pencils and notebooks. They looked at each other in surprise, trying to decode the senator's remarks. He then pushed through the confused throng and walked briskly up the steps of the Senate building, pausing to speak to the security guards and pointing back to Ginny throughout the conversation. They would not let her enter. Then all of a sudden, several of Grivas' political friends joined him and after a few minutes so did the unmistakable figure of the Chief of Staff Fred Spiker strode through the entrance towards them. There was a lot of hand waving and discussion, but the arrival of Spiker seemed to calm matters. He spoke earnestly to the security personnel and they turned without further ado, began to raise the paperwork necessary for Ginny's entry into the building. Spiker and Grivas stood looking at each other and after a while shook hands, then embraced.

The senator entered the building first. Ginny waited for a few moments before quickly going up the steps, collecting her pass and following her father into the building.

When she reached him inside, he hugged her and said, "The debate that I am due to chair will take place in one of the large committee rooms. The television cameras will be all set up, so there's no problem there. We have to be calm. If I'm a few minutes late Judy Woodruff, who is organising the event, will understand. Okay, let's walk around the long way, that. That will help your nerves."

He bent down and kissed her forehead tenderly. "I love you honey, you're brave and principled and I am a dumb Dad never to have noticed that before."

Ginny looked up at her father, "Love you too Dad."

Together they walked hand in hand through the outside corridors in the Senate building. Ginny just wanted it all to be over. She was tired and was glad to be with her Dad; she felt safe. They walked for a few minutes along some well decorated but dimly lit corridors, and then came across several people crowded around a television set. One of them looked up, "Hey, Senator Grivas, sir, isn't this just awful?"

"Oh, hi Mike, isn't what awful?"

"Sir, you haven't heard? The Hotel Quo Vadis was blown up about an hour ago. Some Polish was guy killed, along with dozens of others, including foreign journalists. They reckon it was a terrorist group with Iranian connections." The man looked mad.

Senator Grivas turned and saw Ginny's face. She was as white as a sheet, put her hands to her mouth and let out a noise resembling a muffled scream and a groan.

She cried out, "Merric, oh dear God, Merric, and Catherine," she put her hands to her mouth and her eyes welled with tears. Then she fainted.

Grivas and some of the younger men picked up Ginny's limp body and carried it to a nearby sitting room where she was gently put into a high-backed leather chair. The room was on the inside of the building and had no windows. It was lit by a single lamp on one of the coffee tables and smelled of leather chairs and cigars.

Grivas stroked his daughter's hair and said over his shoulder, "Okay boys, thank you so much, Mike and I can handle the young lady now."

The men were concerned, but left the room. Grivas then turned to Mike.

"Look Mike, I have to tell the committee that I am about to chair that I will be a moment or two longer, I will go and do that now, look after the kid will you? I won't be long."

Grivas looked at his daughter and didn't want to leave. But Ginny's presence at the committee and her testimony live on television was important to her, to the senator and the nation. As he left he looked over his shoulder, and then walked quickly to the committee room.

Mike looked at Ginny as she began to regain her composure, her eyes watery with tears and her body quite limp. She looked just like his sister, but also strangely familiar.

"Get her some cold water," said a voice behind him.

"What?"

He turned around and saw a tall man in a dark suit standing in the doorway with the light behind him. Quantock walked a couple of steps into the room and raised his pass so that Mike could identify him.

"Get her some cold water. She needs to be brought round slowly. Go on, it's all right, I'll watch her to make sure she's not sick or anything."

Thinking that Ginny was in safe hands Mike easily agreed to run the errand. Quantock stood looking at Ginny. She was certainly a pretty young girl. He remembered her naked body in the hotel room in Benson. It was going to be such a waste to mankind, but it had to be done. He reached into his left-hand pocket and brought out the small pistol, then into his right-hand pocket bringing out a standard issue service handgun. He released the safety catch on the handgun and waited.

Ginny's eyes half opened and she turned her head from left to right. Then, just as she settled down, she stared at the shape in front of her framed by shards of light from the corridor. The shape reached to the left and touched a switch and the main lights went on. Now she could see clearly.

Ginny recoiled in horror and tried to sink into the armchair. Her eyes bulged and her jaw dropped.

"Nice to see you Ginny. My, my, you and Clem led me on a hell of a chase. You know that? Well here we are and it all has to end my child," said Quantock.

"You killed Merric and Catherine and all those poor people. God knows how many more in your rotten life. Why?" said Ginny, putting her hands to her mouth.

" 'Why' is a strange question at the best of times Ginny. Why are there wars, why are there politicians and why do people on drugs drive cars that kill innocent mothers and children? I just survive like anyone else. Just like I'm gonna survive now honey."

Quantock paused for a moment as if thinking twice about something, and then he quickly threw the small pistol to Ginny, "Here catch this," he said.

The silver shape arched almost to the ceiling, sparkling, spinning in the light, moving as if in slow motion, before falling towards her. She instinctively put out her hands and caught the pistol and as she did so she rolled it into her right hand, holding it out in front of her. Almost instantaneously Quantock brought his handgun to the ready position; he cocked and aimed.

Just as he was about to fire he felt a metal gun barrel next to his right temple.

"Drop it!" Said a harsh and authoritative voice.

Surprised, he slowly lowered the handgun and let it fall to the floor. Turning round he saw that it was Jim Sparrow.

"Jim, careful, for Chris'sake, the girl's armed, she was going to kill me, lookout."

As Quantock went to move away, Jim held his collar and pressed the barrel of the gun into his neck. Quantock was transfixed and said nothing.

Then another voice said, "Hello, Dan. The game's up my friend. Jim, good job done. Cuff him."

Quantock stared in amazement. It was Troy Hammond, Head of the FBI. They stared at each other with mutual contempt.

Hammond turned to Quantock and said, "That was interesting. I don't usually get involved in fieldwork. I must confess that Jim was very quick off the mark. He telephoned as soon as he realised Ginny's identity. It was a close run thing. But you should never have killed all those people Dan. That was bad. Real bad." He turned to Jim Sparrow, "Keep him here until we can get him out without anyone seeing him. Ginny, come on honey, get over here and let's get you outta here and home."

Ginny was led out of the room and Senator Grivas joined his daughter in a FBI Cadillac and they went home. The televised Senate committee and CNN joint meeting went ahead as scheduled with Judy Woodruff in the chair. The next few days were frenetic. It took time to concoct stories that were credible to the public regarding Clem and Ginny's survival. It meant setting up a false hideout with provisions and so on in Arizona, then claiming that the teenagers had been held prisoner by Mafia criminals who wanted ransom from the parents and it had all gone wrong. It was just about believable and the relief on the rescue of two of the four teenagers together with the presidential election reduced the level of questioning. The Middle Eastern plot was discredited and tension in the Gulf of Arabia was lessened and troops and ships were brought home. Considerable diplomatic activity ensued and deals were struck, mostly with an emphasis on the withdrawal of US troops and improved trade links.

The scam and its terrible consequences were described to several very senior senators and with the Presidential Election only days away an exit strategy was devised. Under interrogation Quantock revealed the full details of the Kinz scam and provided copies of letters and other details from his office safe. He also produced a copy of Kinz's letter to the president and this was damning proof that the president did know of the scam's terrible outcome and had unwisely been content to use it for his own aggrandisement, happy to reap the benefits of the political fallout. Brannigan was normally fearless even when confronted by his deceits, which wasn't often. But in the face of mounting evidence as to his part in the affair he immediately agreed to step down, stating that it was for reasons of ill health. The Republican Party and indeed America would be damaged to the core if this was revealed.

So it was in the best interests of the nation, that Ginny and her father agreed with a broad coalition of US senators that the whole matter should be kept absolutely secret. In recognition of this it was also agreed to open the door for a Democrat President. Initial Republican reluctance was soon overcome. The Republicans desperately wanted to avoid this debacle becoming public knowledge. If it did, it was likely that they would lose their credibility and remain in the political wilderness for a decades.

Catherine was reunited with Ginny and stayed with the Grivas family for a long time afterwards, before taking up a job with "The League of Women." The American administration put a lot of faith in her and the Grivas' silence. It would have done no good whatsoever for the story to be revealed. But they needn't have worried, the Grivas' and Catherine were patriots and had always put country before self – even if, under the microscope, their approach to democracy had been so very different throughout the course of their lives.

On 5 November 2008, the United States of America elected its first woman president.

Quantock felt light-headed and hazy. His body felt heavy and his arms and legs wouldn't move more than a few inches. He was aware that he was dressed in only a light nightshirt and that the room he was in was very warm and lit by a soft green light. He lifted his head and tried to look around. There was a French window in front of him that was open and the breeze softly stroked the white net curtains so that they moved erratically left and right. He caught sight of green grass outside and trees without leaves.

Then a shape came from behind him.

"You okay honey?" said a female voice.

"Where am I?" he said.

"Now never you mind that. You are in a kind of hospital and the best thing for you is to get some rest. Don't do any thinking. Don't do any moving around, you'll only fall over. It's in your own interest to just stay quiet and calm.

"Are you a nurse or a guard?" said Quantock.

"Now honey," said the nurse with a loud huff, "you're doin' the thinkin' I told you not to do!"

She then reached into a nearby medical tray and slowly took out a syringe.

Back in Quantock's office the daily routine was going on as usual. A cleaner vacuumed the woollen carpet and as she moved in front of the desk she knocked the chess pieces off the coffee table and onto the floor. Already fed up with having to tip-toe around the chess set each day, she picked up the pieces one by one, putting them into a large brown envelope. Then she put the envelope on top of the chessboard after giving the board a quick dust down. When she left the office she was in such a hurry that she didn't notice that she had stepped onto the black king, breaking it into pieces and crushing it into the carpet.

It was a bright sunny day and Clem had just finished his video shoot. He put his camera down on top of a pile of equipment that carelessly lay around him and sat down in a canvass chair that someone had labelled: "Boss." It was the end of a tough recording session. His head ached. Where was he? Oh, Philadelphia, that's it, Philadelphia. Yesterday it was Pennsylvania, before that Wisconsin and before that…..well, he just couldn't remember. The subjects of his video had been hard work as usual. They were always hard work and had to be persuaded to talk; this annoyed Clem. Surely they had something to say? Why did they just sit there and need so much encouragement? Faces, dumb-assed faces, always the same? The left side of his face twitched uncontrollably.

It had been two years since the last minute withdrawal of President Brannigen from the presidential race. Some insiders said Brannigan had stepped down just as the postman arrived at his door with and envelope marked, 'Justice – Open Carefully.' The new incumbent, Democrat Elizabeth Rand, brought about sweeping changes to social programmes of all kinds and had refocused the country's ailing economy and improved America's foreign policy. America was now pursuing more scientific and medical exploration rather than political expansion. Importantly NASA and Medicare programmes were back on track. Things were better, but only just. Clem knew that he and Ginny had something to do with her victory. Damn! She owed them both a lot and he would tell her that when he saw her next.

Clem was proud of his video company. Perhaps it had played its part in the reformation of government afterwards? Everyone told him that this had been the case; well everyone he knew anyway. He wanted to be one of the very best at producing 'fly on the wall' documentaries, exposing corruption and maladministration in government as well as business. Clem accepted that big business continued to provide the lifeblood capital, but his mission was to make social responsibility part of the 'American Dream.' His video of that title would be dedicated to Senator Randolph Kinz. Kinz would've liked that. It was just taking a bit of time that was all.

Sometimes he heard Kinz's voice, as clear and loud as anything, but he wasn't really sure. He heard a lot of voices. It only happened when he had a headache or he got upset. He felt agitated today. His mind was in a whirl; it was always in a whirl these days. President Elizabeth Rand was visiting the shoot today, or was it next week. Why couldn't he remember? He must be ready to meet her. He began to brush his clothing

276

with his hands and straighten his hair, and was so agitated he nearly knocked his spectacles off.

Just then Ginny Grivas walked through two double doors facing Clem some twenty yards away. She was flanked by two women in starched white uniforms and shoes that clicked as they walked over the brown shiny parquet floor. They walked past side rooms and received polite whistles and shouts from a number of men. Clem stopped rubbing his head, looked up and laughed nervously.

"That's steel-workers for you," he said loudly as he saw her coming and he stood up slowly, tears falling down his face, "sure it is, red blooded Americans...good guys all of them..."

His voiced trembled and faded and he stared wide-eyed at the approaching women. He shuffled forward slowly, squinting, with his hand outstretched for a handshake. His dressing gown fell open and his slippers flip flopped on the floor.

"Madam President. I'm so glad you made it, so very glad," he said.

As Ginny reached him he fell to his knees and buried his face in her stomach. She was never able to convince him that she was not the president and her stomach never failed to knot up when she was with him. She stroked his hair and face gently, softly, until he quietened down. Ginny was now an experienced senior case worker for the American Civil Liberties Union and was able to schedule regular visits to see Clem at the Brunswick Nursing Home in Portland. She would never stop visiting Clem.

One of the nurses reached for a syringe and Ginny glared at her and said, "It was the drugs that did this in the first place, does he have to have more?"

The nurse shrugged and reluctantly moved away from them both.

Ginny held Clem's head as she had done on every visit for almost two years now, each one unrecognised or not remembered and always confused.

She cupped his head in her hands and whispered in his ear. "The American Dream is doing okay Clem, just okay, don't you worry."

The End